Jo Thomas worked for ma
producer, including time
and Radio 2's Steve Wright

Jo's debut novel, *The Oyster Catcher*, was a runaway bestseller and won both the RNA Joan Hessayon Award and the Festival of Romance Best EBook Award. Her book *Escape to the French Farmhouse* was a No. 1 bestselling ebook. In every one of her novels Jo loves to explore new countries and discover the food produced there, both of which she thoroughly enjoys researching. Jo lives in Pembrokeshire with her husband and three children, where cooking and gathering around the kitchen table are a hugely important and fun part of their family life.

Visit Jo's website: jothomasauthor.com
or follow her on:

X Jo_Thomas01
f JoThomasAuthor
Instagram JoThomasAuthor

www.penguin.co.uk

Also by Jo Thomas

THE OYSTER CATCHER
THE OLIVE BRANCH
LATE SUMMER IN THE VINEYARD
THE HONEY FARM ON THE HILL
SUNSET OVER THE CHERRY ORCHARD
A WINTER BENEATH THE STARS
MY LEMON GROVE SUMMER
COMING HOME TO WINTER ISLAND
ESCAPE TO THE FRENCH FARMHOUSE
FINDING LOVE AT THE CHRISTMAS MARKET
CHASING THE ITALIAN DREAM
CELEBRATIONS AT THE CHÂTEAU
RETREAT TO THE SPANISH SUN
KEEPING A CHRISTMAS PROMISE
SUMMER AT THE ICE CREAM CAFÉ
COUNTDOWN TO CHRISTMAS

Ebook short stories:
THE CHESTNUT TREE
THE RED SKY AT NIGHT
NOTES FROM THE NORTHERN LIGHTS

Jo Thomas

Love in Provence

PENGUIN BOOKS

TRANSWORLD PUBLISHERS
Penguin Random House, One Embassy Gardens,
8 Viaduct Gardens, London SW11 7BW
www.penguin.co.uk

Transworld is part of the Penguin Random House group of companies
whose addresses can be found at global.penguinrandomhouse.com

First published in Great Britain in 2024 by Bantam
an imprint of Transworld Publishers
Penguin paperback edition published 2024

A CIP catalogue record for this book
is available from the British Library.

ISBN
9781804993859

Typeset in ITC Giovanni Std by Jouve (UK), Milton Keynes.
Printed and bound in Great Britain by Clays Ltd, Elcograf S.p.A.

The authorized representative in the EEA is Penguin Random House
Ireland, Morrison Chambers, 32 Nassau Street, Dublin D02 YH68.

Penguin Random House is committed to a sustainable
future for our business, our readers and our planet. This book is
made from Forest Stewardship Council® certified paper.

To Francesca Best. One of the very Best of editors.
Thank you.

1

'*Putain!*' I hear the smash of glasses and the shout. I race through the swing doors from the kitchen into the little restaurant, leaving the bouillabaisse I'm preparing for today's lunch service. The front door slams, creating a huge gust and a cacophony of crashing. Glasses on the tables topple and roll this way and that. More hit the floor.

'*Putain!*'

'Stephanie!' I chide, with a smile in my voice. 'You're a mother of two now! Mind your language!'

'*Oui*, Del. *Je sais, je sais*, I know!' Stephanie replies crossly, as we run to the door, turn the worn brass handle and dash out onto the small terrace. Its red and white awning is flapping up and down in the wind, and the new sign for Henri's bistro, over the door, is swinging enthusiastically on its hinges. It matches the

1

freshly painted gold writing on the window, ready for the summer visitors to the town, who are starting to arrive. June always sees visitor numbers pick up. They come for the sunshine and cicadas, the slower pace of life, the cobbled streets and the smell of Provence in the air as the lavender starts to bloom.

Stephanie rushes forward to gather up the glasses that tipped over on the tables, muttering more expletives. No matter how often I correct her bad language I don't think it will ever change. For such a slight figure, she has a very commanding presence. It comes with a lift of her chin and a lioness's passion to protect her young. Stephanie has had to learn the hard way in life. A single parent when I first met her, she did whatever it took to provide for her child, Tomas. Sometimes it's easy to forget the road she's travelled, and how far she's come, when I see her now, running her own business, making the lavender bakes she sells at market and provides to cafés in the area. She has a smart new house where she lives with her husband, JB, and their now two children.

Stephanie is like family to me, as I am to her. We were there for each other when life hit rock bottom. It hasn't been an easy road back up, but we made it together. I gave her somewhere to stay when she and Tomas needed it, and she taught me French. Together we grew the market stall, baking from the kitchen in my old farmhouse, Le Petit Mas de la Lavande. Since then she's moved the business into a purpose-built unit, and I run the bistro in this little side-street off the main square. I'd say life is pretty much exactly where we want it to be. Except for the mistral wind we have in the South of France, which likes to shake things up every now and then. But I smile as a chair swings to and fro and falls over, sliding across the terrace. Nothing we can't manage. I grab the handle to wind in the awning as it flaps up and down, threatening to take flight.

'*Merde! Merde!*' Stephanie expands her profanities as she gathers glasses to her chest, the little vases that were filled with dried lavender strands from last year's harvest, and a red-and-white-check tablecloth doing its best to take off on the strong cold north-westerly wind.

'It's just a little mistral mischief,' I say, turning the handle swiftly to get the awning wound in, telling Stephanie what she already knows. Then I'm helping to gather more fallen glasses and rescuing more tablecloths – even though they're pinned down with ornate dragonfly weights at each corner. The little vases of lavender are tumbling about as the wind whips down the alleyway. I snatch up the rest and Stephanie adds them to the others she's collected and runs inside, letting out the scent of the simmering bouillabaisse, steeped with saffron and fennel. It mingles with the aroma of pines and wild herbs, blown in on the wind, the smell of Provence in summer, the smell of my home. I stack the metal chairs against the window as the wind roars up the narrow street past the restaurant, and bring in the rest of the tablecloths and condiments, rescued from the mistral, which steals hats from heads, ruins wedding days and turns life upside down.

A door slams upstairs in Henri's apartment, which has been unused since he and my best friend Rhi got together and went travelling while time was still on their side. A shutter bangs against the stone wall. A dog barks in one of the nearby narrow streets that all lead to the square, just along the way from me. I lift my head to the wind and feel the memories it left that summer. I remember the havoc the mistral caused for me, turning my life on its head, the first time I encountered it, three years ago now.

2

It was moving day. We were leaving France, my then husband Ollie and I. Everything was packed and ready to go. I remember the removal people fighting against the wind to close the truck's big doors and finally succeeding. And there it was, my life in a van, heading back to the UK, just six months after we'd made the big move to France. The wind laughed and howled, teased and tormented me. I felt it chill my bones, even though it was summer in the South of France. Ollie and I were going back to how we were – or not quite: this time we didn't have a home to call our own. And the one thing really missing? The love we had once shared was now lost somewhere between the hospital appointments and failed IVF treatments. In moving to France we had tried to rebuild something that had disappeared and couldn't be retrieved through fresh baguettes and croissants for breakfast.

Once the adventure of the move had died down and everyday life kicked in, with the lack of internet connection, our poor French and worse DIY skills, what was left? It hadn't been the sticking plaster on our dying relationship we'd hoped for. Instead the sticking plaster had had to be ripped off. It was the only way.

I decided not to leave. It wasn't that our life in France didn't work. It was our life *together* that didn't work, in France or in the UK. Call it mistral madness, but as I stood on the front steps of the farmhouse, the shutters slipping loose from their moorings, with Ralph, my dog, at my side, I knew I wouldn't follow that truck 'home'. It wasn't my home. My home had been with Ollie, but that had gone. Our marriage was over. He knew it and I knew it. It was just that one of us had had to say and do something about it.

I stayed on the steps until the truck had gone, followed by a furious, uptight Ollie. As there wasn't a stick of furniture left in the house, I slept the night in the bath, my bra holding together the shutters until the wind dropped, and had big daft Ralph as a blanket. When morning came, I pulled the bra from the shutters and pushed them open on a still day, the sky bright and blue, with barely a cloud. It was a new day. I had nothing. But it was a blank canvas to start again.

Ollie went back to the UK into the waiting arms of

the lover he'd left behind, when he was trying to hide from what had really been going on: she was pregnant and ready to start a family with him. I grieved for my marriage and the child I would never have as I began to bake with Provençal lavender that had once grown in the fields of our . . . my farmhouse. I kept the house, he got everything else. It worked out for us both that way.

After he'd sent out my best friends to check that I hadn't gone mad with the mistral (which they say can drive you mad) and finally realized we were better off apart, Ollie announced that his child was on the way, and I went on to . . . well, to become a partner in Henri's bistro. Henri was one of the first people I was introduced to after I'd met Carine, the estate agent, and Fabien, who ran the *brocante*, when I started trying to make a life for myself here. Henri was a big character, running his bistro, offering a *plat du jour* for which locals flocked to his place at lunchtime. He ordered lavender bakes from me for the bistro when business was slow at my market stall, which gave me the start I needed. As it turned out, I wasn't the only person he helped: he looked out for people when they needed it most.

It was because of Henri that I'm working in the bistro and that I met Stephanie. Henri and Fabien have known each other since Fabien was a young man helping his grandfather at the *brocante*. When his grandfather died and he took over the business, Henri became a father figure to him . . . and to me, to us all.

Stephanie was another he looked out for, making sure she had a hot meal whenever she needed it. After some persuasion, she finally moved onto the farm with me, escaping dreadful living conditions and a life of petty theft, with her young son Tomas. Stephanie began to work with me making lavender bakes and delivering them to Henri, then other restaurants. She sold them in the market, too.

We all helped Henri with his riverside project, delivering the *plat du jour* to the clearing there where people paid what they could afford, if anything, for a meal at the end of the day. Once Henri had had a heart attack, though, he knew it was time to take life a little easier. He and my friend Rhi went off travelling together, and I stepped into his shoes at the bistro, learning to make the dishes he cooked for his customers and the riverside project. I'd found my home in that little bistro kitchen. And I finally allowed myself to find love again, with a man ten years younger than me: Fabien. That mistral changed a lot three years ago.

Now I let the wind whip around me and think of how far we've all come in those three years and smile. Stephanie has had her second child and married her childhood sweetheart, JB, Tomas's dad. We became a close little family, the children loving Fabien and calling him Papi. Stephanie is still running the lavender baking business, delivering to shops and restaurants and doing the weekly market. JB works with Fabien at the *brocante*. And I'm here, at Henri's, where I've never been happier, making the local dishes he taught me. I wrap my arms around myself against the wind and turn towards the restaurant door.

Stephanie is coming out with an empty basket, her ponytail dancing in the wind.

'I've put the desserts in the chiller. I have some more deliveries to make.' She nods to the van, parked by the *brocante*. She's holding two-year-old Louis's hand, his white-blond hair whipped up by the wind, his arm covering his eyes against the dust. 'I'll be back to help with lunch service,' she says, just as she does every day. Each morning until recently, Stephanie arrived at my farmhouse, Le Petit Mas de la Lavande, in her little van, painted with lavender flowers down the side, her branding for the lavender baking business. Before Louis was born she lived in the Romani caravan in the garden, which was an empty shell at the time. Just like the main house. She needed somewhere to stay and I needed to find my way through French life. I suppose we saved each other. Now she bakes early in the morning, in her purpose-built unit, makes her deliveries and comes to help me at the restaurant. I'm so proud of her.

'*À tout à l'heure*,' she says, guiding Louis along and holding her basket on her hip. With his eyes screwed shut, Louis stops, his hands to his face, refusing to move. He begins to cry.

'Oh, Louis, *doucement*,' I say, and step forward but tears are falling. I bend to pick him up. Stephanie wedges the basket back onto her hip – it was slipping off – and her bag onto her shoulder. It's stuffed with everything a toddler needs to see him through the day. I may not have had children of my own, but I was there for Louis when he was a baby.

Louis curls into the crook of my neck and holds his fists to his eyes. No amount of cajoling will cheer him.

'You could leave him with me,' I say, 'while you do your rounds.'

'But you have work to do,' she says. 'Come on, Louis, we're going in the van and you love the van.'

He shakes his head and kicks his feet. By the look of it, he's not going anywhere until the mistral has passed.

'Whoa!' The familiar voice makes me smile and Fabien is jogging towards us from the *brocante*. He slides his arm around my waist and kisses my cheek. 'You left early this morning, before I had even woken.'

'I had so much to do, clearing up from last night at the riverside and getting today's bouillabaisse on the go. It's always busy when I cook Henri's bouillabaisse.' I kiss him. '*Bonjour*, good morning.'

'Good morning.' He kisses me back. 'I just wish I could have said it to you in bed,' he says quietly, with a grin.

'Me too.' I smile back. 'Perhaps I could say good morning to you later.'

'Ha!' He laughs. 'Or we'll be asleep in our chairs like an old couple after a busy day.'

'No. I'm going to cook for you, something special. Remind me what you look like! What was your name again?'

'It's a date!' he says.

'No deliveries to make this evening?' I ask.

He shakes his head. '*Désolé*.'

'It's fine,' I try to reassure him.

'Nothing so far today. Sales are slow. If I sell anything, I'll have to deliver it. Or get a house clearance. But so far nothing. I think people buy less when the weather is against them,' he says, of the wind.

'Good,' I say, raising my voice above the whistle as the mistral tears down the street again, like a youngster racing their bike and forgetting where the brakes are. 'I mean, not good that you've had no sales today, just good that I'll see you tonight. We have enough from the bistro right now. And soon we'll have the harvest and the lavender to sell.' Stephanie sells it on the market stall, in bunches and lavender bags. If we had a still we could turn it into oil. That's the plan, when we have the time and the money. 'In the meantime,' I smile in the face of the wind, 'I get to see you!'

'It comes to something when I need to book a date with my partner!' He chuckles, then looks down at

Louis. '*Qu'est-ce qui se passé*, Del? What's happening here?' he says, cocking his head to one side.

'Papi Fabien!' Louis lifts his head. 'Papi!' he shouts, a smile spreading across his face as he reaches out for Fabien, who takes him into his arms.

'Oh, we all know who's favourite around here.' Stephanie smiles.

Fabien has slipped into the role of surrogate grandfather effortlessly, even though he's nowhere near old enough: he's ten years younger than me and ten years older than Stephanie. The age gap used to worry me but not so much, these days. Life is so busy there isn't time to think about it. Our little stuck-together family seems to work and that makes my heart swell.

'Okay! You going in the van with your *maman*?' Fabien asks, and Louis nods. 'You're going to ride in the van? *Au camion!*' Fabien shouts, and bounces the little boy up and down. 'I came to see if you needed help with the tables and chairs, but I see you've already done it.'

'All sorted,' I say, touched by his thoughtfulness. 'But *merci!*' That's Fabien. Always thinking of others. I sometimes worry we forget to make time for ourselves.

'Well, in that case, if you're all sorted here, I'll help Stephanie to the van, with this little man.' He kisses Louis's little fingers, which are tightly wrapped around his own. This family may not be conventional but I love it. Fabien kisses me gently on the lips and I wish that I was still wrapped around his warm body in bed. But life doesn't allow for lie-ins. The bistro is busier than ever, with holidaymakers and second-home owners arriving in the town and wanting tables. I'm getting in earlier to check my deliveries – things get missed off the orders from time to time. And Fabien finds it hard to say no to house clearances, which means the *brocante* is full. Almost too full for people to browse. But holidaymakers aren't here for the *brocante*. Sales will pick up again in the autumn, when it's cooler, I'm sure, but for now, we're dependent on what I bring in from the bistro. And that's fine. Even if we're like ships that pass in the night. We'll make more time for us when the swifts start to leave, when the harvest is over, the visitors head home and the restaurants quieten down. I watch Fabien giving Louis a piggy-back, Stephanie by his side, hurrying up the lane to the main road where the van is parked, his arm protect-ively around her.

I look up and down the small street, at the basket and bag shop opposite, whose proprietor has taken in everything that was hanging outside; the clothing shop, whose owner has hurried in her linen dresses on a rail, and the ceramics outlet. I grab a couple of little vases and a remaining tablecloth and turn back to the bistro where my bouillabaisse is still simmering.

'*Bonjour, Madame!*' I turn.

'*Bonjour, Monsieur.*' I raise a hand to the mayor as he passes, holding his briefcase tight to his chest as he battles towards the *mairie* just off the square.

'Ah, *le mistral*, eh?' He shakes his head. 'Causing trouble where it's not wanted!'

'*Exactement!*' I call back. 'Let's hope it leaves soon and takes its trouble-making with it.'

The mayor shrugs good-naturedly. '*Le mistral* always leaves chaos in its wake.' He hurries on.

I place my hand on the brass door handle into the bistro. But not this time, I think. Life here is sorted. I'm happy. We're all happy. This time the mistral is just passing through. 'Do your worst!' I say, and push open the door, drawn back to the kitchen by the enticing smell of the rich broth on the stove, and to my happy place, this little bistro kitchen where everything feels safe. I go to step into the restaurant, when a sudden huge gust, bigger than before, is trying to lift me off my feet.

'Whoa!' I push against the door that's trying to slam shut. 'No, you don't, Mistral!'

Behind me, there's a loud slow crack. I whip my head around to see where it's coming from, and as I do it's followed by an almighty crash.

3

I drop the vases I'm clutching, which smash on the ground, scattering white china shards and lavender stems. My hand with the tablecloth flies to my mouth. The olive tree that has stood outside the bistro for years has cracked and fallen to where I was just standing with Fabien, Stephanie and Louis. I'm rooted to the spot. The dogs bark louder. There are shouts from neighbouring shop owners asking if everyone is okay.

'*Oui, oui,*' I finally manage. '*Tout le monde va bien.*'

But I can't move. I stare at the tree and at the smashed front window, now with a pattern on the glass like one of the cobwebs on the lavender bushes on an autumn morning. The tree is resting on the chairs I've just stacked by the wall.

People are coming out of their shops.

'*Oh, là là!*' someone calls to another, who's summoned the police and the fire brigade.

I turn back to the big solid door with the brass handle and hold onto it, steadying myself, resting my forehead on the cold metal, catching my breath, centring myself. That is what this place does for me. It centres me. It's just a window, I tell myself. No one was hurt. It's just the mistral causing mischief. The window can be fixed.

I push open the door and look back at the branch that's cracked the glass and its lettering. At least no one was hurt. The window can be fixed. I walk into the small kitchen and turn off the gas under the bouillabaisse. There won't be any lunchtime service today. I take a deep breath, close my eyes and breathe in the herb- and fish-scented broth. I put the lid on the big pan. At least there will be plenty to take to the riverside project this evening. Fabien had put furniture under the big larch tree there, with festoon lighting, and it has become quite the place to go. Anyone in need of a meal mixes with locals, who are happy to contribute and help. People play chess, talk, and once a month a local hairdresser comes and gives haircuts and manicures for those who need it, those with no home to go to. I wouldn't like to be out tonight, I think, looking at the leaves stripped from the plane trees careering past the window.

The *pompiers* arrive quickly, with the local *gendarmes*, and check no one is hurt and no one is inside the building. I'm still rooted to the spot on the threshold, thinking of what might have been if Fabien, Stephanie and Louis hadn't left when they did. Everyone steps back a little as they discuss taking down the stricken tree. I feel this huge sadness for something that has stood at the heart of the community for so long. It's about to leave a large gap in the street where it stood and shaded my diners when the awning didn't cover them, shielding them from punishing summer sunlight and creating a cosy corner in autumn, covered with the fairy lights I'd hung there. Now something that made this place special is missing. I'll have to think of something to replace it. But first I need to get the window repaired.

I text Carine, my friend and the local estate agent, tell her what's happened and ask for the name of a handyman. Then I text Fabien and tell him about it, but not to worry, no one was hurt and I'm fine. At least, I think I am. I look at my shaking fingers hitting wrong letters on my phone's tiny keyboard. Life was much easier when we all just picked up the phone, I think, knowing I sound old. But life has a way of galloping away with you. When I moved here and set up my life with Fabien, I promised myself we'd make the most of each day. Enjoy each other's company. Coffee in the morning on the terrace overlooking the fields of lavender we'd planted, with people coming on Work-away schemes to help, staying in our converted barn and shepherd's hut. Some pickers bring their own tents and motorhomes, while others prefer to stay in our barn. They'll be coming again soon, for this summer's harvest. Even though it's a juggle, I love it when the farm is in full swing. As does Labradoodle Ralph. A boisterous young pup when we first moved here, now he sits in the shade watching the action from the cool terracotta-tiled terrace beyond the French windows from the kitchen.

Don't get me wrong, I'm content. But the more I enjoy the routine of our lives, the busier and busier Fabien and I have become, rarely having time for coffee on the terrace. Days turn into weeks and months, the seasons change and life moves on. The cycle of life continues, spring turning to summer and summer to autumn. Winter will be brief, which also serves as a reminder that life is moving on – quickly.

Carine messages back with a glazier's number and a message hoping I'm okay. I let her know that all is well. I'll message Henri later, tell him what's happened and ask about buildings insurance.

I walk back to the kitchen and, on auto-pilot, switch on the coffee machine, ready to serve coffee, with lavender biscuits, to the *pompiers* and *gendarmes*. Stephanie made them for today, to accompany the ice cream that won't be eaten.

I may as well finish the bouillabaisse and cancel any bookings for lunch. I head for the reservations book on the desk in the corner of the restaurant. We don't take many, just a few for regulars who know when I'm cooking what, like mussels after the market on Tuesday, steamed in white wine and served with a splash of crème fraîche and parsley, and on Wednesday a tomatoey beef *daube*. It's fish on Fridays, like today's bouillabaisse, made with chunky monkfish. I also serve salads, Niçoise, with flaking tuna, green beans, hard-boiled egg and salty black olives in a thick vinaigrette, or a *paysanne* salad, with chunks of crispy pancetta and croûtons. Steak *frites* is a regular on the menu, with homemade aioli, which is garlicky mayonnaise, and thin French fries. Fluffy omelettes cooked in butter, with grated cheese that strings from the plate when you eat it and home-cooked ham, with seasonal salads, slices of plump tomato scattered with fresh basil, circles of sweet white onion and a crisp green salad with a dressing of oil and vinegar, mustard and garlic. Come the cooler months, there will be thinly sliced black truffle and rich ratatouille. And, just as Henri did, I take the leftovers of the *plat du jour* to the clearing by the river. I always make sure there's some left. Just like Henri taught me. I smile thinking about the people waiting for me to arrive.

I hear the front door open.

'Sure everything is okay in here, Del? No one hurt?' It's Marcel, the local *gendarme*.

'I'm fine, Marcel, and no one is hurt.'

'When they start to take the tree away, I will need you to either come outside or stay in the kitchen, okay?'

'*Oui. Bien sûr.*' I look back at the diary. At least with the bistro shut today I'll have more time to make the beds in the barn for the lavender pickers arriving later in the week. I hear the door open again, letting in another blast of manic air.

I look out from the kitchen. It's the mayor.

'Will you be open later?' he asks in French. 'You know I love your bouillabaisse!'

I shake my head. 'Not today, Monsieur. But I have plenty to take to the river clearing later.'

'I'll be there!' He smiles. '*Bonne chance!*' He nods to the uniformed men with chainsaws revving up and shuts the door. I hear him talking to the firemen and police about what a shame it is, the old olive tree gone, and how the mistral has certainly caused mischief this time.

It certainly has. I pick up my phone and start texting the regulars.

The bell over the door rings.

'*Désolée*, we're not open today,' I call, presuming someone is asking whether I'll be open for lunch again. I carry on texting and listen for the bell to tell me they've got the message and are leaving. But I don't hear it. In fact, the wind whips around inside the restaurant, causing more mayhem, lifting tablecloths, knocking over glasses on the shelves, catching the corners of the reservations book and flapping over the pages. It's like they have a life of their own. As if some kind of a spell has been stirred up from its pages. I tut.

'*Désolée. Fermé aujourd'hui!*' I hope they'll get the message and shut the door behind them. Still no bell, and still the wind whistles around, rattling bottles and clanking pans.

I crane my neck to look out of the kitchen and into the dark restaurant. Someone's standing in the doorway.

'*Excusez-moi?*' I call. Still nothing. '*Fermé aujourd'hui!*' When the silhouetted figure doesn't move and the door stays open, I head into the restaurant. '*Âllo?*' I say. Finally I recognize the person standing there, among the chaos going on outside, *gendarmes* calling to each other to close the road, the windswept restaurant and the front window, which looks like a fractured frozen lake.

'Rhi?'

It's her. My best friend is standing in the doorway. 'Rhi!' I hurry towards her, circumnavigating the tables and chairs in the compact restaurant, my arms flung wide. 'You should have rung! Come in! Don't mind the commotion outside. It's all in hand.' She's here!

Just when I need her. She's always here when I need her most.

She doesn't move towards me or open her arms to hug me back. It's then I take in her sagging shoulders, drawn face and thinner-than-usual frame.

'Rhi?' She still doesn't move and neither do I. 'Is . . . everything all right?' The chill in the air is now running up and down my spine, making me shiver, telling me it's not.

She looks up at me.

'Is Henri with you?' My mouth feels like it's full of sawdust.

Just then I see Fabien rushing in past the *pompiers* and *gendarmes*, bizarrely shaking hands with those he knows, which is most of them, and the gathered shop-keepers standing by the fallen tree. 'Hey, I just got your message,' he says from the doorway, behind Rhi, not noticing her. 'Are you okay?'

'Yes, fine. No one hurt. Just shocked.'

He lets out a sigh. 'Thank goodness.' He goes to step inside the restaurant.

'*Pardon*,' he says politely.

Then he does a double-take, seeing Rhi on the threshold, blocking the entrance. Not moving one way or the other, in or out. 'Rhi?' he says, then smiles widely and wraps her in a huge Fabien hug. That's one of the things I love most about him: his hugs make you feel everything will be just fine. But still she doesn't move or hug him back. He pulls away, looking at her face, then at me, as if I have the answer. And I think, by the chill in my bones, I do.

'Rhi?' I ask again.

'Henri,' she says, and swallows, the words catching in her mouth. Then she takes another run at it. 'Henri's . . . dead,' she manages, as the wind screams down the narrow cobbled street, around the town square and out the other side.

4

Her voice is thin and trembling. 'I didn't know where else to go.' Rhi's face is haunted. 'Oh, Del . . .'

I step forward and in two big strides I'm enclosing her in a hug. It's the only thing I think of doing, just like Fabien did. I hold her tight.

'You came here. Henri's home. It was the right thing to do,' I say, into her thick, soft hair.

She's tense in my arms, clearly still trying to hold it all together.

'Come in,' I say, above the noise of the tree being sawn up by a local tree surgeon, assisted by the *pompiers*. The *gendarmes* are looking on and accepting coffee from the shopkeepers.

I raise a hand to them, acknowledging them, as does Fabien, thanking them for coming so swiftly. He follows us inside and shuts the door.

I lead Rhi through the kitchen to the narrow wooden stairs up to Henri's apartment. It's quieter than downstairs, I think, away from the bustle of the tree removal outside. We climb up, past all the framed photographs on the walls of Henri as a younger man, holidays in Brittany with his family, life here at the bistro in the early days, friends and special guests who have visited, then of him and Rhi in the setting sun. We step onto the landing and into the big open-plan room over the kitchen and restaurant, zoned into the salon, with a sofa, the dining area and the kitchen, with a separate bedroom and bathroom. It's a lovely light space. But perhaps it wasn't the best idea to come here.

Everything is how it was when Rhi and Henri left, only occasionally returning to check in with us and plan their next adventure.

She looks at the big wooden desk, then at the captain's chair, with Henri's indentation on the worn tapestry cushions where he would sit to do his paperwork. Not that he enjoyed paperwork, but he did like sitting at his desk, with the long shuttered window in front of it, looking down on the street below.

Rhi walks in slowly, then goes to rest her hand on the back of the chair, as if imagining him there. Then, as if the reality hits her, she dissolves into tears. I lead her to the sofa that's positioned to look out of another window, to the cream stone apartment opposite over the bistro. Cheerful voices from below rise to us, in contrast to the feeling in the room right now.

I sit beside her and look up at Fabien. His face shows his shock and I can't work out who to comfort first.

'Perhaps a cognac?' I say quietly to Fabien. He nods, goes down to the restaurant and returns with three glasses and a bottle of Henri's favourite on a wooden tray.

'It was very quick and peaceful at the end,' says Rhi, clutching a fistful of tissues, her nose red and eyes swollen. We are all sitting in the salon, around the circular golden-edged coffee table, with the bottle of cognac on it. We have a glass each, and some coffee, from the brew I put on to give to the *pompiers*. No one has touched their coffee or the biscuits I insisted Fabien bring up with it. It was more of a knee-jerk reaction, an attempt to take the edge off the pain that's almost palpable.

'You should have rung,' I say gently.

'I wanted to,' Rhi says, shredding the tissue and taking a large gulp of her cognac, 'but I couldn't say the words.' She coughs and blows her nose on the shredded tissue. Fabien silently passes her another. 'The hospital contacted his children obviously. They are his next of kin. I spoke to them briefly, told them he hadn't been alone, but I felt like I was talking about someone else. Not Henri. My Henri. I didn't know how to say the words . . . Until now.' She takes a deep breath, says, 'Henri's dead,' and dissolves again. I watch helplessly as my friend's heart breaks in two.

'Where is he now?' I ask, hoping that practicalities will help us negotiate this huge sorrow.

She puts her hand on her large handbag. 'In here,' she says.

'In your bag?'

She nods.

'Like I say, I didn't know what to do. I told his son I would bring his ashes home. We were in Bora Bora at the time. Had to get to New Zealand . . .' she stumbles, swallows '. . . to bring him home.'

'Well, you got yourself here. That was the right thing to do. Do you want to stay here in the apartment or come back to the farmhouse with us?'

'I . . .' She looks as lost as I know she's feeling.

'Stay with us at the farmhouse,' I say, taking control of the situation.

'Oh, I don't know . . . Maybe I should go back to the UK. Back to where I left off before . . .' She takes a shuddering breath.

'Stay,' I insist, wanting to take care of her, wanting us to be together while this news sinks in. 'Stay, just for a while. At least until after the harvest.' I'm thinking on my feet. 'The pickers are arriving soon. I need all the help I can get. Please do.' I try to smile, hoping I'm helping, but it hurts.

She nods and sniffs.

Fabien's phone rings. He looks down at it, rejects the call and pockets the phone.

'I'll give you some time. Maybe have a rest,' I say to Rhi, despite the chainsaws and shouts from the street where I can hear that the olive tree is being removed from the front window. I'm not sure rest will be possible, but maybe some time on her own, with her memories here . . .

I reach out to touch Fabien's hand as I cross to the stairs, trying to process the news. Henri's gone yet everything feels as if he's here, all around us. I run my hand along the wooden wall, almost feeling his presence. Henri is the beating heart of this place, not just of the bistro but of the town. Everything good that happens here is down to Henri. How can he not be alive?

I hear Fabien speak to Rhi, then follow me downstairs, giving Rhi the time she needs in the apartment on her own.

'She's going to have a lie-down and then I'll bring her to the farmhouse,' he says, as he reaches the bottom of the stairs. The smell of the bouillabaisse, which Henri taught me to make, is like a hug. And I feel like falling into Fabien and letting the world around me disappear. He hugs me. A Fabien hug. I want to collapse into sobs and stay in his arms. But I can't. I have to be here for Rhi. And to let others know. He kisses the top of my head, then lifts it a little so our foreheads meet, comforting each other. The time will come soon when we can take in this news together, talk about it, cry, rage at the unfairness. But, right now, we're not ready.

I lean against him. *'Merci,'* I say. Thoughts are whirling in my head. People we need to inform. People who will want to grieve for him, shopkeepers and suppliers, those he's helped, like the people at the riverside clearing. His community.

'I'll go and speak to the mayor and Carine. Do you want me to tell Stephanie or will you?' asks Fabien.

'I will,' I say. I pull out my phone to message her and ask her to meet me at the farmhouse.

'Okay.' He kisses the top of my head again, leaving his lips there for a few seconds. I want to stay in the moment for ever. I close my eyes tightly. But I have to move. There are people who need us right now. We have to stay strong.

He pulls away and, with a glance back at me, leaves from the front door. The tree surgeon and *pompiers* are packing up, pulling off their helmets and jackets as the cold wind has dropped. The air is warmer.

Let's hope the mistral has done with creating havoc now, I think, as I watch him go. My aching heart wants to hold on to everything dear to me, including Fabien.

That night, I fall into bed, exhausted. Rhi is tucked up in the farmhouse too, back in the room she stayed in when she first visited and met Henri. I can hear her snoring – the medication the pharmacist suggested for a good night's sleep must be working.

I could barely get myself to bed. Ralph is curled up in the kitchen. I keep remembering the shock and pain on Stephanie's face when I told her about Henri. She may not be my daughter or younger sister, but she's as close as it gets. She's family and I'm hurting for her. She's lost the man who was a rock for her when she had no family at all. I wish I could take away her pain.

I slide under the light covers, the window open, and outside just the merest whisper of wind in the trees. I can smell the ground where the lavender is planted. It's nearly in flower and the fragrance will soon be here, a scent that never fails to calm me, even the thought of it. But tonight is different. I lie there, thinking about Henri, Stephanie and the shopkeepers who came to speak to me once word had started to spread through the town.

Fabien slides in beside me. I'm usually asleep before he comes to bed, after dropping off a house clearance at the *brocante*. I'm exhausted after an early start with another in the morning.

He runs his hand down my arm, and then across my stomach. But I feel nothing. I know he's trying to comfort me, but I don't know what I want. I feel numb. His hand moves across my body. I'm usually excited and energized by his touch, but not tonight. I kiss him

lightly on the lips and tell him I'm tired. Like so many
other times recently, I turn away, expecting sleep to
come quickly. But not tonight. Tonight I curl into a
ball trying to stop the words running around my head:
Henri is dead. Nothing can change that. Fabien eventually turns away from me, his back against mine.
Something I thought would never happen. Later that
night, when neither of us is sleeping, I hear him leave
the bedroom and head for the spare room next door. I
feel wretched for me, for Fabien, because of Henri.
Maybe Fabien needed holding, comforting. Tomorrow
I'll put it right with him. Tomorrow I'll show him how
much I love and appreciate him. Because I do and I
need to make time to tell him. We need to be there for
each other. I can't let the mistral make any more
trouble than it already has done. They say trouble
comes in threes, but tomorrow I'm going to make sure
nothing happens to affect Fabien and me.

5

I'm awake early. Actually, I'm not sure I've slept. But the first thing I think about is Fabien, who is not beside me. Usually I'm first to slide out of bed and creep away in the early mornings. Then I think of Henri . . . and Rhi. It wasn't a nightmare. Henri really is dead and Rhi is here without him. Then I remember that the pickers will soon be arriving at the farm, and the harvest will begin any day now. I throw back the covers, then the shutters on the window, and breathe in the scent of the early-morning earth, the lavender that is nearly ready to pick.

Then I smell something else, something just as welcome as lavender blossom. Coffee, coming from the kitchen. Someone has beaten me to it. I grab my silk dressing-gown and slide into it as I head down the stairs to the kitchen, drawn by the need to put things right with Fabien.

In the kitchen he's standing with his back to me, on his phone, texting. Ralph jumps up to greet me and I ruffle his big head. He follows me as I walk over to Fabien and slide my arms around his waist.

'*Bonjour*,' I say huskily, my eyes sore from lack of sleep.

He turns to me and I wonder whether there'll be any awkwardness between us, but he puts his arms around me, his face softens, and I reach up to kiss him, then lean my head against his chest.

'I made you coffee. I was about to bring it to you,' he says.

I spot the two mugs on the work surface. '*Merci*. Fabien, about last . . .'

'Sssh, no need for words,' he says, and kisses me again. I start to stir, wishing we could fall back into bed, like we used to if it wasn't a work day . . . sometimes even when it was a work day. It's been a while since we've done that, though.

'Oh, sorry, I didn't know anyone was up already. I just fancied coffee.'

I spin round at the sound of Rhi's voice. 'Come in, grab a seat.' I let go of Fabien, pick up the mug of coffee he's made for me and place it in front of her on the wooden table in front of the French windows.

'I don't want to be in the way here. I could always go and stay at Henri's. Or go back to the UK, stay with one of the kids.' She sits down tentatively, her eyes drawn out towards the rows of purple lavender in the fields outside.

The kids Rhi is talking about aren't kids, even though they're her children. It took Henri's first heart attack, not long after they'd got together, for Rhi to grasp that her grown-up children needed to stand on their own two feet and were perfectly able to do so. She put a manager into her hairdressing salon, then later sold it to her, with the accommodation above, and became nomadic, Henri by her side. The first heart attack had made them realize life was precious and they made the most of it.

I want to make sure Fabien and I do the same. Life has been too busy recently, what with my job at the bistro, his *brocante* business, the lavender farm and helping Stephanie with the children. We need to take some time for ourselves. Once the harvest is in, I decide.

At that moment Stephanie arrives, still visibly upset, and the two children career into the kitchen, one to hug Ralph, the other heading straight for Fabien.

'Oooof,' he says, as Tomas throws himself at his legs, then starts a game of gunfire at him.

Stephanie puts two baguettes and a bag of croissants on the table and gathers plates from the cupboard. 'I saw the bakery van so I brought *le petit déjeuner*,' she says, in her usual no-nonsense, straight-to-the-point way. But I can tell this is her way of coping right now. Sticking to routines. It was the same when Ollie and I split up and I was here alone: routine helped – the bakery van arriving each day, walking with Ralph, then trying to make the next recipe in the lavender cookbook.

Rhi stands up to help Stephanie. Ralph stands by the French windows and I open them to let him out.

I look back at the busy, early-morning kitchen, then to the fields of lavender, nearly in full bloom, and breathe.

It's a clear, bright early morning, as if someone has taken a duster and cleaned the window on the world. It's why painters like Picasso came here to work – the bright colours after the dust has been blown away by the mistral. I step outside and watch the mist creep and curl through the rows of lavender in the field, breathing deeply, trying to control the anxiety that is bubbling just below the surface every time I think of Rhi's words. 'Henri's dead.'

I look towards the orange-tiled roofs in the distance, the town I have come to love, as the church bells ring out for seven o'clock. I watch Ralph bouncing through the lavender field without a care in the world. Then I feel Fabien join me, while inside

Stephanie is preparing breakfast before heading to the unit for a morning of baking. I can hear her occasional sniffs as she makes hot chocolate for the boys, busying herself in the kitchen, where she clearly feels she needs to be.

'I made you more coffee,' Fabien says, in his deep, husky voice, handing me another mug, and I breathe in its aroma, which mingles with the early-morning fragrance. But there's something else in the air, something I can't put my finger on. Words that seem unspoken, hanging between us. Is it still about last night? Or is it that we're lost in our own worlds, which have been shaken, rocked and tipped on their axes by Rhi's news, and we don't know what to say to each other to make it any better? The world seems to have stood still and I'm not sure how we'll get moving again.

'*Merci.*' I smile and take it, grateful for his thoughtfulness.

'Rhi is helping Stephanie with breakfast and the children. Do you want something to eat? You should eat,' he tells me.

I shake my head and rest it against his chest again, breathing in the heady mix of him, already showered and dressed, the lavender and the soil.

'The pickers start arriving over this weekend. It looks like it's going to be a good harvest,' I say. 'I'm just grateful you'll be on hand to oversee them. What with the pickers arriving and Henri . . .'

His phone beeps with a message. I lean away from him and he pulls it out, reads it, types a reply and pushes the phone back into his pocket.

'Who was that?' I ask.

He shakes his head. 'No one.' He looks at the view.

'No one?' I'm intrigued.

He turns his head back to me. 'No one important.' He tilts my chin and kisses me lightly. The phone beeps again.

He tuts.

'Well, it must be someone.' I laugh softly.

He pulls out the phone and types another reply, shoving it back into his pocket. 'Just some old friends.' He waves a hand dismissively. 'Nothing important.'

There's another ping from the phone.

'Well, it must be something fairly important for them to keep messaging you.'

He tuts again, pushes his unruly hair off his face and pulls out the phone once more. This time he switches it off.

I look at him inquisitively.

'It's just . . . the band.'

'The one you used to be in?'

He nods. 'Before I took over the *brocante*. They are re-forming. They have a tour booked. Lots of festivals over the next few weeks. Don't worry, I told them I couldn't do it.'

I smile at the thought of him playing guitar. One of the many we have in the farmhouse that arrived with him when he moved in. He has barely any time to play these days.

'*C'est dommage*,' I say. 'A shame.'

'They got someone else to fill in for me.'

I nod, understanding and feeling disappointed for him.

'But that person has had an accident, broken their collar bone, so,' he holds up the phone and taps it into the palm of my hand, 'they have been . . .' He searches for the right word.

'Badgering you?'

'Badger?' He frowns. 'You and your English words!'

I remember how language was part of the barrier between us when we first met, but also part of the attraction.

'They are chasing me to join them on the tour. They cannot find anyone else.'

I can see he's disappointed, but resigned.

Suddenly I have a flash of, I don't know, inspiration or maybe madness. I think of Henri, how quickly his time was over. Gone. Just like that. The lights have gone out.

'Well, can't you go?'

'What?'

I start to warm to the idea. 'Just for a bit? Until they find someone else? You'd love to play with them again, wouldn't you? You often talk about those days. What is it they say? You only regret the things you don't do.'

He laughs. 'No, I'm needed here. We have the *brocante* and the harvest. And now with Henri . . . there will be a funeral.'

The mention again of Henri's passing makes me even more determined that we should seize the day. I don't know if I'm feeling crazy because I'm sad, in shock or angry, but I suddenly feel really strongly about this. 'You should go!' I say urgently.

'What? No!' He shakes his head. 'We have too much on. You can't do it all by yourself!'

'You loved playing in the band. It was one of the happiest times of your life. You told me!'

He tucks my hair behind my ear. 'Before meeting you, of course.'

'Of course!' I smile.

'That was then, when I was younger. Things are different now.'

But he shouldn't be held back because of me or the farm.

'Fabien. You should go. Text them. Even if it's just until they find someone else.' I point at the phone.

'That's mad!' He laughs. And I feel a little mad. Just like I did when I decided not to return to the UK with

Ollie. But it was absolutely the right thing to do. I've never regretted it. What if Fabien doesn't go and spends his life regretting it?

'Look at Henri! It took his first heart attack to make him realize he had to live life for the now. We have to grab life with both hands! We only live once!'

He's staring at me as if I've gone actually mad now, and that's a little how I feel. I'm furious that Henri isn't here. He's gone. And there was so much more he and Rhi wanted to do. They'd only just met and got going on life. Now Rhi is here, left behind, lost without him.

'He'd want you to go. Henri would be the first person to tell you to do it. I can just hear him telling you to live your best life.'

'But I am, here with you!' He holds the tops of my arms, but I can feel his infectious excitement at the idea of him joining the band, just for a while, one last blast.

I don't know what else to say, so much is going through my mind – the pickers arriving, the harvest, the bistro, Rhi, how we should prepare the funeral . . . Maybe Fabien's right. I'm being ridiculous. The timing is all wrong. Timing usually is. But his eyes are suddenly bright and twinkling, the prospect of what-if. We stare at each other, at a crossroads, a moment in time . . . a sliding door. A what-if. Then his eyes soften, the excitement seeping away. He shakes his head, his dark hair flopping over his forehead.

'Of course I can't go. We have far too much going on here.'

'And what if you don't go? Will you always wish you had?' I say. Will he always resent that he gave up the chance to go back on the road one last time? Last time he gave up life with the band to take over from his grandfather at the *brocante*. This time it's because of me. He can't be with the band, on stage, playing music, because of life here at Le Petit Mas. I can't let him do that for me.

'It's fine. They'll find someone else.' He gives a little laugh. 'I'm not indispensable as a bass player.' He holds his hands across himself as if playing air guitar.

There's only one thing I can say. 'Of course you have to go!' I give him a little shove. 'We need to take something from what's happened to Henri. You have to seize the day.' The tears are backing up behind my eyes but they don't fall. They stay there, making everything blurry and skewed. 'Are they paying? The money will be useful,' I say, a little more bluntly than I mean to. 'When do they leave?'

He looks at me as if I'm joking. 'If it's about the money—'

'No, no. But you said hardly anyone is buying while the town is full of holidaymakers and it's so hot.

People are putting off house clearances until it cools down. It could be useful!' I'm wondering if I've just put my foot in it and made him feel bad about his income. I didn't mean to. 'It's not the money.'

'But it would be useful,' he repeats. He pulls out his phone and switches it on. Another couple of messages come through. 'Yes, they're paying. It's not a lot, but as you say—'

I cut across him. 'It's about seizing the day!'

'But,' he types, 'as you say, I could do with bringing in more than I am right now. Especially with JB's wages to pay.' He types some more, then throws up a hand.

'It's today. They leave today,' he says, with disappointment. 'See? It just wasn't meant to be. They're leaving as soon as they can.'

'Well, then,' I take a deep breath, 'what are you waiting for? You'd better go and pack. And don't forget your guitar!'

'What?'

'Go!' I give him another gentle shove.

He throws his arms out, laughing. 'But the harvest! Henri's funeral!'

'The harvest will happen, one way or another. Isn't that what you've always told me when I get panicky? And it does. And, no, it's not about the money,' I say firmly. 'It's about remembering to enjoy life. To live it! While we can! And once I have the details of the funeral from Rhi, I'll let you know so you can come home for it. No point us both waiting around here for the date.'

He frowns. 'But you need help.'

'I've got Rhi!'

'What's that?' Rhi steps out onto the terrace.

'I was saying I've got you here to help with the harvest. You've done it before.'

'I have, and you have,' she says, roughness in her voice, tiredness. She sips her coffee. 'No plans to go anyway just now. Get up, get through the day, go to bed. Repeat.'

'Fabien is going to rejoin his old band,' I explain to her. 'They're going on tour. They had a replacement bass guitarist, but they've broken their collar bone. So Fabien is going to join them until they find someone else to step in.'

Rhi looks as surprised as Fabien does. 'Good for you! Do it while you can!' Her eyes fill with more tears. Mine sting, but no tears fall. I nod a lot to agree with what she says.

'It'll help with the finances. The *brocante* is very slow at the moment.'

'Good to take the work when we can.'

'It's not about the money!' I say, slightly tetchily. Then, with a deep breath, 'Go, just enjoy the ride.'

Fabien looks at me, then at Rhi and back at me for reassurance. 'You're serious, aren't you?'

'Go!' I say.

He smiles widely and hugs me hard. 'You are incredible, you know that? You are telling me to do this mad, crazy thing because Henri would want me to?'

'Yes! Exactly! You're seizing the day,' I say, barely able to breathe.

'I love you!' he says into my hair, kissing the top of my head.

'And I love you,' I say, slowly releasing him.

'I'll be back for Henri's funeral,' he says, and turns to go inside.

'Just don't stay away too long,' I add quietly, so that only Rhi can hear me as doubt tumbles in and he heads to the stairs. What if I can't do this? What if I can't do everything I need to do?

'That was good of you,' says Rhi.

I hold the back of my hand to my mouth and nose, wondering what on earth I've done. But I know it's the right thing. We have to grab our moments.

'You want him to be happy.'

I nod a lot, unable to speak.

Suddenly there's a cry from inside the house, one of the children.

'Del!' Louis calls out.

Rhi smiles. 'You're needed.'

Inside, Stephanie is trying to tidy and go to work, get Tomas to school and Louis to childcare, and the children are squabbling. I step in to sort out the quarrel over who gives Ralph his morning biscuit. He has two, just to make things fair. By the time Stephanie is ready to leave in the van, with the children ready, Fabien is back downstairs with a battered old holdall and his favourite blue guitar. I explain to her that Fabien has to go away for a bit, but he'll be back soon, in time for the funeral. A little taken aback, she and the children kiss him through the van window and she sets off for town.

I walk with Fabien to his truck. 'I'll leave it parked by the *brocante*,' he says. 'The tour bus will pick me up there.'

I gaze up at him as he wraps his arms around me. I wish we'd made more time for each other before now. I wish I hadn't been too tired last night. I wish we could have comforted each other. I'd thought we'd have time tonight.

'I could stay,' he checks. 'I don't have to do this! It was a crazy idea, but it doesn't have to happen.'

'There's nothing you can do here to make this situation better. I'll find out about a service or funeral. In the meantime, the pickers will be here. Henri would be furious if he'd stopped you doing this. You have to go.'

He nods. I know he feels the same. Just sitting around here waiting for a service to be organized isn't going to help. Doing this will make him feel he's still alive, when his friend isn't.

'I said I'd leave as soon as I could,' he says.

'Yes, of course,' I say, patting his chest softly. 'You need to be on your way.'

'Come with me!' he says, his eyes wide with excitement once more.

'What?'

'Come with me on the tour. You and me, on the road!'

I can't help but laugh. 'Fabien, the pickers! I can't just go!'

'Ask Stephanie to look after them maybe.' He tilts his head and I know he's clutching at straws.

'I can't. She has so much on with baking for the restaurants, the market stall, the little ones to look after and get to school and childcare. And she needs me. She's still in shock about Henri as much as the rest of us. And there's Rhi.'

He nods.

'I know, I know.' He kisses me. 'You are good to them all.' Then he looks me straight in the eyes. 'Will you be okay? You need to take care of yourself too. It's not just the others who will miss him.'

'I'll be fine. I have Rhi here to help. The harvest will be a good distraction for us, just like you going on tour will be for you.'

Suddenly doubt taps me on the shoulder again.

'You'll be fine. You know what to do,' he reassures me.

'But you've always been here before.'

'I will be . . . here.' He holds my hand to his chest, over his heart. 'You can do this.'

'Can I?'

He nods, and gently smiles. 'You can.'

'I wish Henri was here,' I murmur, as the sun begins to rise in the sky. A big ball of orange.

'He will be proud of you.'

'And you!' I smile again.

He pulls open the truck door with a squeak, throws in his holdall and places his guitar on the passenger seat.

There seems to be so much I want to say. Thoughts are tumbling over each other in my head. I want to talk about Henri – I want to ask him more about Henri before I came here. His life before the bistro, his wife, children, the riverside project, and remember how wonderful it was when he and Rhi met. I want to talk about last night: how I felt numb. How I'm scared that we haven't made time for each other lately, that we could drift apart where family life has piled into the space between us. I want to reassure him, be reassured, that we are still us. That we are still the couple who fell in love three years ago. That he's still happy here with me. Maybe I shouldn't have told him to go.

'Maybe you're right. Perhaps I could come with you. Cancel the harvest, forget about it for this year.'

But Fabien is shaking his head gently. 'No, Del, you

were right, it was a silly idea. There are people coming who depend on you. You're needed here. You said so yourself. Henri would hate to think you'd cancelled the harvest because of him.' He repeats my words back to me. 'But, honestly, I don't have to do this.'

'Yes, you do. And you need to go. Life must go on! Henri would be the first to say so. It will be good for both of us. Absence makes the heart grow fonder!' I say, with forced jollity, but knowing it's right. I sniff and rub my itching nose and look up at him.

'This is ridiculous!' he says quietly. 'We have the harvest, businesses to run. Our close friend has just died . . .'

'That's exactly why you should do it! Because you can!'

'Sounds like you want me to go. Is that what you want, for us to be apart?' He looks me in the eye. 'Del, are you asking for a break?'

'No! That's not what I want. I'm trying to do my best here for everyone,' I say. 'Just go! Go! Live every minute!' I'm trying to smile, but the knowledge that Henri isn't able to is building in me like a wave gathering in strength. 'Henri can't. But we can. You have to go because you can.' I'm being torn in two, selfishly wanting him to stay and desperate for him to take this chance. I wish he wasn't going. But I'm also glad he is. It's an adventure. An opportunity. And it would only be a regret if he didn't take it.

'Message me when you get there. Hang on, where is "there"?'

He shrugs. 'No idea. It's all been so quick, I'm not sure of the venues. But I'll let you know.' He leans in and kisses me, tentatively, as if, once again, he's checking in on us. 'I'll be back as soon as I can,' he says, and climbs into the truck next to his guitar. Ralph barks, enraged at not going along for the ride. Fabien calls to him to be quiet and behave, then turns on the engine and reverses. He blows me a kiss as I wave to him, Ralph barking, and leaves in a cloud of cream dust.

'I'll be back as soon as I can,' he says. Something tells me that it won't be soon. It's the right thing, I think. So why do I feel like I've pushed him away? Something is troubling me and making me anxious as I watch the truck disappear, slowly lowering my hand.

He's gone. And I want to call him back to be here beside me for the harvest. To make time for us to be together. But it looks like Fate has other plans right now. There is so much I want to say, so much left unspoken . . . I realize I'm reminded of Ollie driving away from Le Petit Mas. We'd come to the end of the road and it took me insisting that he left and I stayed for him to realize it. What if I've just done exactly the same to Fabien, told him to leave, and he doesn't come back? But this is Fabien, not Ollie. Ollie was having an affair. He went back to another woman. That won't happen with Fabien. I just don't want him to have any regrets about us. Life suddenly seems to have tilted on its axis.

Damn you, Mistral! Damn you!

6

The following morning, Sunday, there's a loud farting, belching noise from the road outside the farm. I don't pay it much attention – there are lots of old tractors about at this time of year. Ralph jumps up from his position in the sun on the floor in the converted barn accommodation where Rhi and I are making beds together. It's a single-storey building with basic bedrooms, a shared bathroom, and a large open area to one side with simple cooking facilities and seating. Fabien and I did most of the work ourselves two winters ago and I'm so proud of it.

My heart twists thinking about Fabien, his text when he arrived at his first gig last night. He sent a selfie from a festival site, somewhere in the Dordogne. He was hoping he could remember all the chords to the songs, and wasn't looking forward to a night in a tent.

He also hoped he could remember how to put up a tent. A lot has changed in his life since he was camping at festivals, he said, and signed off with kisses.

A lot *has* changed, I think. Life has a habit of doing that when you're not expecting it. Just when it seems to be finding its groove, something makes you stop to look back and realize how much has changed. Five years ago I would never have thought this would be my life now, that I'd be divorced from Ollie and living on a lavender farm with a man ten years younger than me, practically a grandmother to two little boys and running a bistro. Things change so quickly, whether you want them to or not.

Working side by side, Rhi and I are lost in our thoughts, hers mostly about Henri, I suspect, and the hole he's left in her life, and mine about how I knee-jerk insisted on Fabien going off with his old band-mates. How could I have been so stupid? It's the last thing I want. I was in shock at Henri's death. And now Fabien's not here when I really, really need him to tell him I love him and love our life together. That's what we should be celebrating, not trying to recapture the past but living in the now. Although he kissed me and told me he loved me, there was something poignant in that moment. Just like when Ollie left. It was as if things were changing for good. I'm wishing we could have tonight to talk about Henri, and about us. I want to know he's happy with me here at the Le Petit Mas de la Lavande. I don't want him to stay with me if he has any doubts about us or the future. I want him to be happy. If I had to, I'd let him go. I'll call him later, tell him how I'm feeling, talk it through with him. I'll feel better once I've done that.

Occasionally a tear falls from Rhi onto the clean white bedding and one or other of us sweeps it away.

It's what Rhi and Henri found in each other that was so special. No long-term promises, just living in the now, no matter who disapproved, like their grown-up children for a start. Rhi's children came round to the idea of her giving up the business and spending some of her hard-earned money but I don't think Henri's ever did. He spoke very little about his children. I don't think he was in contact with them much. Clearly there was history – hurt and sadness on his part.

There's another farting sound and this time Ralph is standing at the door to the room we're in, barking. I go to the open window where the early-morning mist has dispersed, leaving a brilliant blue sky, the sun pushing gloriously upwards. There, coming in through the gate-way at the end of the long drive, I see a little turquoise VW camper van, swaying and lurching, clanking, grinding and pushing out plumes of smoke. Just the sight of it makes me want to cough. Rhi joins me in the doorway of the little bedroom looking out onto the yard.

'Pickers! They're here!' I say, panicked by their arrival.

Although I'm expecting them, I'm not as organized as usual.

'You go. I'll carry on in here,' says Rhi, picking up the mop and cleaning fluid to give the tiled floor a last going-over.

'Thank you,' I say gratefully, totally wrong-footed. Everything would usually be ready in their rooms, towels on the beds, little gifts of cookies, lavender in vases. I would have planned meals for the week too, including the first-night welcome dinner, and have a schedule for the harvest printed, showing where to start picking and more. But between Rhi arriving, Fabien leaving and Henri . . . I haven't planned anything. And I still need to chase up the window repairer for the bistro. I hope nothing's happened to the place over the last couple of nights.

I take a deep breath and step out into the brilliant sunshine, feel its warmth on my skin, comforting as ever, as the vintage camper van crunches and grinds its way to a halt in the middle of the drive.

'Think the clutch has gone,' says a woman of about my age with wild curly hair, leaning out of the driver's window.

I wave a hand, trying to dissipate the smoke coming from the vehicle. Ralph is barking, like it's a great game, and running around it.

'Where shall I park? Not sure it'll move for a while once I cut the engine.'

'Over there.' I point to a space a little further on in the corner of the parking area. 'Do you think you can make it?'

She nods and, with more smoke and grinding and crunching, the van limps and lurches to the spot under the apricot tree where she cuts the engine. Everything goes quiet, apart from the cicadas chirping in the June heat.

'Sorry I'm early,' she says, as she gets out of the van and shuts the door with a bang, making herself jump. 'Just wanted to make sure I actually got here, so I left at first light.'

'Have you come far? I'm Del, by the way.' I hold out my hand to shake hers, then notice mine is quivering and whip it away. 'Sorry, been cleaning.'

'I'm Jennifer. Jen. I was staying on a campsite not too far away but wanted to leave time in case anything happened with the van. Given the number of times it's broken down and I've been delayed for a day or two, I like to plan ahead and keep moving. I worry that if I stop too long, I won't get the old girl going again.' She laughs. 'I mean the van, not me! Already looking into places to go for the autumn and then it'll be Christmas.'

Christmas? It's only June. It's like this woman is wishing the year away.

'Well, I'm glad you've found us,' I say. 'And you're here to help with the harvest.' I'm trying to slip into farm-manager mode. 'It's going to be a hot few weeks, so make sure you're armed with sun cream, water and a hat.'

'I follow the farm on Facebook. I love your posts from here – it's just like I imagined – so I was delighted when you said you were looking for pickers.'

I look back at the farmhouse, a smile tugging at the corners of my mouth. I love this place too. 'Yes, this is the farmhouse. I've been here for three years now. And this is the lavender we're harvesting.' I point towards the field on the other side of the accommodation and the drying barn. We walk slowly towards the field as if drawn by its colour and scent.

'This is beautiful,' she says. As with most people who visit, I see her shoulders drop and relax when she looks out over the field. I do it every morning as the sun rises, heralding a fresh new day.

We stand looking out, just beyond the drying barn, at the deep purple plants, which resemble an intricately embroidered quilt, softly undulating down the hillside, offering comfort and peace. Right now, I could just lie down, shut my eyes and wait for some of that comfort and peace to assail me.

'How does it work?' she asks, breaking me from my thoughts.

'Well, you and the other pickers will be here in the field. We start early in the morning, when the blooms are at their perkiest, to capture all the fragrance. We cut the lavender stems, collect them in bundles and take them to the drying barn just there.' I point to the weatherworn building, dark but with plenty of holes between the joints. 'It looks a bit sorry for itself, but it's perfect for drying the bundles, which need darkness and ventilation. Some people use fans. I just have holes that let in the breeze!' I smile and so does she, staring out across the field to the town beyond, where we can see the church spire, then the terracotta roofs of the houses and shops around it.

'And what about oil? Do you make that? How about soap?'

'Not yet. That's next. We hope to get a still, maybe for next summer if this harvest does us well. Then we'll start to do oil, candles, soap and cleaning products. Lavender is so good for so many things . . . Well, make yourself at home. We're expecting people to arrive at any time from now until tomorrow, ready for the picking, which should start any day.' I step forward and break off a head of the lavender. *Nearly there*, I hear someone say in my head. *You've got this*. And I swear it's Henri's voice. I give a little cough and clear my throat.

'I'm going to have to find out what's happened to my van and how to fix it.' Jen looks back at it. 'Maybe try to order a new clutch online.'

'That's impressive,' I say.

'Necessary! Giving up your house to be a digital

nomad in a 1950s splittie isn't for the fainthearted. And you're happy for me to park here and settle in?'

'Of course. This is where the camper vans usually are. Some people come with tents and set up over there.' I point. 'But this has the best views.'

'It certainly does.'

'Well, I'll leave you to it,' I say. 'My partner, Fabien, is the one who knows about cars and the like but he's . . .' I search for the words '. . . away at the moment.' And that's perfectly reasonable, I tell myself. He's just away for a bit, until a new guitarist is found. He's working away from home. It's all fine. And it's not like the money won't be welcome. It will. He said so himself. I know he'll feel better about earning something, with the *brocante* bringing in so little at the moment. He needs to pay JB's wages. Without my wages from the bistro, things would be very tight. So . . . Del, stop worrying about Fabien. He's just away for a bit. He'll be home soon, with no regrets, and life will get back to normal.

'Is there anything you need or that I can do to help?' I ask, trying to focus on my guest. 'Although, as I said, cars and what goes on under a bonnet are not my forte!'

'I have everything I need in here. My whole life in one place.' She smiles, although this time it doesn't quite reach her eyes. 'Plus I have Google, and a fair bit of experience of this old girl!' I watch her open the side door, then bring out a small folding table and a chair, a washing-up bowl and a drying rack with her washing on it, settling in, like Stephanie did in her caravan, bit by bit.

'I'll leave you to it,' I say.

'Got everything I need. I won't be any bother. Look forward to meeting the others when they arrive tomorrow. I've plenty to be going on with.'

I'm not sure what she means, but I leave her to it, relieved to get away. I don't have any small-talk just now. What could I say? One of our best friends has just died, and I sent my partner off to join the band he used to play with in a moment of madness and grief?

With that, Rhi and I finish off the bedrooms in the barn. Later, as the day starts to cool, I check on the lavender again, Ralph bounding through the rows as the sun sets over the purple fields. I bend to break off another stem and examine it. I hear his voice again: *Nearly there.* The buds are just starting to flower, so that by the time we pick, some will be fully open and others not quite. This field will be ready first, and the second lot on the other side of the slope. When we finally get a distillery, I'll keep half of the field for drying and half for turning into oil. But not yet. There's no spare cash to buy the still or create a workshop for a bottling unit. Who knows? Maybe after Fabien's stint on the road with the band, a good harvest, and a busy summer at the bistro, things will look better by the autumn and we can think about it then for next year. Something to look forward to!

I pick off another head of lavender, roll it in my palm and hold it to my nose as I walk back to the farmhouse. *Nearly there*, I hear again, and this time I know he's right. It's nearly there. This is where I need to be right now. Here, among the lavender plants. And the lavender needs me. Right now, it feels good to be needed.

Come Monday morning, it's a rush. Jen spent yesterday lying beneath her camper van raised up on axle stands in the shade of the apricot tree. She's barely surfaced. I've offered her drinks and baguettes, but she hasn't left the van. This morning she's searching the internet, apparently for a new clutch.

'I have to go to the station soon to pick up some others,' I tell Rhi and Stephanie, who is there with the children, 'and meet the glazier at Henri's. The blooms are nearly ready for picking and drying. We'll need to start tomorrow. Maybe I should get Serge to check them.' He had taught me about lavender. He had a farm in the area but wanted to retire and had passed on plants, with advice, to me. Fabien had introduced us. 'God, I wish Fabien was here. I wish Henri was here, too.' I feel a wobble. 'He'd know!'

Rhi steps forward. 'He'd tell you to trust your instinct,' she says, taking my elbows.

My hands fly to my eyes, which bunch tightly shut. I push my fingers into the sockets to stop any leakage. I can't crack now. Rhi puts her arms around me, as does Stephanie, then Tomas and finally little Louis. We stand for just a moment and I pull myself together. I remember being in the field yesterday and hearing Henri's voice.

'Look at what you've achieved here! When you realized you and Ollie were over and, rather than returning home, you stayed with nothing,' Rhi says. 'Just the empty shell of a house in a country where you barely spoke the language. With a daft dog for company. Look at how you dug deep then, made a life for yourself, Stephanie and Tomas.'

'She's right,' says Stephanie, in her usual no-nonsense way. She's packing her bag before she takes Tomas to school. She's already been baking at the unit, ready for the market today. 'You should listen to Rhi.'

'Remember when Lou and I came to find you to see if you'd gone crazy?' Rhi says. 'And there you were, firmer in your mind than I'd ever known you! You were divorcing Ollie and staying put. Then you started baking with the lavender from the cookbook.'

'It was the cookbook that saved me. One recipe, one day at a time. And Henri who sorted me out with the market stall.'

'And then me,' says Stephanie, waving the lavender cookbook I'd found in Fabien's *brocante* when I was trying to source cheap furniture, something to sit on, sleep on and eat with. I couldn't afford the book, or the dressing-gown I'd seen, but Fabien gave them to me as a moving-in present.

'It was the lavender that saved us both,' I say to Stephanie, and once again, I feel a swell of pride for the woman she has become.

'And now let's hope it sets us on the right path again, starting today,' says Rhi, gently.

'You have a harvest to bring in,' says Stephanie, less gently. 'We need the lavender for the baking.' Without it, she will have to buy in lavender from elsewhere. The whole business is reliant on the farm and the lavender we grow here, which we sell to tourists at the market, to the restaurateurs and cafés who provide baked goods to their customers. Stephanie makes ice cream and sorbet, biscuits and desserts. We need the lavender. I pull myself up as tall as I can.

'Big-girl pants on!' I say to Rhi.

'Absolutely! You can do this! Just tell me how I can help.'

'And me.' Stephanie softens.

'*Et moi*,' says Tomas.

Tears prick my eyes as I bend to hug him. This is what I need. I can do this, I hope. Everyone else seems to think I can. I'm not so sure . . . With Fabien away for

I don't know how long, and without Henri to guide and help . . . The only thing I can do is give it my best. I told Fabien I could. And I will.

Suddenly the day is busy, collecting pickers from the station and walking them back to the farm, fetching others from the bus stop, and booking a taxi to wait for a delayed flight.

They're an eclectic bunch, I think, as I hurry from the farm to meet the glazier, who is to price up the new window, and explain to the signwriter the lettering I want to replicate what was already there, in gold, *Bistrot Henri*. I visibly reel when the glazier tells me the cost of the new window. I have no idea where the insurance documents are. I left those details to Henri. They'll be in his desk somewhere, I suppose. I should've asked. He kept saying he'd sort it all out when he was home next. Everything happened so quickly when he left and I took over the kitchen. His paperwork is a shocking mess. It all needs to be gone through. But the window has to be done. I need it replaced quickly so I can be up and running again. Maybe there won't be a still for making oil this year. I'm using all of my savings, my safety net, to fix the window. I'll look out the insurance paperwork once the window is in.

I'm standing on the street outside the bistro, looking down at the quote in my hand. The glazier is

Jo Thomas

packing away his tape measure and making a final note on his iPad.

'Del!'

I look up the cream-stone-lined cobbled street and see my friend, the local estate agent, walking towards me holding her little daughter Clémentine's hand.

'Carine!' I call. We kiss each other warmly. The little girl asks to be picked up and sits on Carine's slim hips.

'How is everything?' Carine says. 'How are you?' she adds, concerned. 'Fabien said he was going on tour with the band.' She frowns. 'Surely it's not a good time for him to be away.'

I take a deep breath. 'I told him to go. I thought it was what he wanted. To rejoin the band one last time. It was . . . What with Henri going, just like that, I thought he should grab the chance.'

She raises her eyebrows and pouts. 'He loved the band. He hated leaving when he came here to take over the *brocante*. But he loves the *brocante* too. I suppose he must miss the music, though. I can feel Henri smiling at the idea of him playing again.'

I nod a lot. 'That's what I thought. At first he wouldn't go. But I told him he had to, for Henri, and . . .' I trail off. She raises a perfect questioning eyebrow again. 'I just thought it would be good for him to check in on himself. Isn't that what they say, these days?' I give a little laugh. 'I worry. Worry about, oh . . . you know, lots of things. I wish I felt I wasn't holding him back in

64

some way. Most of Fabien's friends are only just getting married, having babies. He's skipped that part and gone straight to being a sort of grandfather.'

'And he loves it!' She puts a hand on my arm to reassure me. 'You have to stop over-thinking this! He wouldn't be with you if he didn't love you. What's brought this on?'

'I don't know. Life just seems to be going so quickly at the moment. I want it to slow down. I want Fabien and me to take some time for each other, just to enjoy life.'

'You need to get yourself to Beatrice at the chemist. Get some peri-menopausal treatments, start taking collagen.' She nods sagely. 'It'll be your hormones. For sure.' She looks down at my nails. 'And get a manicure too.'

I laugh. 'I have the harvest to bring in. After that I'll get my nails done. I promise.'

'Good. And get some treatments from the chemist. They will help.' She shifts Clémentine effortlessly to the other hip. I love the way this single woman about town has slid into motherhood. Mother and daughter, they're like something out of a photoshoot for a magazine.

'I never heard the band,' I say. 'He was finished with it by the time we met. He only plays guitar for fun these days, and there's not much time for that with the businesses. What are they like?' I ask.

'They're great! Well, they were. A really tight group.

Mostly jazz, and jazzy versions of newer songs. Jean Paul is on the keyboard, Dante on double bass, Monique on saxophone and vocals, she's amazing, and Fifi on lead guitar. Fabien plays bass and . . . how do you say? . . . mouth organ.'

'Ah, yes, the harmonica! He loves it, and Tomas loves to hear him play it. He's been teaching him too.'

'That's sweet. Good for you persuading him to go. Especially with . . .' She indicates the boarded-up window, and a wave of loss washes over me. 'With everything going on at the moment, it's good to keep busy.' She shifts Clémentine on her hip. 'What about Rhi? And you? You okay?'

'Well, I think Rhi is still in shock. She's staying with me for the harvest. The pickers are here, all except one whose flight has been delayed.'

'So the harvest will happen.'

My chest tightens. Suddenly everything seems impossible. Things I took for granted. It'll be an uphill struggle.

She reaches for my hand, understanding how I feel. 'And tell me, the pickers, are they a nice group?' she says, as if she's trying to dissipate my rising anxiety.

'They seem so. We have Jen from West Wales. She's a digital nomad.'

'What's that?'

'It means she travels and can work from anywhere, as long as she has good Wi-Fi.'

'Good job you got yours upgraded at Le Petit Mas.' She giggles.

'Then there's an older couple from England, Graham and Keith. They got the train. They're on a gap year, apparently.'

'Isn't that something young people do between leaving school and going to university?'

'Yes,' I agree. 'They're Interrailing, like when they were young, or maybe it was just one of them.' The facts are a bit blurry from the conversation we had on the walk from the station where I met them.

'Then there's a young woman, Maria, whose flight is delayed. She's always wanted to see Europe, according to her emails. She's flying from Australia with her boy-friend. I've given her instructions to get here. They'll take a cab and I've told her their accommodation is ready and waiting for them. And there's Ed, who I met from the bus stop. He made his own way here from the airport. Not sure where he flew in from.'

'That's quite a mix! What are you cooking for their welcome dinner?' she asks.

'Oh, God! Dinner! I still haven't thought about it!' I clutch my hands to my head. First-night dinner is a tradition. But, somehow, the excitement isn't there like it usually is. It's different.

'What? But you always plan a first-night dinner!' Carine and I stare at each other, dismayed that I could have dropped such a big ball.

She steps forward and hugs me. 'It'll be fine. You'll think of something. You always do.'

I hug her back, the kind of hug that says so many things yet to be voiced.

Back at Le Petit Mas, it's quiet. Everyone is settling in and taking in their new surroundings. It's hot. People are in their sleeping quarters, perhaps having naps after their journey. I put down my bags in the kitchen where Ralph is lying on the cool, tiled floor. I check my phone for messages and find one from Fabien, letting me know about the festival and where they're moving on to next. I send kisses and love, happy that he's happy, spending time with his old friends in the band. Then I check the weather forecast on my phone. It's hot and getting hotter over the next week. We'll have to pick early in the mornings while it's still cool. At least there's no rain in sight.

Then I unpack the shopping. I look at the ingredients on the work surface and, once again, my brain turns to mush, like wet newspaper.

'Beef thingy!' I say out loud, trying to shake the fuzz that's descended. 'This is ridiculous,' I say, more quietly, to myself. 'Beef *daube*. Come on! You make it every week!'

It's always beef *daube* for the welcome dinner. Just as Henri taught me. Feeds a crowd, filling and restorative for those who have had long journeys.

I put my head in my hands. Just start, Del! But I can't. I'm just staring at the ingredients in front of me. And I should have put it on hours ago. What was I thinking? Clearly nothing! I have to do something. I can't remember how I usually make this. I go to Google and follow a recipe from a well-known site there. It's not the same, nowhere near, but at least it's something. I mix the ingredients together and put it into the oven, then head upstairs for a short nap, closing the shutters, turning on the fan, and fall into the heaviest sleep.

I wake feeling totally bleary. My brain's a fug. I'm disoriented. Like I've climbed out of a deep pit and am trying to work out where I am. I'm in my bedroom. It's late afternoon. Fabien is away and Henri is dead. Then I smell it . . . I throw back the thin sheet I've been sleeping under, rush downstairs, open the oven door and pull out the casserole. The lid clatters to the floor.

'Ouch! Bollocks!' I shove my burned hand under cold water. Smoke is pumping from the oven and the pot and the smell of burning fills the air. And then the smoke alarm goes off.

I wave a tea-towel vigorously with one hand, as Ralph barks and the alarm beeps at me, telling me what I already know. I've ruined dinner. It's a disaster. My other hand is wrapped in a second, damp, tea-towel. I pull over a chair, climb onto it and wave again at the smoke alarm. Eventually it stops. I sigh and climb down, my whole body feeling like a lead weight.

I look at the clock on the wall, another of Fabien's *brocante* finds. It's nearly six. The pickers will be arriving on the terrace any minute. I told them to come for drinks at six, dinner at seven. And now I don't have the makings of dinner at all.

'Think, Del! Think!' I say out loud, annoyed with myself.

Rhi comes into the kitchen. She's clearly been out walking – there's lavender in her hand – and her eyes are red.

'You okay? You're hurt!' She rushes to get some ice from the freezer, puts it into the tea-towel and hands it back to me. 'What happened?'

I nod to the dried-up burned offering on the side, creating an imprint of its own on the wooden surface.

'You burned it?' She looks confused, then changes tack. 'Everyone can have an off day. There's a lot to think about,' she continues. 'We're all in shock still. It's not just me.'

'Yes,' I say, trying to work out what I can rustle up to cook. But it's like wading through mud in wellies.

'What can I do to help?' Rhi asks. I hear doors closing from the stable block and voices coming towards the house.

'Um, give everyone a drink. I told them to meet up on the terrace at six. Make sure there's wine and beer . . .' I say distractedly, still unsure of where to start with dinner.

'It'll be fine. We can do this together. As Henri would say,' she says, and at the sound of voices arriving on the terrace she hurries out to serve drinks.

'Blimey, something smells burned! Hope that's not dinner!' I hear a young Australian male voice. That must be Marco.

Followed by a shush.

'He's not wrong. That doesn't smell good!' says another, more English, voice. I screw up my eyes, wishing the tears would just come and fall. But they don't.

I look at the mess in the casserole.

Rhi comes back in from offering drinks. I'm still staring into the pot.

I open the fridge for inspiration. It doesn't come.

'I'm starving.' I hear Marco's voice again. 'Hoping for some proper French nosh.'

'I've got some crisps in my backpack,' someone else says. Maybe Maria, his partner.

I look back at the stew and wonder if I can rehydrate it with wine, maybe some tinned tomatoes. I try it and put on rice to steam. Rhi pours me a glass of wine and I drink it quickly. She refills it, and I drink that too.

'Best top them up outside, so they don't notice,' I say, as I chip at the *daube*. It's almost beyond resuscitation. I stare into space, just glued to the spot. 'Come on, Henri. Trust my instinct – isn't that what everyone keeps saying? I'm trying here!'

It's gone eight by the time I put some overcooked stodgy rice and my attempt at rehydrating the *daube* on the table to everyone's dismayed faces.

The young Australian frowns as I serve up plates of gloop. 'We were promised home-cooked meals! Who made this? It looks cooked to death!' he says, glaring at me.

'Sorry, there's been a—' With that Rhi flees the table, a few glasses of wine and a bucketful of grief swilling around inside her.

'Actually, I'll just have rice,' says Maria, glaring at her partner.

'Well, you can't say this was what was promised on the website.'

'I'm sure it'll be lovely,' says Ed, the Englishman, bravely attempting it.

'More wine, anyone?' says one of the gay couple, picking up the jug and pouring it into people's glasses.

The meal, if you can call it that, is awkward and silent as I attempt to scrape the meat from the bottom of the pan.

'I'm sorry,' I say. 'I haven't organized a dessert. I would usually.'

'No problem,' they all say, standing quickly, ready to leave as soon as politely possible.

'I've got a Twix in my van,' says Jen. 'Happy to share.'

'I've still got those crisps,' says Maria.

'Think I could do with another glass of wine to wash away the taste,' says her partner.

'I have maple cookies,' says Keith.

'Right, well, thanks for the meal,' says Ed, standing. 'I'll turn in.'

'Yes, and us,' says Graham, also standing. He's very tall. His husband is very short. Graham is thin and neatly dressed. Keith is wearing a Hawaiian shirt that strains over his round belly.

'And me,' says Jen, sounding concerned.

With that, they take their plates to the kitchen, then wish me a good night and go to their accommodation.

And suddenly it's just me, sitting on the terrace, looking at Ralph. 'Well, I think we can safely say that was an utter disaster,' I tell him. I wish Fabien were here. It would have gone so much better. And Henri. Why the bloody hell did he have to leave us like this?

I pour another glass of wine, then abandon it and decide to go to bed. So much for trusting my instincts. I clearly can't. I change my mind about the wine and drink it anyway.

In bed, my phone lights up with a message from Fabien. *How's things? How was welcome dinner? X*

Could be better, I manage to reply. *How's things with you?*

Good. Great even. How is Rhi? He adds a sad emoji.

Not good. She left dinner early. Went to bed. But I don't think she's sleeping. I can hear her moving around.

Then I start to type. Delete it. Think. And start to type again. I'm going to have to tell him. *I can't do this on my own, Fabien. I'm going to cancel the harvest.*

He replies straight away: *You can't. You have to do it. Keep going. People are depending on you. You know that's what Henri would say. The harvest is the one thing we can all rely on right now. You've got this.* Before I can type back, he sends another message: *I have to go. Off for a catch-up with the band xx*

I really haven't got this. And what does he mean, the harvest is the one thing we can rely on?

I hold the phone to my lips, wishing he was here to ask him.

I don't know if I can do it. But there's no reply, he's clearly put his phone away. And there in the dark, to the sound of the cicadas outside, I'm ready to cry until there are no tears left, the pillow wet. I don't know if they're for Henri, or for Fabien, who is a million miles away right now. But they don't come. And that's how I spend most of the night, staring at the ceiling, wishing the wretched tears would fall.

7

The next morning I have no idea if I slept at all. I'm awake with the birds. My pillow is dry as are my tired, sore eyes. And I have a banging headache. But I can smell the lavender. I slide out from under the light covers and walk to the window in the blast of air from the fan and push open the shutters, just as I do every morning. The warm, scented air fills my lungs and my soul. I think about Rhi, and Stephanie, both hurting right now, and Fabien too, missing such a big person from their lives. I look at the lavender and the early-morning mist weaving its way through it. It helped me through a difficult time once before, I remember, breathing in its heady fragrance. Let's hope it doesn't let me down now.

I have a farm full of pickers, waiting to pick. Fabien is right. I can't let everyone down. It's the last thing

Henri would want too. These people deserve an explanation about last night.

I get dressed in an old T-shirt and shorts, working clothes for the day ahead, and go down to the kitchen. I pour a large glass of water, take two painkillers and swallow them. I turn on the coffee machine, then grab my purse and run down the long drive to meet the bakery truck.

I buy an armful of baguettes and a large bag of freshly baked croissants. The bakery-van owner, Adèle, talks about Henri and how much a part of the community he was. She asks me to let her know when the funeral will be. 'We must live every day to the full,' she says to me, 'but also be prepared for life to be turned upside down.'

I head back up the track, the lavender either side of me waving in the light breeze as if it's cheering me on, putting purpose into my steps.

Back in the kitchen, the coffee is nearly ready, filling the kitchen with some sense of normality. I grab a pile of plates and cups and take them outside to the terrace.

Stephanie arrives in her van and walks over to meet me on the terrace.

'*Bonjour!*' We kiss each other and little Louis. Tomas has gone to school with JB, his father.

'I came to see how you are,' she says.

I shrug. 'How are you?'

'Sad,' she replies.

'I know.' And I hug her. 'Me too. But he's here with us. He'd want us to get this harvest in, and that's what we're going to do.'

She nods. 'He would. I'll come to help after I've done my deliveries.'

'You don't have to. You could have some time off, with the bistro still closed.'

'I want to. Like you say, it feels as if he's here, with all of us, and I want to hold on to that. With the bistro shut, this seems like the closest I can get to him, with Rhi and his friends, looking at the town he loved.' We gaze out at the roofs and the bell tower on the church where the bells chime.

My throat prickles, but still no tears come. 'Let's get the pickers ready. Breakfast, then work.'

We go round and tap on all the doors of our pickers in the barn and Jen's camper van to let them know that breakfast has arrived.

'Hi, Ed. Breakfast on the terrace.'

'Maria? Marco?'

'Keith and Graham?'

I knock on each of their doors in the barn.

They all seem wary, and I'm guessing they're wondering what kind of burned offerings I'm going to serve up this morning. Hopefully, the buttery, flaky croissants, still warm baguettes, with pale unsalted butter and homemade myrtle and apricot jam, will be just what they need.

'I feel I owe you an explanation,' I say, holding my coffee cup against my chest, which is still tight with tension. I breathe in the restorative steam, which evaporates like the early-morning mist as the group sit around the table, helping themselves to the croissants and bread.

'Not for me. I think I'm slightly gluten intolerant,' says Graham, holding up a hand as the basket is passed round.

'Oh, sorry, I should have asked,' I say, kicking myself. Usually I would.

'It gives him gas,' says Keith, matter-of-factly.

'Keith! Do you have to be so graphic!' snaps Graham.

'Mind if I have yours, then, mate?' Marco says politely, and reaches for another croissant. 'Starving after missing dinner last night.' And I see everyone cringe at the reminder of last night's disaster.

'I was just explaining!' Keith looks hurt, and Graham is cross as he brings out a packet from his rucksack.

'I have my own crispbreads, thank you,' he says, ignoring Keith. They shuffle on the bench, turning slightly away from each other.

'I should've thought,' I say again apologetically. Keith and Graham look like they're not speaking to each other. I want to make this better – make it fun, like it always has been.

I look at the dissipating mist from the lavender. If only my brain fog would clear in the same way. 'Like I said, I owe you an explanation for yesterday.'

'No, no, really,' says Maria.

Ed shifts uncomfortably in his seat.

But I know I owe them an explanation. Before I can say anything, though, Marco butts in. 'Well, you did promise on the Facebook page we'd be fed well,' he says, smiling, clearly trying to make light of the situation and tossing a hunk of buttered bread into his mouth. But far from making things better I feel everyone shift uncomfortably. Graham and Keith scowl at him.

He's right, though. And usually they would be. But nothing about these last few days has been usual.

'The thing is, we've had some bad news. A member of our community. A friend. A partner.' I look at Rhi, who's very pale. 'A soul mate.' We manage a tiny smile, a reminder that it's okay to think happy thoughts about Henri, not just the big sad one. 'You could say our family. He's died.' My throat tightens, and I take a big gulp of coffee. For a moment no one says anything.

'Does that mean you're going to cancel the harvest?' says Marco, tossing more bread into his mouth. 'I mean, I'm sorry and all that, only we've got a schedule we need to stick to.'

'Oh, no!' says Keith, looking as upset as if he'd known Henri personally.

'We'd totally understand if you did,' Graham says,

spreading butter on his crispbreads and putting his knife neatly beside his plate.

'I need to get the new clutch sorted before I can move on.' Jen is clearly worried.

'Our next stop isn't for another three weeks,' Marco says. 'But there doesn't look like there's much to do around here if we're not picking.'

'Sssh.' Maria taps his forearm. At first he seems bemused, then slowly reads the others' faces and closes his mouth.

'No, no.' I raise my hands. 'Someone pointed out to me that the one thing I should be doing right now is the harvest. It's the one thing we can rely on at the moment.' I look at Rhi and attempt another smile. She sends a watery one back.

'So, have breakfast, drink your coffee and meet me up there.' I point to the field where the mist is lifting and the sun is rising. 'There's a hut where I'll hand out secateurs and explain everything to you. We'll be cutting the lavender into bundles, tying them and getting them up to the barn where we'll hang them to dry. I think a morning in the lavender field could be what we all need. It's a beautiful place to be,' I say, with a smile. Because it is.

'Yes!' They seem cheered.

I stand up and take my coffee to the edge of the field to inspect the blooms there. Rhi follows me. 'It's time,' I say, running my hands over them. I lift my hand to my nose, remembering what Serge from the neighbouring farm had taught me when I started with a few of his plants here. 'Too early and we won't get the full scent. Too late and buds will drop from the dried bundles,' I say, picking one of the stems and sniffing it. Everything is changing. Serge has retired and Henri has gone.

'The harvest is the one thing right now we can rely on. Come rain or shine, good year, bad year, it will keep coming round,' I say, still inspecting the blooms, putting all my focus there, in the moment. It's the only way forward.

I hear Fabien's voice in my head: *Henri wouldn't have wanted you to let these people down. They've come to work . . . food and lodgings. Where else would they go right now?*

I'm clutching my cup. Ralph barks.

'It'll be fine,' Rhi says.

'I know. Fabien said so too.'

We wander slowly over the stony ground between the rows of lavender.

'Is everything all right between you two?' she asks.

I stop and turn to her and she looks at me, puzzled. 'I . . .' I hesitate. 'I'm not sure,' I finally answer. This harvest, this sunrise, are the only things I'm really sure of.

'I wish I hadn't told him to go. It's my fault he's not here. I pushed him away, told him to go on the tour.

And I really wish I hadn't. I told him the money would be useful and I didn't mean it like that. I was just looking for a way of persuading him that it was okay to go.'

'And now he's there?' she asks.

'And now he's there . . . I think he quite likes it.' I look at Rhi. 'I miss him. I want him to come home.'

She stares at me. I know she doesn't have the answers.

'Come on,' says Rhi, eventually. 'Let's get this harvest in. It's the only thing we can do. We'll do it together. It's what Henri would have said.'

8

'So, we're picking this section first.' I gesture to the sunniest spot at this time of the morning, at the bottom of the undulating field that rolls from the farmhouse, the terracotta terrace, towards the river. I can hear it murmuring as it meanders towards town, out of sight from here, but in the distance, I can hear the bells telling us it's time to work. The smell is amazing, filling my head and lifting my heart. 'It's just about to bloom. We'll collect it into bundles and they will go into the barn to be dried. It'll be used as food flavouring and sold in bunches at the market.' I pick off a few heads and pass them around for the pickers to smell. There, among the rows of lavender, with the early-morning mist lifting, the sun climbing into the sky, the scents of the warming soil, the lavender, the wild rosemary along the border, and the swallows circling overhead, I feel centred, where I belong. 'Lavender is good for so many things, not just as part of the *herbes de Provence* we use in cooking here that give the local food such a distinctive flavour. It's also good to aid sleep, but also for headaches, burns, spots, stings and bites. It's used in creams, lotions, bath products, and even gets rid of the smell of pets in your home.' I manage a smile as Ralph barks, then pants, as I give my usual talk, everything I learned from Serge and the internet. I can feel the sun on my face and the joy in my heart that this place has brought to me. It feels good to be here, doing the harvest, focusing my energy on it.

Stephanie waves as she leaves the farmhouse via the terrace to head out for her restaurant deliveries. I wave back, as if this was just another harvest. Although I know it's not. The mistral seems to have changed that.

'You use the secateurs to cut. Cut about an inch up the stem. That way, the lavender will grow back and keep blooming.'

'How big is an inch?' I hear Marco ask. 'And how long are we going to be out here?'

'Ssh.' Maria frowns.

'Drink water, wear hats, and ask me if you're not sure about anything,' I tell them. 'I have to go into town, but text me if you need me. We'll finish at lunchtime. It'll be too hot to pick then. The afternoon's your own.'

*

As the pickers start working in the field with Rhi as part of the gang, gathering the cut lavender into bunches ready for hanging along the beams in the barn, I tell her I'm going to nip into town to pick up lunch – cheese, pâté and ripe tomatoes for a salad. At least I can't get that wrong.

But, after the walk into town, when I'm standing outside the greengrocer, I'm staring into space again. Nothing excites me. I have no appetite. I pick up the tomatoes, lift one after another to my nose, but can't seem to enjoy their grassy scent. I'm met by sad eyes and condolences from Gilles, the shopkeeper, asking if I know the arrangements for Henri's funeral service. I offer him the same condolences. Henri was everyone's friend as well as mine. It's the same in the cheese shop: they want to know when and where the service will take place and ask after Rhi. I need to talk to her about what should happen. Everyone wants to know about the funeral. It seems the town will be at a standstill until we can have a service and come to terms with him being gone.

With a basket full of cheese, pâté and ham, the makings of salad and more bread, my feet automatically lead me to the bistro.

I come to a stop outside, my shopping trolley standing beside me, a faithful companion. The window is still boarded up and I check my phone. No news on when the window will be fixed. I've agreed to the estimate, even though it made my eyes water and cleared out my bank account. I need to get into Henri's desk and start looking for the insurance paperwork.

I rummage for my keys in my bag and let myself in. It feels dark and cool, against the heat of the day outside. The boarded-up window makes it darker than usual. It feels . . . dead, without the usual smells coming from the kitchen, the sound of pots and pans in use, the deliveries arriving and people popping in for coffee, a glass of *petit rosé*, then lunch starting at midday. It's like a shell. The sooner I can get the window sorted the better.

I walk upstairs to the apartment and go to the desk. I open one of the drawers. Chaos. Papers, paperclips, a packet of Marlboro cigarettes and a half-eaten chocolate bar. I pull out the other drawers. They're in much the same state. It'll take a lot of work to go through Henri's 'filing system'. But not now. I can't get lost in his papers now, or I'll never be back in time for lunch. This is something Rhi and I should do together.

I go back downstairs, staring at the photographs on the wall. In the restaurant I pick up the reservations book and put it into my bag to take home with me. I'll make sure I contact everyone in it. Henri's is closed for the time being.

I go to the freezer and pull out the bouillabaisse I didn't use when the olive tree hit the window. At least there will be dinner for the pickers this evening. Then

I find a piece of paper and a pen and write on it: '*Fermé pour les vendanges*. Closed for the harvest.' I add my mobile number for enquiries. At least by the time the harvest is done, the new window should be in place and we can reopen. I'll need to. With the window to pay for, until I can find the insurance details, and the pickers to cook for, my bank account is stretched and I'm using the small overdraft facility. I need to get back into that kitchen and start bringing in some money.

I write out another sign, step out of the bistro and pull the door to behind me. Then I head up through town, past the *brocante*. I check in on JB, Stephanie's husband, giving him a baguette for his lunch from the local sandwich shop. It's filled with sliced salami and salad, which I know he'll pick out. I tell him I'm not sure how long Fabien will be away for but reassure him that it won't be long.

'Everyone is asking about a funeral for Henri,' he tells me, picking out the salad, then biting into the salami sandwich.

'That isn't far away either,' I tell him. 'I'll get Rhi to start sorting things. Give the children a kiss from me,' I add, as I leave the walled courtyard where furniture and bric-a-brac are piled up. They will be moved into the building at the end of the day and put out again tomorrow morning. It's heavy work for little reward at the moment, but Fabien would never think of closing.

Part of me starts to feel better. He'll be back soon and the bistro will be open again. Everything will soon return to how it was. Then, with my full trolley and the bouillabaisse, I stroll along the riverbank to where the project began, to the little hut there, the blue velvet sofa that I thought was an art installation and has now been replaced by various other chairs that people wanted to pass on to those who were without a home of their own. It looks beautiful, with festoon lighting hanging from the huge branches of the larch tree.

A couple of people are playing chess in the shade of the tree. I greet them and they say how sorry they were to hear about Henri and ask about the funeral. I tell them I'll let them know as soon as I can. Then, wishing them a good day, I pull out the note from my handbag and pin it to the shed door, explaining that the riverside kitchen will be closed until after the harvest. Once the bistro is open again, I'll be back, bringing the daily *plat du jour* after service has ended. Until then, with no food coming out of the bistro, there's no leftover *plat du jour*. I feel wretched, but with the bistro shut, there's nothing I can do. It won't be for long. Just until after the harvest.

Then I return to the farm to serve up bread, cheese, pâté and tomato salad. I cringe at the memory of last night's dinner. At least tonight will be better, with the pot of bouillabaisse in my shopping trolley.

*

After lunch the pickers help to clear up. I don't eat much, and neither does Rhi. But the pickers enjoy the food. The rest of the day is theirs as it's far too hot to work in the field. Jen heads for her camper van, puts her laptop on the little table and sits on one of the chairs she placed under the tree. Graham and Keith head for their room for a siesta. Marco, the Australian, wants to find a bar. Ed is heading into town too. Maria looks up bus timetables. She wants to explore the countryside.

'There's my old bike, if that's any help?' I offer. 'But I only have one.'

'That would be great!'

Marco rolls his eyes. 'Can we just go and have a beer or three? I'm parched,' he says testily. 'All this tramping around the place, it's doing my head in.'

To be fair, he worked hard this morning, bringing the trolley up to the barn from the bottom of the field when it was full.

Maria looks embarrassed. I wish she didn't. It's fine.

'Maybe tomorrow,' she says, and follows him as he sets off down the hot, dusty driveway, talking with Ed, who's joined them. I can't help but wonder about Maria and Marco. They seem to want different things from the trip, as if they're not quite on the same page. But, then, maybe people wonder about me and Fabien. What's he doing with a woman ten years older than him, when he could be with someone closer to his own age? I think of him back with the band and wonder how he's getting on.

I head up for a siesta, in the cool of my bedroom, missing Fabien. I decide to call him to check how he is.

The phone rings and he picks up. 'Hello, *chérie*,' he says, and I love hearing the smile in his voice.

I think I hear someone teasing in the background. He's with the band. On the bus, I assume. There's music playing, and lots of chatter.

'How is everything? How are the pickers?' he asks, clearly trying to ignore the noise around him.

'We've started so that's good.'

'And the children?' he asks.

'All fine. Stephanie is sad, but she's doing okay.'

'Give them all a kiss from me. Say Papi loves them,' he says.

Then I hear, '*Grandpère*,' and laughter in the background.

'What's that?'

'Oh, it's nothing, just banter,' he says, with a tiny edge in his voice.

'Is he calling you "Grandpère"?'

'It's just a joke, Del. Look, I'll call you later, when it's quieter.'

I can barely hear him but tell him that's fine and hang up.

I imagine the teasing now, calling him 'Grandpère'. What do his friends think of him giving up music to work in a *brocante* and be a grandfather? More to the point, what does Fabien think of it now he's back with the band? I shut my eyes to try to nap, but all I can think of is the age gap between us. It seems to be widening with every day he's away.

At dinner that evening, on the terrace, the sun is setting over the lavender fields that slope away from the house. Everyone is seated at the table, glowing after a day in the sun, showered and refreshed. Except Marco, who just has glowing cheeks.

I serve up the bouillabaisse to appreciative murmurs.

'This is more like it!' Marco grins and rubs his hands together. Maria looks embarrassed again, but he's not wrong and I take it as a sort of compliment.

'What is this?' asks Ed eagerly, his enthusiasm surprising me.

'It's bouillabaisse. I make it in the bistro. Nearly every week. It has, erm . . .' I try to recall the ingredients in the order that I use them. I'm imagining myself back in the bistro kitchen, back to the day the olive tree fell into the window when I was cooking it. But my mind goes blank. Is this what they mean by brain fog? Is this the peri-menopausal thing that Carine suggested I get some supplements for?

'It's fish stew,' cuts in Rhi, and I smile gratefully at her.

I watch Ed write something on his phone, then lean

over the bowl and inhale it, as if it were a fine wine. Then he opens his eyes and smiles. We're all watching him.

'Sorry . . . It's just it smells amazing! I'm thinking fennel and saffron . . . and a bit of orange?'

'Yes!' I say. 'That's it! And something else. But I can't remember . . .' The brain fog descends again.

'So, how about we get to know each other?' I say, as I dip my spoon into the bouillabaisse and lift it to my mouth. Just for a moment I'm back to when I first ate this at the bistro, when I thought life around me had been turned on its head and I'd done a totally mad thing by staying here. And that centred me, sitting at the table outside the bistro, having just started to make new friends in Henri and Carine and, of course, meeting Fabien. It was the start of a journey, a new chapter. I take a mouthful of seafood and garlicky rouille, then look around the table. The diners are a couple of mouthfuls in and all look around waiting for someone to start. I swallow, and smile.

'As you know, I'm Del,' I tell them. 'Moved to France three and a half years ago. My husband, now ex, went back to the UK and I stayed here. I started making lavender bakes from a recipe book I found, sold them at the market and to restaurants in the town. Stephanie does that now and I run Henri's bistro in town.' This time I manage to say his name without a crack in my voice. Progress, I think. Thank you, bouillabaisse. Thank you, Henri.

'And Stephanie is your daughter?' Keith asks, leaning over his bowl, his ears sticking out like two little wing-nuts, keeping his glasses on. There is kindness in his voice, which I like.

'She's . . . It's complicated. But, yes, she's practically family. As are her husband and the two children. My partner Fabien is away at the moment. And you've met Rhi, one of my closest friends.' I nod to her. 'She's one of the few friends who believed in me when I decided to stay on in this town. Others thought I was making a crazy decision.' I smile at her and we take a moment to enjoy the memory.

Then there's a lull.

Some are mopping up the juices of the bouillabaisse with chunks of bread, loaded with rouille, and taking sips of wine, poured from the jugs of red and rosé on the table.

'I'm Maria.' I can tell she wants to be brave and make others feel comfortable. 'Marco and I are travelling, trying to decide where to settle. We're looking at our options. We're from Australia. Marco's Australian through and through, from the Gold Coast. Me, I'm a bit more complicated. Adopted in the UK, my birth mother was possibly a Traveller. My adoptive father was Greek, my mother of Indian heritage, and we moved to Australia when I was eleven.'

'They don't need our family history. Next you'll be telling them how many times a day I go to the dunny!'

Marco is laughing, and everyone else laughs with him. He's certainly a character, I think, as he leans into Maria, giving her a playful nudge. She smiles away her initially hurt expression, as he reaches across her for more bread to soak up the juices in his bowl. He puts the bread into his mouth, chews, swallows and grins. 'This is good!' he says, pointing to his bowl. 'Is there any more?'

I smile. '*Merci* – I mean, thank you. It's one of Henri's specialities.' I look at Rhi and give her a little smile, which she returns. That's good, I think. It's good to talk about him. I reach to take Marco's bowl and ladle in some bouillabaisse. 'Anyone else?' More bowls are offered up.

'Henri taught me all his recipes. Never wrote anything down. All done on instinct, taste, touch.' Just like when I met Fabien. It was instinct that brought us together. 'It's how we live around here, following our hearts.' The words catch in my throat and I cough. 'Who's next?' I ask, handing over another bowl and encouraging people to fill their glasses.

'We're Graham and Keith,' says Keith, the shorter, more rotund of the two, with the sticking-out ears and glasses. 'We've decided to tour Europe. Interrail. We've been together for twenty-one years.' We all say things like 'brilliant' and 'congratulations'. They smile, Keith a little more widely than Graham.

'How long are you planning on travelling for?' asks

Marco. 'I mean, presumably it's like a holiday for you guys.'

'Well, more like a gap year. Keith didn't do that as a youngster. I did. Travelled all round this area,' says Graham, 'but Keith went straight to work in a care home. This is our time to do what we never did as youngsters.' Keith swallows and coughs on a bit of bread. Graham pats his back swiftly and sharply, looking concerned. When he sees Keith's fine, he puts his hands back into his lap and continues. 'So, we're taking in Provence, seeing the sights and enjoying the adventure.' He smiles, but Keith doesn't and suddenly there's a moment's awkward silence.

I fill it. 'Great! Seize the day and all that.' My heart twists as I remember pushing Fabien to go out and seize the day, when I should've kept my mouth shut. The atmosphere has dampened.

'I'm Jen,' she jumps in. 'Fifty-two, widowed. I sold up and am living van life as a digital nomad, so to speak.'

'Wow!' says Maria.

'That's brave,' I say.

She shrugs. 'No. It was always sort of the plan to do something like this. My husband Trefor and I had talked about living in a motorhome. Throwing caution to the wind.' She sips some red wine. 'He just didn't get to do it with me. I wanted to do it despite everything. So, here I am,' she says, 'looking for a new clutch. Seizing the day, as you say.'

'What do you do? As a digital nomad?'

'I work in marketing, getting opportunities for clients. I can do it from anywhere.'

The tension that has been hanging in the air since they arrived at the farm, when we'd just heard about Henri, and Fabien was leaving, seems to dissipate a little more. Refreshing, like a breeze after a punishingly hot day in the fields, as the cicadas set about their evening song.

'I'm Edward. Ed. I'm on a gap year . . . first time round!' He smiles at Graham. 'Just taking some time out before I start work. I was supposed to be with someone but . . . they didn't come. So I decided to go ahead anyway!' He gives a short laugh. 'But now I'm here I'm wondering what on earth I'm doing. I mean, I'm the sad single bloke!' He's trying to pick up the laughter again, but he looks a bit lost.

'It's excellent you came. Shows real strength of character,' says Maria.

Marco frowns at her. 'Strength of character?' he scoffs.

'Yes,' she says. 'When you don't know whether you'll fit in. It's brave.'

He dips bread into anything she's left in her bowl, and I can't decide how I feel about him. On the one hand he's fun and entertaining, but on the other, I'm not sure.

'Well, I for one am really pleased you're here. I need

you,' I say. 'All of you! Let's raise a glass to the harvest.' And we do.

'I'm Rhi.'

I didn't think she'd want to talk. She's been so quiet. She worked quietly, collecting and bundling the lavender, then hanging the first day's harvest in the barn, keeping going, slowly and steadily. The group fall silent. 'And I'm here because . . . because my partner Henri has died, and this is where I feel close to him.'

We nod.

'To Henri,' we say, and raise our glasses.

The pickers fall quiet, as the cicadas sing, lost in their thoughts. Looks like it's not just me and Rhi who need this harvest and time on the land. Perhaps my other pickers have a reason for being here too. Once again, Henri is bringing people together. We may be starting this harvest on a better footing than I'd thought last night and I'm hoping for another good day tomorrow.

9

'*Putain!*' I find myself saying under my breath, borrowing Stephanie's favourite expletive. It seems to help and sums up exactly how I'm feeling. I slam down the pen on the blank page of my notebook and clutch my face.

My head is pounding with the rising heat of the day and tension, despite another successful morning's picking. Fabien and I exchanged a few messages last night. He was busy at a festival. There was hardly any signal, so I just told him I missed him. And he misses being here, he says, but there's nothing we can do about the miles between us. He's promised to stay on with the band until they can find a new player, and they can't. I wish he sounded a little more frustrated about it, but he seems to be enjoying himself. Exactly what I wanted him to do when I told him to go. So why am I feeling so scratchy, wishing he was here and not there?

I mean, things have been busy of late. Sometimes at the end of the night, we come together in the kitchen and share whatever I've been cooking that day before we go to bed, sliding under the covers where, more and more, we're too tired to do anything more than fall into a deep sleep. But on lots of days we're like ships that pass in the night, though I know he's there for me, and I hope he knows I'm there for him. We have to make more time for each other. I just wish I knew if he was worried that we've let things slip. Or is he ahead of me on this? Is he feeling this is the beginning of the end and taking the chance to make a getaway plan? Maybe they're not looking for a replacement guitarist at all. And why did I feel I was being made a fool of with the shouts of 'Grandpère!' on the phone call?

Did I push him into this to test him? To see if he really wants this life here with me?

But what if he realizes just what a crazily busy life we have on the farm, in the *brocante*, at the bistro, and it's just too much for him? What if being back with the band he discovers there's more to life out there and this isn't what he wants?

I always worried that the age difference would be a problem one day. What if he's wondering about us, and if we really have a future together?

'*Putain!*' I slam my fist onto the kitchen work surface.

'Hi!' says a voice behind me, making me jump.

I turn, quickly slamming my empty notebook shut. 'Hi,' I say, as if I'd been caught revealing my innermost thoughts. 'Sorry if you heard me swearing.'

'It's fine,' says Maria, at the terrace doors to the kitchen.

'Come in, it's hot out there,' I say. 'Do you want some water?'

She steps into the cool of the kitchen.

'No, I'm fine, thank you.' She holds up a hand, but I'm on automatic pilot and don't register her response.

'Help yourself,' I say, filling a jug, popping in some ice cubes from the freezer, grabbing a glass and placing it on the table in front of her. She pours some water, probably out of politeness. I have no idea why I didn't take no for an answer. Clearly I think I know better than everyone else. Maybe it's time I learn to stop interfering in other people's lives.

'I just came to see if I could borrow an adaptor. I haven't brought a French one with me. Well, I thought I had but Marco has the only one we own. I'll get one in town, but if you have one maybe I could borrow it for now?'

'Yes, of course.' I step aside, pull open a drawer and see her eyes drawn to the debris on the work surface where I've been trying to recreate my usual weekday menu.

'You're cooking?' She scans the work surface, which is scattered with flour. 'What are you making?' she says.

'It's not going to plan. Not like it usually does.' I look down at the sorry mess and press my palm hard onto the empty notebook. If only I can remember the recipes and write them down, so this brain fog clears. It's like I have stage fright of some sort. Not that I've ever been one for the limelight. I feel completely paralysed when I get out a pan to begin to cook. It's usually my favourite time of day when I gather my ingredients from the market or other suppliers in town, shut myself into the kitchen at the bistro and make a start. I step into my happy place. But now . . .

'I don't know what's going on. I cook this every week!' We stare at the shopping on the work surface. 'I just don't know where to start. It's like I've forgotten how to do it. Which is stupid. How can you just forget what is second nature to you? Perhaps I should bring Stephanie up to cook for you all,' I say. 'But she has enough on her plate. She's got a small unit in town to bake from. I should be helping her, really.' I'm rambling. 'Especially as she has the two little ones, and with little Louis missing Fabien so much . . .' I straighten and gaze at Maria, who is standing with the adaptor in her hand.

My mind is still whirring. I can't ask Carine to help, even though I know she'd do anything for me. She barely eats let alone cooks. I let out a long sigh.

'Could I help?' Maria says slowly. 'I cook at home. A lot. For my friends.'

My head is still swimming. I stare at her, as if I'm walking the route I've always walked but have lost my bearings. To be honest, I'm scared. I have no idea what's happening to me.

She steps in beside me, picking a knife from my hand that I'm turning over and over. I can't help but feel grateful.

'I can make something from this, if you want.' She looks at the ingredients, the white onions, scented tomatoes and plump peppers.

I nod slowly. 'Enough for all of us?' I'm concerned. It's like she's thrown me a lifeline but I want to check it'll bear my weight.

'Plenty, with leftovers.' She rolls up her sleeves and washes her hands.

Ralph looks up from where he's been lying by the door, clearly missing Fabien. He has found his way back to my bedroom at night. That hasn't happened since Fabien and I first got together and he moved in here.

'You know, if you don't mind me saying . . .' she says, hesitating over chopping an onion.

'Go on.' I pour myself a glass of water, my hand still shaking slightly.

'Grief can come out in different ways.'

I sip the water. Is that what this is? Grief for Henri?

But if it is, that means he's really gone – and I still can't believe it. I pull out a chair at the table and sit down, feeling as if I'm having an out-of-body experience as I watch and allow someone, a virtual stranger, to make themselves at home in my kitchen.

'If you don't want to talk about him, it's fine, just say. Marco says I always ask too many questions, talk to strangers too much.' She shrugs. 'Maybe I do. I can be quiet if you'd prefer.'

'No, it's fine.' I smile at the lovely young woman's infectious and enthusiastic interest. 'I'm happy to talk,' I say, pouring more water.

'Were you and Henri related?' she asks, chopping fast.

I shake my head. 'No. Although it feels like we were. He's – he was,' I correct myself although it feels so strange, 'a dear friend. He helped me when I first came to live here. He was my first customer when I started baking with lavender. He helped Stephanie too, when she was a young single mum. In fact, Henri had a knack of being there and helping when you needed him.'

'Looks like you do the same,' she says.

'Oh, I don't know about that.' I stop and think about Fabien. Maybe I do. Maybe I spend too much time putting others first and forgetting the most important ones. 'Wow!' I say, as a punch of powerful spices fills the kitchen.

'Oh, it's my spice box, my *dabba*. My grandmother

gave it to me. I take it everywhere,' she says, holding it up.

'It smells amazing.'

'I hope they like it.' She stirs the spices into the big pot.

'Why wouldn't they?' I ask.

She pauses and drops her head. 'It's hard sometimes. Feeling different.' She's stirring as she adds onions, garlic and ginger to the pan. 'This is the paste, after the spice,' she says.

'What did you mean about being different?' I say, going to the fridge and finding the jug of rosé there, cold and inviting. I pull it out and pour two glasses, passing her one. 'I don't know about you, but I think we deserve it,' I say.

She smiles and thanks me. 'When I was growing up, there was a boy who used to tease me, and say I smelled. Others would join in.'

My stomach twists.

'It was the smell of my grandmother's cooking. I loved her cooking. It hurt. I just always felt a bit different. And then when kids heard I was adopted, they could be cruel. But when I'm cooking I feel close to my grandmother. After she died, we moved to Australia and that really mixed things up. I have no idea what or who I am.' She laughs. 'But the cooking takes me back to my grandmother and helps me.'

'People thought I was mad,' I say, 'when I refused to leave here and return home with my husband. He sent

Rhi and my other friend out to see if I'd had some kind of breakdown. But I felt I belonged here.'

We continue chatting, in the kitchen with the French windows open, and the sun begins to dip in the sky. Mostly we talk about food, and I tell her about the bakery business I set up with Stephanie. As we drain our glasses, she holds out the wooden spoon for me to taste.

'My take on coq au vin, chicken with spice,' she says shyly, as if waiting for approval.

I taste it, the spicy heat hitting me in the mouth, then warming me from the inside, reviving me. 'It's fantastic! Thank you so much for doing this.'

'It was my pleasure. I don't get to cook much at the moment, what with us touring around. I'd better be getting back. Marco will wonder where I've gone.' She takes her phone from the charger. 'Oh, yes, plenty of messages from him!'

'Maybe I should just buy ingredients, put them in the barn kitchen and let people cook for themselves of an evening. It's got to be better than the beef I served on the first night,' I wonder.

'Well, it would take the pressure off you. And you have a lot on your plate right now, so to speak. Presumably sorting out Henri's funeral.'

Rhi still hasn't mentioned a funeral.

'Things are often clearer after the funeral,' Maria says.

'Did you lose someone close?' I ask.

'Just my grandmother,' she says. 'The one who gave me her tin.' She holds it to her chest. 'When I smell these, wherever I am, I feel at home,' she says, and smiles. 'My mother didn't cook. She runs a business, an estate agency, with my father in Australia. Everything changed after my grandmother died, and this tin sort of helps me navigate that.'

'Well, your food is amazing,' I tell her.

'Not everyone is as appreciative as you.' She laughs, and I'm not sure why but I laugh with her.

At seven o'clock, we take the big pot of spiced chicken out onto the terrace where the other pickers are waiting. Graham is pouring wine and Marco is telling an amusing story, making the rest of the group laugh. I can see why he'd be fun to be with.

Maria waits for him to finish his story, then puts the big pot on the table. Suddenly I think about Fabien and the nights we spent in our early days together eating out on this terrace, when I fell in love. When did we last eat out here, just the two of us, with him looking at me over the candles and a bottle of chilled rosé? I can't remember.

'So, this is Maria's take on coq au vin . . . with her own twist on things,' I say, putting down the rice she's also cooked and the basket of bread I sliced.

'Has she been taking over in the kitchen again? She can be very bossy!' Marco chuckles.

I see Maria blush. 'No, not at all,' I say firmly.

'I offered.'

'And I was very grateful. We thought it would be fun to share someone else's food,' I say.

'Well, it smells delicious,' says Jen.

'It really does,' agree Graham and Keith.

'Oh, yes, she's a great cook,' Marco says, holding out his plate as she poses with the serving spoon.

Maria's smile returns and so does mine, but I still can't get over what happened in the kitchen this evening, how I froze. The first time, the burned beef, I put it down to shock. But tonight? What was that about? I've made coq au vin time and time again. Henri taught me what to do. What if I've forgotten it for good? I pick up the glass in front of me and watch the water wobble in my shaking hand. I take a sip. Then put it down and pick up the glass of rosé Ed's poured for me, as Maria puts down a plate of chicken. When everyone is served, Maria sits.

We lift our knives and forks and dip them into the glossy spicy dish. She's even made chapatis – I watched in awe as she toasted them over the gas ring.

'I saw my grandmother doing this for years until finally she felt I was ready to learn. But it's not something you can just expect to go right,' she said, explaining why she didn't need the help I offered. 'My dad's more of a barbie man. Never happier than with long tongs in one hand and a beer in the other. And Mum is always watching her weight.'

We eat the chicken, the spices reaching the corners of my mouth and reminding me of how long it is since I've eaten like this. 'I don't think I've eaten curry since I moved to France,' I say. 'We used to have a fantastic Indian restaurant where we lived before we moved out here. I think it's the only thing I miss.'

We all laugh. And that feels good, really good.

Later that night, I stand by the window, staring at the lavender fields. It's warm and the mosquitoes are determined to feed off me tonight. But I've covered myself in lemon juice and that seems to keep them at bay.

The sky is laden with stars, and I think of Fabien. He'll be on stage now. I try to imagine him as I gaze upwards. The nights we've sat under the stars, a quiet time after a busy day. When did life get so frantic for us that we stopped having time to sit under the stars like we did on the night he convinced me to take a chance on us?

When I arrived back at the farmhouse from the riverside clearing, the night after Henri had come home from hospital after his first heart attack, I remember Fabien waiting for me on the terrace where we watched the stars. Henri and Rhi had decided to change their lives, to stop focusing so much on their businesses and their grown-up children and see the world while they could. That was when Henri had offered me the partnership in the business. I agreed to stay and work in the bistro, whether Fabien and I had a future or not. But he was ten years younger than me, and I knew the one thing he wanted was a family, which I couldn't give him. I'd had all the tests and treatments. I'm not sure if that had finished my marriage to Ollie or we realized we wanted different things. Or, in his case, a different partner. But that's water under the bridge. Fabien's happy and so am I – at least, I thought we were – but I can't remember the last time we did something as simple as sit out under the stars.

That night, there had been so much going on at the riverside clearing. Henri was home from hospital and stepping back from the bistro. I looked for Fabien and he'd gone. But when I got back to the farmhouse, there he was, the terrace lit by candles, the bats flitting to and fro, and a cold bottle of rosé waiting with two glasses. It was there he told me that the age gap made no difference. I was enough for him. Our stuck-together little family, with Stephanie and Tomas and now JB and little Louis, was enough for him. I was everything he wanted. That was enough for me too. He was everything I wanted, and that night meant everything too. No marriage vows, just those words to each other as we went to bed and started our life together here.

What would it have been like if I'd gone with him on tour? Should I have let the harvest go for this one year?

I turn from the window above the terrace, overlooking the lavender fields and the town in the distance, lit by the silver light of the moon. I turn back and look over the barn from the other window. There's a light on in the little kitchen. With sleep doing its best to avoid me, Ralph clearly interested, I say to him, 'Need to pee?'

Together we head down the stairs, him for a quick wee while I go to switch off the lights that someone must have left on.

I head over the gravel towards the barn kitchen. When I see someone there I jump, startled, making Ralph bark.

10

'Sorry, sorry! I didn't mean to scare you!'

'Don't worry,' I say to Jen, who is standing in the open-side area of the barn where there is a table, chairs, a soft red sofa and an outside kitchen. It's rough and rustic but I love it. She's standing by the little stove.

'I couldn't sleep,' she says.

'Snap.' I smile.

The smell from the kitchen is amazing!

'I really didn't mean to disturb anyone,' she apologizes again.

'You didn't. I just saw the light and thought it had been left on by mistake. I had to let Ralph out too.' He has lain down by the table and chairs. 'What are you cooking?'

She looks at the pan. 'I hope it's okay to do this.'

'Of course it is. This kitchen is for you to use. In fact,

I was thinking everyone might prefer to cook for themselves, after my disaster the other night.'

She doesn't say anything. There's a pop, and another, and then what sounds like a round of gunfire echoing around the barn, coming from the pot on the stove.

Jen looks aghast, putting her hands on the lid as if she's trying to silence it. But in the quiet of the night, it seems even louder.

I'm trying not to squeal with laughter as the pot keeps popping. Just when she thinks it's nearly done, it pops some more, making us laugh although we're trying not to.

I'm scrunched up, clasping my stomach, weak with laughter, when the popping to match any fireworks display draws to a close. We sit at the table, wiping the tears from our eyes, as the local dogs start barking. But none of the other pickers have woken. Or if they have, they thought it really was a fireworks display, or an armed raid, and stayed put in their rooms.

'What is it?' I ask, as Jen brings the pan to the table, the odd pop still going off, like a petulant child trying to have the last word in an argument.

'It was Maria, this evening, cooking something that made her think of her past, a happy place. This was our budget treat, my first husband and I, when we had no money. We'd buy a big bag of popping corn, then caramelize some sugar, add salt and butter, then bicarbonate of soda and mix it together. We'd pop the corn, then stir in the caramel, sit on the sofa and pretend we were at the cinema. Lights off, curtains shut. Popcorn and a can of Coke each. Sometimes we'd cook hotdogs too, the ones from a tin. I loved the squeezy mustard on softened onions. He had ketchup *and* mustard.'

'Wow! And you just had a craving for this now?' I indicate the pot of fluffy popcorn. 'Do you make it a lot?'

She shakes her head. 'I had the ingredients in the van. Thought I might at some point, but never did until now.' She takes a handful. 'It was tonight, Maria making that dish with the spices her grandmother used, the happy memories it brought her. It reminded me of this. Those early days when we were newly married, then taking the brave step to move to Spain. They were good years in Spain, running the bar. Busy. We were rushed off our feet. Barely had time for each other. And then I ripped a hole in our lives and left him for someone else. A moment of madness, some called it.'

Suddenly her eyes are full of tears.

'He must have been special if you gave everything up for him.'

'I thought so, at the time,' she says quietly. 'We hurt a lot of people and I regret that so much. My first husband, his wife and daughters. The guilt doesn't go away.'

She reaches for a smaller bowl, scoops some of the popcorn into it, takes a moment to smell it, closing her eyes, then puts it on the table in front of me. 'Help yourself. Would you like something to drink?'

'Isn't it me who should be asking you?' I smile.

'You weren't the one who got up with a craving for salted-caramel popcorn,' she says, producing a can of Coke, opening it and pouring it into two tumblers from the dresser. 'This is beautiful. Did you buy it here?'

'Fabien, my . . . partner.' The word isn't enough to explain what Fabien means to me. 'He owns the *brocante* in town. He took it over from his grandfather, saw the dresser and brought it here, rubbed it down and painted it. He has an eye for what works where.' It's so typical of Fabien's style when it comes to repurposing old pieces that come into the *brocante*.

'And he's . . . not here?' She pushes a handful of popcorn into her mouth, some falling onto the floor that Ralph happily hoovers up.

I sip the Coke and shake my head. 'He's playing with what used to be his band. He hasn't been with them for years, but the bass guitarist broke his collar bone and they needed him.'

'Ah,' she says, understanding. 'That's hard, him

being away. It's a busy time for you, and what with your friend Henri . . .'

'Yes. I wish Fabien was here. But I'm also glad he's doing something he used to love.'

'At least you know it's not for ever. He'll be back.' She smiles.

And that's when I feel my insides start to churn, like a washing-machine. What if . . . what if he decides he wants to stay away? That he wants to go back to life on the road?

'Here,' she says. She tilts the bowl towards me.

I take a handful and put it into my mouth. Delicious. 'Tell me about your husband – if you want to, I mean,' I say to Jen, feeling some kind of comfort in the low light of the barn.

'The first or the second?'

'Either or both!'

She takes a deep breath. 'Well . . .'

'Wow!' says a voice, making us jump. 'That smells amazing!' It's Keith.

'Sorry, did we wake you?' We look guiltily at the popcorn pan.

'No, no.' He ruffles his hair. He's wearing SpongeBob boxers and a matching T-shirt. 'Graham was snoring.'

We fall silent and then we hear it. It's like a wart-hog's snorting.

'You see?' he says. 'No one believes that a man with a beautiful face like his can snore so loudly!'

115

We laugh again. I cover my nose and mouth with my hands, as does Jen.

'Join us,' I say quietly. 'We've got Coke.'

'I can do better than that,' he says. 'I have vodka in our room!'

He slips back in. For a moment we hear Graham snoring, then the door shuts and Keith returns waving a bottle. Jen grabs him a glass from the dresser and he offers the vodka over our glasses. We nod.

'Oh, God! This popcorn is amazing!' he says, munching a handful, then washing it down with vodka and Coke. 'This is like a sleepover party!' He beams.

'How's your gap year going?' Jen asks.

Keith's smile slips. 'It's okay. Frankly, I'd rather be at home,' he says, then adds apologetically, 'Not that it isn't lovely here. It is!'

I wave a hand. 'Home is special. And when you find it, it matters.'

I see Jen look down.

'It's not just the house, really,' Keith goes on. 'It's, well, our son. He's gone to university, and Graham had the chance to take early retirement, so here we are.' He sips his drink. 'But I'd rather be back to where we were before our son left home. I loved it. I baked on my days off from the care home so there was always a tin of cake and biscuits on the side when he got in from school.'

'I'm sure he'll be back soon, wanting a taste of your cooking,' says Jen.

He shakes his head. 'I think . . . I think he's embarrassed by us.'

'Surely not!' I frown.

'I'm certain of it. He's hardly been home all year and now, this summer, he says he's going travelling with friends. I was hoping for plenty of time with him at home, going to the beach and for meals out. He was offered a really good job at the local pub for the summer. But he's taken off. He has new friends and we're probably a bit of an embarrassment in our small house.'

'Oh, Keith, I'm sure that's not the case,' says Jen, putting her hand over his.

'So Graham decided we should do something. Get motorbikes or climb a bunch of mountains. I agreed to go Interrailing and stay on farms. At least I know I'll get fed.'

'How much longer will you be away?'

He shrugs. 'Until . . . I don't know . . . until it doesn't hurt any more? It's amazing how time flies.'

Jen squeezes his hand. 'So . . . what about favourite films?' She puts us back on steadier ground, clearly used to doing so.

'*National Lampoon's Christmas Vacation*,' says Keith.

'Love it!' I say. 'And *The Holiday*!'

'Give me a Bond any day!' says Jen.

*

With the popcorn eaten, we say goodnight.

'See you in the morning nice and early. As usual, we'll pick before it gets too hot, once the dew has dried,' I say, feeling more confident.

'I was thinking . . .' Jen hesitates.

'Yes?'

'. . . maybe we should take turns to cook,' she finishes.

'What? Everyone does a night?' asks Keith. 'I do a brilliant fish-finger sandwich! And my cinnamon swirls . . .'

'We could all pitch in. Only if everyone wanted to,' says Jen.

Does she know I'm struggling? Is she just being kind? Or is this a really lovely idea?

'Sometimes a change of location can help us when we're feeling stuck,' Jen says, and I think about her on the road after her husband died. 'We could eat out here in the barn kitchen.'

I look around. It's lovely with its thick beams, furniture that Fabien has put in from the *brocante*, and festoon lighting strung across the ceiling.

'I'd love that,' I say quietly, standing. 'Although I'm not sure how Marco will feel about it.'

'I think as long as Marco is fed, he won't care,' says Keith, and Jen laughs. I wish them *bonne nuit*.

Maybe we can make this work after all. Maybe

moving out of the kitchen is what I need for now. Just until the bistro is up and running again. I head back to the farmhouse with Ralph at my side, following me upstairs to bed. I really don't have the heart to tell him no.

11

As the heat of the day sets in, I call time on the pickers in the lavender field.

'That's it for today, guys.' I stand up straight, back aching, hands stiff from the secateurs. The sun is packing a punch as it reaches higher into the sky.

'Everyone, grab some water. I've put it with the bread and cheese in the barn kitchen for lunch.' We leave the field where we've made great progress and amble towards the barn.

Inside, everyone helps themselves to a bottle of water and drinks. Then we use the outside tap to wash our hands and faces, splashing water onto our hot cheeks. As I shake my hands to dry them, I decide to tell the pickers Jen's idea for a new eating arrangement.

'Erm, about dinner tonight—'

'If it's okay with everyone,' Ed cuts in, taking me by surprise, 'I'd like to try to make something. I didn't know if you'd be interested, but I loved what you did yesterday, Maria, with the chicken. I just . . .' he says, and then, a little shyly, '. . . I wondered if I could share this dish with you all.'

'We'd love that,' Jen and Keith say together, clearly delighted, and I wonder if they've spread the word about taking turns to cook.

'Only if you're sure,' I say.

'Of course I am!' He grins, and it's as if he's suddenly come to life. 'In fact, I'd like to very much.'

'I'll organize a kitty for ingredients,' I say quickly.

'As long as it's not burned beef, like we had on the first night,' says Marco. 'I ended up with a sour cream and onion Pringles sandwich.'

'You're lucky!' Keith joins in. 'We had stale baguette dipped in wine to soften it!'

They laugh, but not unkindly. Marco has managed to break through my embarrassment and I like him for that. 'Clearly if I was left to my own devices right now, you'd be on the same again tonight!' I joke.

'Like I say, I loved what Maria did.' Ed smiles at her.

Marco looks up from his phone. 'What's that?'

'Your girlfriend is one heck of a cook!' Ed tells him.

'Oh, yeah,' he says, and returns to his phone. 'She's the best, if you don't mind spice all the time.'

*

After lunch, I plan a shower and a siesta. Some are walking into town. Maria decides to go for a bike ride in the countryside. Ed is going shopping in town and Marco decides to join him. Graham is off for a walk. Keith is emailing their son, he tells me, just like he does every day, keeping him up to date with their adventures, but he doesn't hear back very often.

I lie on the bed after my shower and attempt to Face-Time Fabien, hoping now is a good time to talk.

The phone rings and rings . . . but finally he picks up.

'Hey, how's it going?' he says, and my stomach flips.

'Better. You?'

'Great! I'd forgotten how much I missed this. I even remember the chords and which order they go in!' He laughs. 'Thank you for making me come. I didn't think I'd ever do this again, but now I have, it's like riding a bike!' He looks really happy, and so attractive. 'And how is everyone there? Any news of a funeral for Henri yet?'

I shake my head. 'No. I've been giving Rhi some time, but I think I need to say something. Everyone is asking.'

'Yes, it would be good to get it sorted. People want to talk about him, make it real, and then, I suppose, start to move on.'

'Fabien!'

I hear a call from outside his tent. 'Who's that?' I say, my interest piqued.

'Just Monique, our lead singer. We're going to get something to eat in the town here. It's a cute place. You'd love it.'

'I'm sure I would.'

'I've got to go,' Fabien says. 'Speak soon.' He's getting ready to head off and there's only time for me to say a brief goodbye.

As I hang up, I pause. I vow things will be very different when he's home. We'll make time for each other. Visit the little towns together. Take time to go out and eat. Before it's too late.

By evening, I'm drawn to the outside kitchen by the beautiful smells coming from it. I can hear chatter and laughter too. The kitchen in the farmhouse seems very quiet and empty. I fill two jugs from the wine boxes, the red that's sitting on the side and the rosé in the fridge, and take a deep breath. For a moment I wonder whether to call up to Rhi but decide that space is what she needs. She's done an amazing job of bundling the cut lavender today and hanging it in bunches in the drying barn. Working slowly, steadily, alone with her thoughts.

'Ed, this smells amazing,' I say, arriving from the stone-covered driveway with the jugs of wine, one in each hand, and Ralph bounding happily around me, excited by the company.

'I hope you like it. I saw the recipe on the Food

Channel and just wanted to give it a go. The town here has amazing produce! I went in this afternoon. I could have just stayed in the one shop all afternoon tasting cheese and wine.'

'Have you always cooked?' I peer over his shoulder at the pan on the stove and breathe in the scent of slow-cooking duck, *herbes de Provence*, green olives, celery, bay leaves and thyme.

He laughs and shakes his head. 'No. My parents didn't spend a lot of time in the kitchen. It was only when I got to uni I started to cook, tried to make things go further, that kind of thing. But, well, I don't really have anyone to cook for at the moment.'

This is a completely different Ed from the guy who's been here so far. He's hardly said a word, but over the stove, he's a changed man. It's like the tongs he's holding have magic powers. He's lit up.

'What were you studying?'

'Law,' he says, focusing on the food.

'What kind?' asks Graham, pouring drinks and handing them round.

'Conveyancing,' he says, losing his spark.

I chew my lip. 'Is that what you plan to go into?' I ask, picking up an olive from a bowl on the table. I think Jen may have put it there.

'Erm, yes. I start with a law firm when I get back. I just needed some time away.'

'I didn't mean to intrude,' I say, throwing the olive stone onto the driveway.

'No, it's fine. I might as well tell you. I was coming here with someone. I told you. My . . . fiancée,' he says.

'Wow!'

'Everyone I meet says we're young to be engaged. It just sort of happened. We were together from the sixth form, went to the same uni and both stayed at home to save money. My parents were so proud. Then a house came up for sale in the same street as them. They used their savings to lend us the deposit to buy it. It was all sort of mapped out. We went on holiday to Center Parcs and everyone expected us to get engaged so we did. When we came back, the house had been decorated from top to bottom by our parents to celebrate.'

'Whoa . . .' says Jen, eyebrows raised.

'They meant well,' he says, clearly understanding our reaction but also feeling for them.

No one speaks.

He sips some wine. 'Then the wedding plans started. All I'd done was buy a ring. I thought that would be it for a couple of years, but it was like this whole big machine whirred into action. Venues, dates, register offices, licensed premises, guest lists, themes . . .'

'God, what a waste of money. Just have a party and spend the money on a good trip, like we did,' says Marco. Maria's looking thoughtful. 'Marriage is for mugs!' he adds.

'But we plan to do it at some point,' she says firmly, putting a large bowl of green salad on the table.

'Not for a while. A long while,' says Marco. 'I mean, I just wanted a holiday. It was you who wanted to do all this picking.'

'I wanted to be a part of a community, not just sit by a pool, eating all-inclusive meals and drinking cheap beer all day,' she says quietly.

'She's got this mad idea that if she keeps travelling around Europe she'll find out where she really belongs.'

'I was adopted,' Maria jumps in quickly, 'by my parents, obviously, so I don't know much about my background. European is all I have,' she tells Jen, Graham and Keith. 'Then, growing up in the UK, when my grandmother died, as I said, we moved to Australia. I'm kind of a mix of all sorts.' She tries to smile. 'But what about you, Ed? Where's your fiancée now?' she asks.

He takes a deep breath. 'I'm not proud of it, but . . . the closer the wedding got, the more I knew I couldn't go through with it.'

We all hold our breath.

'I had to get off the bandwagon. It was the petits fours that did it. I mean, they were lovely – but the wedding was all about everyone else. What they wanted. We'd just become bit parts in this huge event. I couldn't do it. So I told Kim, my fiancée, and then my parents.

I may have broken their hearts.' He goes red and wipes his eyes.

'And the job?' Graham asks.

'Gave me a sabbatical. Said I needed time for my mental health.'

'So . . .'

He shrugs. 'I couldn't bear it, everyone looking at me. The one who'd walked out on his wedding, the big plans. I sat inside, watching cookery programmes. I didn't even know I liked cooking. But it seemed to get me through the day. That and Facebook. To be honest, I wasn't in a good place. So I booked to come here. Even asked Kim if she wanted to come, just some time on our own, without wedding talk. She thought about it, but turned me down. Said it was probably right for both of us, and I just needed some time out. Work out what happens from here.' He goes back to focusing on the pan in front of him.

I'm about to ask him what will happen when he goes back when I hear a car coming up the drive. My heart doesn't so much skip as practically trip over itself as I turn, hoping to see Fabien's truck, hoping they've finally found a replacement bass player and he's come home.

But it isn't Fabien. And my heart dips lower than before. I think about what Ed said, about getting off the bandwagon and letting the world slow down.

Maybe this is what we need, some time apart, I tell myself. I need to focus on what has to be done here. And being apart is reminding us of what we need for ourselves. But the age gap between us seems to taunt me as much as the physical distance between us. Suddenly Fabien seems closer in age to Ed than he does to me and I feel . . . How do I feel?

I watch the little white car pull up. Carine slides out, effortlessly stylish, despite bringing up Clémentine on her own and running the estate agency in town. She waves and I wave back. She and Fabien were best friends when we met. At first I assumed they were a couple, growing up together and staying close. But they weren't. Carine kept her lovers close to her chest. Still does. But Fabien wasn't one of them.

I walk across the white stones of the driveway to meet her. She kisses me on both cheeks. 'Where's Clémentine?' I say, looking into the car.

'With her father and his wife,' she says, as if it were the most natural thing in the world. It might not have been what Carine was expecting after a long-term relationship with the mayor, but they have worked things out and all seem happy with the arrangement. What works for one couple may not be right for another. Look at me and Fabien. Again I think of Fabien at Ed's age and everything he may have hoped for the future, the band, his lifestyle. His commitment to the family made him give up life on the road for the *brocante*, and then he threw in his lot with me. Does he regret it? I remember Monique calling to him to go out and eat. He sounded relaxed, able to enjoy some time in the sun . . . I shake off the thought.

'How are you?' Carine says to me, pushing her sunglasses to the top of her head.

'Hmm.' I tilt my head from side to side, as I've learned to do here when things aren't going as well as we'd like. 'How about you?' I ask in return.

She lets out a long 'Phffffffff,' then follows it with, 'It still doesn't seem real. Everyone is talking about Henri in town, wanting to pay their respects. Like, they can't believe it's happened. It seems he's still just away, travelling.'

She looks out at the fields of purple, undulating down the hill towards the river. In days gone by a still would have been taken to it and oil made there with water straight from it. One day, there will be another still at the farm. I wonder if this was how Henri and Rhi felt when they gave up everything to go travelling. 'One day' became 'today'.

'I know what you mean. I think it's the same for Rhi. She's still in shock. And Henri is still in her handbag.'

Carine sucks the end of an arm of her sunglasses. 'I have a question to ask you – and Rhi, of course.'

'Okay,' I say, intrigued. 'Come in, she's here.'

We walk around the farmhouse and stop to take in

the beauty of the setting sun over the purple field and enjoy the warm lavender-scented air.

'How's the harvest going?' she asks.

'Good. The weather's just right. We're picking in the morning, and we're on schedule to finish on time.'

She nods approval in typical Carine style.

Rhi is sitting on the terrace, freshly showered and alone. She stands to kiss Carine on both cheeks.

'Wine?' I ask them.

'*Oui*,' Carine says, in her strong southern accent. The word sounds more like 'whey'. '*Un petit verre.*' She takes a seat, sits back, crosses one leg nonchalantly over the other and swings her sunglasses from her hand.

Ed arrives on the terrace. 'Hi – oh, sorry, am I interrupting?'

'Not at all,' I say. 'I was just pouring wine. Would you like some?' I raise the jug at him.

'Actually I was wondering if you had any parsley I could use.'

'Of course. Here, you pour the wine and I'll get it. I've got some growing out here.' I point to a terracotta pot on the far side of the terrace.

He takes the bottle and glasses from me and pours, handing one to Rhi and one to Carine, who looks at him with interest, I note, as I come back to the table and hand him the parsley pot. Ed is evidently nervous.

'Keep it over there. I can get anything else we need for the outdoor kitchen. Just let me know.'

'Are you not cooking?' Carine attempts to raise her eyebrows, but they stay where they are. She must have had some recent treatment there.

'Ed is,' I say, smiling. 'He's making duck and green olives.'

'I saw a recipe for it and wanted to give it a try here, with the fresh ingredients.' He seems to be blushing. Carine can have this effect on men.

'It sounds good. Did you add orange?' she questions.

He smiles. 'I did.' He's seemingly finding his feet again. 'Are you staying to dinner? Perhaps you could tell me what you think.'

I still can't believe this is the same quiet Ed who has been here for the past few days.

'Oh, yes, do, Carine!' I say.

'Well, if there is enough . . .' She smiles back at Ed.

'There's plenty,' he says.

'Let's go and join the others,' I suggest. We stand and walk slowly with our wine glasses. The sun is starting to set over the lavender field. The view comforts me as it always does, filling my head and my soul.

'What were you saying, Carine? You wanted to ask Rhi something?' I ask, as we walk. We stop, our heads slightly lifted to take in the heady scent of pine, wild rosemary and lavender, the sound of cicadas, the sight of the swifts dipping and diving over the cut lavender plants, and the cooling air on our faces.

'It's just that people are asking about a service, a

funeral for Henri. Everyone wants to come together to grieve.'

I look at Rhi. 'It's been on my mind too,' I say. But I'm glad it was Carine who brought up the subject. I haven't felt able to mention it yet when Rhi's just getting upright again.

Rhi takes a sip of the light rosé. 'You're right. He can't stay in my handbag for ever,' she says, and we all laugh.

'I can make the arrangements, if you like. Speak to whoever. He wasn't one for church, but it would be good to have some kind of a formal send-off,' Carine says.

'It would,' agrees Rhi. 'Thank you. I'll let his family know once the arrangements are in place. It would be great if they came. I know Henri didn't see eye to eye with his children but he never stopped loving them. You don't, do you?'

Everyone agrees, reminding me of the children Fabien and I never had. I feel the tiniest of holes for them that I try to forget about, but every now and again it lets me know it's there and will never completely go away, no matter what. I wish it would. We agreed it didn't matter. It shouldn't matter. It doesn't. We have each other and it's all we need. We are a family and I'm grateful for that. But every now and then I grieve for the baby I never held in my arms. But that time has gone. We have more than enough on our plates and hardly see each other. That's what needs to change when – if – he comes back.

'How's Fabien?' Carine asks, breaking into my thoughts.

'He's fine.' I stumble over my words. 'The tour's going well. But they're trying to find a bass guitarist to take his place so he can come home. But he's really enjoying it. Even if his back is aching from sleeping in tents or on the bus. And he's enjoying being with old friends. It's good for him, I think.'

'Ah, don't tell me. Monique!' Carine shakes her head.

'Monique? The saxophonist and singer? Yes. She's on tour with them.'

Carine tuts.

'What's wrong with Monique?' I laugh, but it sounds forced. I think back to his phone call, Monique calling to him. They were going out for lunch. They're just friends, I tell myself. So why am I suddenly feeling . . . jealous? Is it her or the band he's enjoying being with, making him feel young again?

Carine's still sucking the arm of her sunglasses, a habit she's got into since having Clémentine and cutting down on her smoking.

She gives another tut and a phffffff. 'Monique and Fabien were together for a while in the band's early days. Just sort of casually. But she never really got over them finishing, him coming to live here and take over the business.'

Suddenly my heart is thundering. 'He didn't mention that,' I say.

She waves a hand. 'It was ages ago. She's probably married with children by now – and, besides, Fabien is with you.'

I think briefly of Carine's relationship with the mayor but I don't mention it. It does nothing to put my mind at rest.

'So, Henri's ceremony,' says Rhi, moving the conversation onto safer ground.

'Yes, the ceremony. We'll make it a town event.'

'Fabien has promised to be back for it.' And now, no matter what's happened or been said, that is exactly what I want. I want him to come home.

'Now, who's ready to eat?' says Ed, as we head for the table. I try to push away the thought of Fabien with Monique. My earlier ravenous appetite gets up and leaves the table. The sooner we arrange the funeral for Henri, the sooner the harvest is done, we can all get back to normal. Just as we were.

12

The following morning, my phone's ringtone cata-
pults me upright in bed. I try to acclimatize myself
after a night of weird, stressful dreams in which Fabien
was running off with Monique, hand in hand, laughing at me, and I was desperately trying to find Henri
but he kept disappearing.

It was a hot night and I'm sure few of us will have
slept through it. I dropped off in the slightly cooler
early-morning hours, my head churning with so many
thoughts and worries, my mind playing all sorts of
tricks on me in the dark hours before dawn, with
only the cicadas' song for company. Then I slept
deeply, thrashing around in my bad dreams, and
now – I can't believe it! – I've overslept.

I grapple for my phone, hoping to hear Fabien's

reassuring voice. But I don't. In fact, I don't recognize the number. Perhaps it's the glazier.

I dial it back.

'*Âllo? C'est Del ici,*' I reply, when the caller answers. 'Are you ringing about Henri's?'

'*Oui!*' says the man's voice at the other end of the line.

'*Alors!*' I say. 'I'll be right with you. Stay where you are!'

I hang up, pull on a linen dress and slip my feet into my flip-flops.

'Rhi,' I call, rushing down the stairs as I tie up my hair to keep it off my neck. 'I have to go to the bistro. The window men are there. Can you start things off here for me this morning?'

For a moment she's daunted and I worry she's not up to it.

Then she gives a nod and a small smile. 'Of course I can. You go and sort out Henri's. That's the most important thing. We need to get it open and then perhaps we can hold the wake in it after the service. Carine is going to speak to the mayor and the priest.'

'Good idea!' I say, and find myself smiling. 'We can get everyone together there to celebrate Henri.'

'I can hold the fort here,' says Rhi. 'In fact, I'm enjoying the time in the field. Time to think or not, talk or not. It's good. It's helping.' I'd see her and Jen working in the field side by side as they cut the crop, occasionally sharing stories of their past.

'You sure? The bakery van will be here any minute. And the coffee machine needs to go on.'

'I'll be fine. You go.' She shoos me away with her hands. 'Get Henri's place sorted out. That's the best thing you can do. We'll do him proud with a fabulous lunch there for all to say their goodbyes. He would've liked that.' Her eyes sparkle with tears.

'He would,' I reply. And once I'm back in the kitchen there, in my happy place, I know my recipes will come back to me, Henri guiding me as he always has. We need to get the bistro open in time for his wake.

I hurry down the dusty drive from Le Petit Mas, as the mist leaves the fields, and wave to the pickers emerging from their accommodation. Jen appears from her camper van and stretches, as if she has an aching back. But she waves back cheerily. Then I wave to Adèle in the bakery van on its way to the farmhouse and gesture that someone will meet her there. Then I head to the pathway that runs along the riverbank, past the clearing under the big larch tree, by the hut where I've posted my note, which is still there, and where I bid the men sitting there, playing chess, '*Bonjour.*' They call that they hope to see me back at the clearing soon. I hope so too, and I feel a bubbling sense of excitement. With the harvest on its way, and the new window about to go in, we can start to move forward and put the world back on its axis, even if there is a hole in it. This is good, I think. Very good. This is progress. Life has to go on, and reopening Henri's is how I'm going to achieve that.

I reach the end of the river pathway, cross the road, walk up the main street, then down the shady side-street towards Henri's bistro, the square and the town hall beyond it. I'm still finding it odd with the olive tree missing – like everything else it'll take time to get used to its absence. But we'll be opening again soon.

There's a man outside looking up at the front of the bistro. He's not quite as I was expecting. He's there on his own, dressed in light chinos and a white linen shirt. A very attractive man. Well-built and smart. He's on his phone. I can't see any sign of the new window or a team of fitters. I slow as I near him. He spots me and finishes his call, raising a hand. He puts his phone into his pocket and waits for me to come and stand in front of him.

'*Bonjour! Je suis Del.*' I put out my hand for him to shake. I'm still glancing around for a van that tells me he's come with the new painted pane.

He takes my hand.

'You've come about Henri's, *oui*?' I ask, regarding the sad boarded-up window, the closed dark-wood shutters above and the empty space where the olive tree once stood. The chairs and tables that are a feature of this alleyway are still stacked outside where we put them when the mistral blew in and caused its havoc. It's a miracle the board is still there and we haven't had any attempts at a break-in. 'I need to get this sorted as soon as possible. Quickly,' I say firmly to the man. *'Très vite!'*

He nods. 'I agree.' He has sunglasses on but there's something familiar about him. I wonder if he's eaten here before.

'The mistral took down the tree and we haven't been open since,' I say, 'and now we need to reopen.'

Again, he nods.

'People are missing the restaurant being open. It's very popular with the locals,' I insist. 'And we have a special event to organize.'

He nods again, irritating me now. 'It does need to be addressed as soon as possible,' he agrees.

'Are you actually here to fix the window? What was your name? I didn't catch it,' I ask, once again looking for a large piece of glass to replace the chipboard.

He looks at his phone, then up at me. 'I'm not here about the window.' He smiles, pulling off his sunglasses. It's a very attractive smile, and again, I'm familiar with it.

'Oh?' I frown.

'I got your number from the card in the window. You're Del, you said?' He looks almost pleased with himself.

'Yes.' I'm confused. 'I thought you said you were here about Henri's.' I feel niggled.

'I am.'

'Well, I'm Henri's partner in the business. How can I help?'

The smile drops from his lips. 'I'm Zacharie, Henri's son,' he says. I stare at him. It's like a flashback in a film to a younger Henri, before the silver-grey set in, the stomach filled out, the laughter lines appeared and the hairline receded.

'Of course! I can see the resemblance now.' I throw open my arms and step forward. 'I'm so sorry about your dad. We all are. I'm so pleased you're here. We've just been talking about arranging a service for him.'

I wrap my arms around him and wait for him to hug me back. But to my surprise, and slight awkwardness, he doesn't lean forward to me at all. I draw back, and feel as if I've been drunkenly hugging a lamppost. I cough and clear my throat.

'Like I say, we were just talking about arranging a service, so I'm glad you're here.'

He looks at the bistro, then back at me and says drily, 'That's okay. I have it all in hand.'

'Okay, I'll let everyone know. I think everyone needs it. Especially Rhi.'

'Rhi?' He sounds distracted. It's probably grief, I think. Being here, at his father's home.

'Rhi. His partner. She's staying with me.'

'Ah, yes. The woman who was with him when he died. The solicitor told me. I couldn't remember her name. In that case, I'd like to meet with her.'

'Of course. Come to my farmhouse for lunch. She'll

be there. And don't worry about the window. We'll have it fixed in no time. I'm getting the writing done just the same.'

'Don't worry. There's no need for a new sign.'

'Oh, but I think we should have one. It looks so good. And, as I say, I'm a partner in the business.'

He turns to me with piercing blue eyes. 'But not in the building,' he says flatly.

'Pardon?'

'A partner in name only . . . in the business but not in the building. I own that now. Me and my sister.'

For a moment my jaw waggles up and down. I'm not sure what to say or even if I've heard him right. 'Well, no. Okay. If you don't want the name on the window, I'm sure we can work around that. I mean, people know where we are. They know Henri's.'

Carine is hurrying towards me. 'I've been trying to ring you,' she says, through gritted teeth.

'Sorry, I've been here with Zacharie, Henri's son.'

'Yes, we've met,' she says, giving little away.

'You have?' I'm wondering if he is one of Carine's romantic encounters. I look between the two of them. Zacharie is smiling. Carine isn't. Although he's very attractive, it isn't a warm smile. There's an atmosphere that I can't read.

'We were just talking about the business, getting it up and running again,' I tell her.

'You were?' She attempts a frown, not very successfully.

'Actually, you were talking about that,' says Zacharie. 'I was talking about the building. The one I own now. I'm having it valued.'

Despite the heat of the day, I'm suddenly very cold.

13

'Now, you mentioned lunch?' He gives a wide, attractive smile, reminding me of Henri. I thaw a little. 'Give me the address and I'll be there.'

My hands shake as I describe how to get to Le Petit Mas. He's Henri's son, I remind myself. He's in shock. Henri would want me to welcome him.

'I'll see you there,' I say, hoping we can sit down and talk about Henri over a glass of wine and some bread and cheese. I really hope he enjoys hearing how fond we all were of Henri and how much Rhi loved him.

'Oh, and, Del?'

'*Oui?*' I say, turning back to him.

'*Les clefs?* The keys. I'd like to take some time to look around my father's home, if that's okay.' He gives me another smile, reminding me again of Henri, and holds out a hand.

'Of course!' I say quickly. 'Take your time. It's a beautiful home. So much like him.' I rummage in my bag and pull out the keys.

I'm about to tell him there's a spare set under the geraniums to the right of the door, but he turns to Carine and says, 'Will you join me?'

'*Oui, bien sûr,*' she says, shrugs in her usual way and looks at me.

I can't read her expression – perhaps that's down to the Botox. But I wonder if this could be the start of something and back away. 'I'll make myself scarce,' I tell her.

They can spend some time talking about Henri. It'll be good for them. We can discuss his service over lunch at Le Petit Mas.

Zacharie must be hurting. Henri would want us to look after him. He and Carine may be good for each other.

'Your father's things are just as he left them,' I say. 'You can feel Henri's presence as soon as you walk into the apartment, like Rhi did. Finding comfort in just being there. Actually, I need to look through his paperwork, get it into order. Find out who the insurers are for the window.'

He nods. It must be a lot for him to take in right now.

Besides, he probably needs to get the place valued for probate or whatever they have in France. It will all be part of the process. Carine is the best person to be there for him right now.

'Your father was very proud of this place,' I say, feeling comforted by talking about Henri. Little steps. 'I'm looking forward to you seeing it up and running again.'

'Hmm, me too,' he says, this time without a smile. But why would he? His father has just died, and not just any father: Henri.

'I'll see you at Le Petit Mas for lunch.'

'See you then,' he replies, turning from me. And Carine kisses me on both cheeks, with more affection than she would usually show. Usually Carine barely touches your cheek when saying goodbye or hello. This time as she does, I get a slight jab from her high cheekbone against my cheek and I'm hoping that now we can all start to move forward. Get the bistro running again, money, which I really need to keep the pickers fed, coming in, and soon, hopefully, the harvest will be over and Fabien will be home. Little steps, I think again, but good ones, moving forward. I turn up the alleyway, leave them to it.

I text Fabien as I walk, letting him know that Zacharie is here and how I'm hoping this will mean we can arrange a service for Henri and start to move on with our lives. I add that I'm missing him.

Fabien doesn't reply.

*

Lunch in the open-side barn is a quiet affair. It's hot, and getting hotter, when the pickers come in from the field and head to their accommodation for showers. The barn is welcomingly cool.

I've told Rhi that Zacharie is here and excited to meet her. She feels the same. I go to greet him when he arrives.

'Let me show you around.' I hold out an arm to Zacharie.

'This is where we're harvesting first.' I show him the field, wishing once again that Fabien was here to speak to him. He knew Henri for far longer than I did. If Fabien was here he'd find common ground. He has a way of doing that. And suddenly I'm thinking about him and Monique, again, finding their common ground . . . when they used to hang out together as youngsters, members of a cool band. I shake myself. Is this all in my head? Has anything happened to make me think he's reconnecting with Monique? No! She just called him to go for lunch. Just like I'm here having lunch with Zacharie. It means nothing. Stop it, Del! It's the shock of Henri's death, reminding me that nothing is for ever. But we have today! The here and now.

'It was this view I fell in love with,' I tell Zacharie. And I'm transported back to when I first arrived. 'Actually, I didn't think there was any way on earth I could live here. I was a complete fish out of water. But something big, a break from my past, made me see how beautiful this place is. I could imagine the field being full of lavender again. Like this. But it's taken time to get here. Things do, don't they? Little by little. Next year I hope to have a still in one of the barns,' I tell him. I'm determined to make it happen, once Fabien is home and the harvest is over. The money from the sale of the lavender could go towards it.

I have no idea if I'm saying the right things or helping Zacharie in any way.

'I lost my mother just before we came to live in France. Although I was an adult, I felt lost. It made me look at myself, I suppose, and where I was in life.'

He says nothing. Not the common ground I was hoping for. My mouth feels dry. I can't think about my mother on top of everything else right now. I cough to try to ease my tightening throat. 'What do you do for a living, Zacharie?'

He looks at me steadily. 'I'm a chef,' he says evenly.

I brighten. 'Like your dad?'

'No,' he says, stony-faced. 'I said I'm a chef. Trained. In Paris. Not a self-taught cook, like Henri. I offer French cuisine. Not something out of my grandmother's kitchen.'

I feel as if I've been slapped. Tears sting my eyes as my cheeks burn. I'm embarrassed, hurt, shocked and angered by his comments about the food that means so much to me. He's grieving, I remind myself. I swallow hard and point in the direction of the barn where the pickers are gathering.

'We should go and meet the others,' I say firmly, searching for a distraction while I bite my tongue.

'Woof! It's hot out there today.' Marco takes a bottle of beer from the fridge and pings off the cap on the side of the table, making me wince.

'This is Marco,' I tell Zacharie. 'He's from Australia, here to help pick the lavender.'

He raises his bottle and Zacharie nods, seemingly unimpressed with this informal style of greeting.

As everyone arrives and is introduced, they take the bread out of its bag, the cheese and ham from the fridge. Jen washes the large ripe tomatoes and dries them, then slices them, drizzles them with dark green peppery olive oil and tears basil over them. Ed cuts the bread. Maria folds and curls the ham onto a plate and Graham sets up the wine, while Keith makes sure there are enough seats and cushions for everyone. The scent of the lavender is weaving its way to us from the drying barn where Rhi has been bunching it. It's in the cushion covers, our clothes, and on the warm summer breeze.

'Please, take a seat,' I say, pointing to the best chair and cushion. But Zacharie doesn't move. He's watching as everyone puts plates and glasses on the table.

Brightly coloured and mismatched glasses, worn patterned plates and an assortment of cutlery, some of which is heavy and expensive, the rest cheap and cheerful.

'Would you like wine?' Graham asks, holding up the jug and a pretty little one-off glass with a short stem.

Zacharie eyes the jug as if he's been offered cyanide and holds up a hand in refusal. He turns to me and asks, 'Where is Rhi?'

'She's coming now,' I say, pointing to her. She's pushing her sweaty hair off her face, pulling off her gloves and running an arm over her forehead as she comes straight from the barn where she's been hanging the bundles of lavender.

'Rhi, this is Zacharie, Henri's son. I told you I'd met him this morning.' I'm trying to warn her with my eyes that he's a bit prickly.

She stares at him for a moment and then, much like I did, flings her arms around him in his cream jacket and doesn't let go for some time.

Finally, he steps back, peeling her arms from around him with what can only be described as horror on his face, and brushes at his jacket.

'It's so good to meet you,' Rhi carries on enthusiastically, her eyes sparkling, taking in the resemblance. 'I've heard so much about you from Henri.'

'Really?' he says, still dusting at his jacket, and Ralph

jumps around excitedly, kicking up more dust from the driveway. Zacharie waves a hand in front of his face to clear the air. 'In that case, you'll know that Henri and I have been estranged for some time. We were not close,' he says, still brushing traces of her hot, sticky body from his jacket.

'But,' Rhi frowns, 'he was your father. He loved you. Whatever differences you may have had . . .'

'That was between me and Henri, who now can't comment,' he says.

I can see the shock on Rhi's face. His use of Henri's name seems so pointed and wrong. Rhi looks broken all over again. I think she was hoping to find some comfort in meeting Henri's son, a joyous piece of a puzzle to slot into its place and make this easier. But no.

'Here, sit, please. Let's eat.' I'm trying to ease the tension, and the group around the table help me by sitting down, picking up plates of meat and cheese and passing them to each other.

'Actually, when you suggested lunch, I wasn't expecting a peasant's picnic,' Zacharie says. 'Please, enjoy. I can see you have the palates of tourists.'

There's a sharp intake of breath. The pickers look at each other and shift uncomfortably. Suddenly I'm not in the mood for bad manners, however difficult Zacharie may be finding this. We have all been through testing times, but that is no excuse for rudeness. I lift my chin. 'There is no need to be rude.'

He sniffs, infuriating me further.

'These are my guests. You should either sit and join us, or leave, if you can't be polite.'

'Willingly,' he sneers, and I'm suddenly burning with anger. How dare he? I roll my hands into tight balls. I feel hot tears in my eyes.

'Your father wouldn't have wanted this kind of behaviour,' Rhi says.

'And how would you know what my father wanted? You were just his bed-warmer!'

There's another sharp intake of breath and I squeeze my fists even tighter.

'Hey, now,' says Graham, sharply.

'How dare you?' Jen cuts in.

I had not seen our lunch going like this. 'I think you'd better go,' I tell him.

'I shall. Enjoy your picnic.' He turns to Rhi. 'But first – Rhi, is it?' I'm sure he knows her name but is just doing it for effect. 'You have something that belongs to me?'

I glare at him. 'She does?'

He stares at me with ridiculously familiar eyes, the same shape and colour but lacking the maturity, sense and kindness of his father.

'Yes. My father,' he says, and Rhi's hand flies to her

mouth. 'Could you hand him over, please? I'll be arranging a proper funeral. I'd like his ashes.' He holds out a hand.

'About the funeral,' I say, as calmly as I can. 'We will all want to be involved with that. We have some ideas. Favourite music. Perhaps we could get someone to speak about the work he has done in the town, the people he has helped. And open the bistro so that people can come back there for canapés and drinks. Reopening Henri's with Henri right there!' I try to mend the cracks that have quickly appeared between us.

'I have a meeting to be at. Now, his ashes?'

Rhi walks to the farmhouse, and we stand in silence as she returns with the urn, holding it tightly to her, sniffing but more composed.

'As I said, I had some ideas about his funeral. Perhaps we can meet for coffee and discuss them.'

'That won't be necessary. Thank you,' he says.

'What do you mean, it won't be necessary?' I ask.

'I'll be arranging a quick and very private service.' He's prising the urn away from Rhi. She clings to it before she lets it go. He holds it out in front of him, like a piece of decaying fish.

'A private service?'

'Yes, a family one. Just us.'

'Wait. You can't do that!' Rhi says angrily.

'I think you'll find I can. My sister and I want a small, quick service so we can move on with our lives. I suggest you do too.'

With that, Rhi runs into the house, tears streaming down her face.

14

I'm so cross. Cross with Henri's son for his rudeness, cross with Henri for not being here, the voice of reason when I need him. Most of all I'm cross with myself for doubting Fabien. I want to ring him and tell him to take all the time he needs, and to put things right with him.

I've spent the afternoon with Rhi. After she had handed over the ashes to Zacharie, he drove off at speed. I told Stephanie what's been happening, then had little Louis so she could work in the baking unit. And all afternoon my fingers have been itching to call up Fabien's Facebook page on my phone. Just to see what Monique looks like. But why? I ask myself crossly. This is Fabien! He's not going to cheat on me. Maybe not, says another voice, but does he still want to be here with you?

And as the sun starts to set I realize I've dropped another ball. I haven't organized any food for the pickers. We said we'd take it in turns to cook, but I should have gone out and bought what they needed. 'Shit!' I say. Everything at Le Petit Mas is going backwards. Just a few weeks ago I cooked in the bistro every day, spoke French, had a partner I loved and trusted. Now I can't think of a single thing to cook and am wondering if my partner still wants me or if he's hooking up with his ex, a woman ten years younger than me. Everything has gone wrong since the mistral.

'Sorry!' I say, running into the open-side barn where the outdoor kitchen is. 'I just lost track of time. I can go and get us pizzas . . .' I stop in my tracks. I look at the table, which is laid, with jugs of water and wine, and the kitchen area is a hive of activity.

They stop what they're doing and turn to look at me. Maria pours a glass of wine and hands it to me. 'It's a bit of a pick-and-mix this evening,' she says. 'I hope you don't mind but we went through your fridge and cupboards while you were walking in the lavender field with Rhi and little Louis.'

I stare at the table and take in the setting, complete with pots of lavender.

'We thought you might need a bit of . . . Well, we just wanted to help.'

'We thought you could do with a bit of cheering up,' says Keith.

155

'Mind? Of course I don't mind! This is amazing!' I say, tears prickling my eyes yet again. 'And it definitely has cheered me up! Thank you!'

'We couldn't decide what to make, so we all suggested different dishes to bring to the table,' says Ed.

My heart swells. 'This is so kind! So thoughtful!'

'Well, we could see that it was . . . a difficult time for you and Rhi. And what with you having Louis to look after too, it was the least we could do.'

'Yeah, that Zacharie was a right knob!' says Marco. 'Felt like decking him.'

Although I'm not sure I like Marco's approach, I suddenly feel very fond of him. Perhaps I can understand what Maria sees in him, after all. He can be funny, and loyal.

'Indeed,' says Graham.

There's a murmur of agreement among the group.

I feel a bubble of laughter rise in me, dispelling my tension. 'So, what's on the menu?' I clasp my hands together.

'I'm cooking samosas,' says Maria.

'And I'm doing cauliflower risotto, with truffle oil,' says Ed.

'I brought more crisps,' says Keith, 'but I'm doing it like nachos, with melting cheese and salsa. That was Jen's suggestion.'

I love it!

'I haven't cooked since my husband died and I

took off in the van,' Jen says. 'I just live off beans and sausages.'

'Well, that's almost a cassoulet!' I joke, and the cassoulet recipe I've cooked time and time again flashes into my head and out again, there and gone. But it was there, and that brings me a sense of warmth and desperation mixed. A bit like the meal being put on the table right now, a mix that makes no sense, but was born of caring.

'Exactly. That's what I said!' Ed's eyes are glistening with enjoyment.

I hear a car and turn around.

'Papi Fabien?' Louis asks, and points to the driveway.

'Soon,' I say, and kiss the tips of his fingers. 'Soon.'

It's Carine. Clémentine is running around with Ralph.

'I came straight after work to see how things were after your meeting with Zacharie.'

I take a deep breath. 'Not good. He came for the ashes. Didn't even stay for lunch. In fact, he was very rude. How did the valuation go? Did he say why he wanted it?'

Another car comes down the drive. It's the mayor. I walk over to greet him as he gets out. Carine and he kiss each other's cheeks, like good friends do. Clémentine rushes over to greet her papa.

Then Stephanie arrives in her little van, with the

purple lavender sprig painted on the side. Tomas and JB are getting out.

'Fabien?' Tomas looks around and I have to tell him that Fabien is still away with the band. My heart twists. I wish he was here and could see how much the family are missing him. I explain that he'll be back soon. Very soon, I hope.

'Join us,' I say to the mayor, having introduced him to the pickers. Then I look at the group. 'If that's okay?' After all, I didn't cook any of this. 'They made all of this,' I say, with pride.

He peers at the heavily laden table.

I raise a questioning eyebrow at Maria.

'Of course,' she says, and the others move around the table. Keith fetches a chair from the farmhouse, then finds cushions and plumps them, making sure they're comfortable. The mayor sits next to Carine, Clémentine between them, as if this was perfectly normal. But what is normal?

'So, Carine texted me and told me about Henri's son arriving,' says the mayor, accepting a glass of red wine and looking at the array of small plates as they're put on the table.

'Yes, it wasn't an easy meeting. Especially as I thought he'd come to mend the smashed window!' I half want to laugh at my case of mistaken identity, but I can't, not yet, and it's sticking in my throat like a ball of bile.

'And he took the ashes?' asks the mayor, sipping his wine from a turquoise blue tumbler.

'He wants nothing to do with any of us.' I turn to see red-eyed Rhi behind us.

'Come and join us,' I say, budging up on the bench. And Graham stands and pours her wine from the jug, already knowing her well enough to give her rosé.

'And he wanted the bistro valued,' says Carine, giving her usual Gallic shrug.

'But that's the thing, we don't know why,' I say. Then I pause, admiring the full table. 'Thank you, guys, for this. It's fantastic.' I want to make sure they know how much it means to me to be sitting with a table of strangers who are now so much more than that. 'Tell us what's on the table.'

We begin to serve the food, everyone explaining what they've made and why.

'I've made salads, carrot, then chickpea and, last, tomato. The chickpea one is my favourite,' says Maria, 'to go with the samosas.'

'Bet it's got spice in it!' says Marco, and laughs. She doesn't, I notice.

She shrugs. 'It's just one of my favourite go-to recipes. Reminds me of—'

'Now, come on, they don't need to hear about your family and your grandmother again,' Marco says. I want to say, I do. I want to hear whatever you were going to say. 'This is why we've come away. Just to be

159

on our own, without any reminders of home,' he says, and the mood darkens a little.

'Ed?' Jen says kindly.

'I've made cauliflower risotto.'

'Wow! It looks amazing.'

'I could have done some things differently, given the time again.'

'No one's judging here!' Jen laughs.

'I've poured the wine. I'm afraid I don't cook. But I'm really good at clearing up!' says Graham.

'And I've made nachos and cupcakes,' says Keith.

'Keith's always baking,' says Graham.

'Reminds me of when our son was at home.'

'And where is he now?' asks the mayor.

'University,' says Graham.

'He doesn't come home much, these days.' I hear the dip in Keith's mood.

Graham jumps in. 'He's having the time of his life. Which is why we decided to have this adventure. Our gap year!'

But Keith doesn't look like he's enjoying it. I see him wipe what I think may be a tear.

'But he'll be home soon,' says Graham, 'after this year, so we have to make the most of it.'

Carine fills a small plate for Clémentine with salad and the dish Ed has made. Although she didn't think she would be, she's a natural mother, always thinking of Clémentine and putting her first.

I pick up one of Keith's crisp nachos and bite . . . Interesting, paprika Pringles, I think, and something else . . . Maybe peanut.

I contemplate the group around the table. Jen looks like the sort of person who leads from behind. Maria seems tired, confused, and certainly needs to tell her boyfriend, Marco, a thing or two. I get the impression she's the brains behind their trip and he's just along for the ride.

Graham and Keith seem an odd couple. Graham seems to be driving this gap year.

And Ed. Clearly he's unsure where life will take him next.

A small group, none of us having quite what we want at the moment, but with this meal, the company, we all know exactly what we need.

We tuck in.

'This is amazing,' Maria says to Ed.

'I wish I'd been a bit more careful, made it look like fine dining,' he says, excusing it again.

'It really is lovely,' I say, but I don't think he hears me.

'And the spice in the chickpea salad is gorgeous. Just right,' says the mayor.

Graham agrees, 'Yeah, perfect,' and spoons in another mouthful.

There is that wonderful lull in conversation when people are enjoying what they're eating, interrupted only by the occasional crunch of the crisp nachos.

Finally, we're passing round the cakes with a jug of coffee.

'Henri would have loved this,' I find myself saying out loud.

'This is excellent, really excellent. Even the crisps sandwiches. You could charge people to come here and eat at this table,' says the mayor.

We laugh.

'I'm not sure people would pay for crisps sandwiches!' Graham says.

'Or Batman fairy cakes!' Keith laughs.

That night, in the warm, sticky summer air, I ring Fabien. He answers and it sounds noisy again, and fun.

'I can't really hear you!' he says, laughter in his voice.

'I just rang to say I miss you!' I shout.

'Come and join us!' he shouts back.

'I can't. I have too much to do here. We can't all be off having fun,' I say, and suddenly bite my tongue.

'You told me to go.' Fabien sounds annoyed. 'I thought this is what you wanted.'

'I did. But . . . I want some time for us too.'

'You are always too busy, Del. Too busy to make time. You are so busy helping others. You can't help yourself!' The noise gets louder from whichever bar they're in, or whatever festival, and I'm more infuriated with every peal of laughter that floats down the phone. Is that a woman's voice I can hear, right next to him? Is it Monique?

'Just go and have fun, Fabien,' I say, knowing now isn't the time to tell him what's been going on here.

'Wait! This is work! You cook and love it! I play guitar!'

How can I tell him I can't even cook any more?

The signal breaks up and the call finishes. I feel wretched, harassed, my ears ringing from the noise of the festival.

I look towards the barn and see lights. Someone must have left them on again, I think and sigh. Or is it midnight popcorn once more? I enjoyed it last time. I slip my feet into my flip-flops and grab my dressing-gown. I could do with some popcorn. In fact, popcorn could be just what I need. If Fabien is out having fun, I will too. I head away from the terrace and am nearly at the open-side barn when I smell something amazing. Something is cooking, or is it the lingering smell of dinner? And then I hear it. A deep, sorrowful sobbing. I stand, stock still, wondering if I should just turn and leave whoever it is in privacy. But I can't. I can't let someone be that upset and not offer comfort. I step out of the shadows and, to my surprise, see Jen standing over the cooker, crying as she stirs the pot on the stove. She seems so together that it's a shock to see her like this.

I may reconsider and leave her to it. She's here at

this time of night because she wants to be alone. I begin to turn, and Ralph suddenly barks, making me jump, Jen too. She looks up. 'Hello?'

'It's just me, Jen,' I whisper, so I don't wake anyone else. She's trying to wipe away the tears as she stirs the pot and sniffs. I'm not sure what she needs right now. Do I hug her, pretend nothing has happened, that it's perfectly normal for the woman who doesn't cook to be standing here at one in the morning, cooking and crying? I do what instinct suggests and say, 'I thought you might be cooking midnight popcorn again.'

She lets out a big sob.

'Jen, what on earth is the matter?' I hug her as I speak.

'Sorry, I didn't mean to wake you. Again!' She rubs the back of her hand under her nose. The smell of whatever she's cooking is making my mouth water.

'You didn't. I was awake. I just saw the lights.'

'Sorry, sorry . . .'

'Jen, stop saying sorry. It's fine,' I pull back from her. 'But what are you cooking? That's not popcorn. I mean, why are you cooking? You don't cook!'

For a moment she doesn't say anything. Then she takes a deep breath and looks up from the floor to me. 'I didn't,' she says flatly. 'After Trefor . . .'

'Died.' I finish the sentence for her. 'I'm sure Rhi knows exactly how you're feeling. She's in the same boat. I'm glad you have each other right now.'

She takes another deep breath, part sigh, part fortifying herself. 'He left me.'

'Oh, Jen, he didn't mean to go. It's not his fault. No one can help dying.'

She sniffs again. 'He left me, for somebody else.'

'Before he died?'

She shakes her head. 'He's not dead. It's just been easier to say that somehow. And now, what with your friend Henri dying, who I never even met but feel sad for, it feels like an awful thing to lie about. I feel so guilty. And your poor friend Rhi.'

'He's not dead?' I say incredulously.

She steps away from me. 'He left me, just before taking early retirement. For someone else. I had no idea. We were planning the next phase in our lives together. Packing up and going travelling in the camper van.' She juts her chin towards it.

'So . . .'

'Yup, I did it anyway.' She gives a derisory snort. 'It just seemed easier to say he'd died and I was doing what we'd said we'd do. Instead of "He left me, and I thought I'd do it anyway." And now I feel even worse for lying to people.'

'Oh, Jen!'

'I should never have left my first husband. It was a moment of madness. We were busy. We'd forgotten to make time for each other. I was flattered by the attention. I thought I was in love! I wasn't! I loved Dan, my first husband. We just lost sight of that on the way. Life was so busy in Spain. So when Trefor showed me lots of interest . . . I was an idiot. I miss Dan. I was thinking about the popcorn. And this! This is what I used to cook all the time when we were together. It was our celebratory dish. Spanish omelette, like it should be made.'

'I didn't think you cooked at all.'

She looks at me. 'I haven't cooked at all, not for me or anyone else since Trefor left. Gave away all my cookery books, pots and pans when I downsized and moved into the van.'

I look into the pan. 'It smells amazing.'

'I kept the saffron, didn't give that away.'

We breathe in its fragrance.

'Would you like some? I've made a bit too much.'

I smile. 'I would.'

She takes two plates to the table, then places another over the frying pan and flips the omelette like a pro. After browning the other side, she slides it onto the plate under the festoon lighting. The bats flit to and fro, in and out of the barn. She cuts a slice for me and then for her.

We sit, and then we taste.

'This is amazing,' I tell her.

'He always said it reminded him of our honeymoon. When we first went to Spain.'

'And what happened to your Dan, your first husband?'

She sighs. 'He eventually remarried. Had a family. They still have the bar in Spain.' She looks round at the camper van. 'And here I am, trying to make a living by designing wedding invitations and social-media posts and living in a clapped-out camper van. I'd say that was just desserts!'

She makes me laugh.

'I don't think you should be too hard on yourself. I'm quite sure that your partner leaving you is as much like grief as it gets. Especially when there's so much hurt and betrayal in there.'

She looks at my empty plate. 'Thank you. That was the first time I've cooked for someone since I started this whole van-life thing.'

'And how does it feel?'

'The cooking? Fabulous! It's like a little bit of me has come back.'

'And what about van life? Must be great, just you and the road, going where you like, carefree.'

'Honestly?'

I'm running my finger around my plate, then licking the buttery remnants off it.

'I hate it!'

Suddenly we both laugh, which I haven't done for a while. And it feels good.

15

The following morning, I check my bank account. I've drunk far more coffee than is good for me. One thing I know for sure: I need to get Henri's bistro bringing in income. I have to get the restaurant back . . . I have to start cooking again. I haven't come this far to have it all taken away from me now. I need to fix this. Then I need to fix things with Fabien.

If last evening has shown me anything, it's that people will come to the table if the food is good and the atmosphere convivial. That's what Henri's is all about and I have to make some money to help the harvest to the end. Zacharie can't just push me out and cut off my income like this.

I text the number on my phone that Zacharie rang me from. I'm presuming it's his phone. *We need to meet and talk*, I tell him. *10 a.m. at Henri's.*

A reply pings back. *You mean at the restaurant? Because, forgive me if I'm wrong, Henri is dead*. I can practically hear the belligerence in the words on the screen and don't rise to it. We need to find a way to work together, to open the bistro again.

10 a.m., I reply, not getting sucked into anything else.

I dress, lay out breakfast on the terrace, with bread and croissants from the van. Adèle, the baker, asks if there is any news on a service for Henri. I tell her that Henri's son is here. He's planning a funeral for Henri, but family only.

'*C'est dommage!*' she tells me. It's a shame. I agree that it is.

I check in on the pickers and Rhi, telling her I have to go out.

'Okay,' she says, this time not as nervous at being left in charge. 'We'll be fine.' The group around the table are tucking into baguette, butter and jam and another cake that Keith made early that morning in the outside kitchen. The smell of freshly cooked cake, sweet and comforting, fills the air and I've missed it since Stephanie moved into the unit.

'You'll be giving Stephanie a run for her money soon.' I find myself smiling.

'What's this?' Stephanie arrives with little Louis on her hip. 'Wow! That smells good!' she says, leaning over the table. Louis points at the cake.

'*Gâteau!*' he says, and Keith puffs up, like a little fat robin in winter showing his full red chest.

'I'll be back as soon as I can.' I pull my shopping basket onto my shoulder, feeling much more like the old me than I have in days. 'I'll buy some food for tonight while I'm out. We can decide what to make when I get back. Hopefully with good news!' And I feel as if everything is about to get back on track. Henri may not be here but we will carry on as if he is. The same for Fabien: I want everything to be back on track for when he gets home. His home as well as mine.

'Is everything okay?' Stephanie asks.

'It will be. Just something I need to sort,' I say, then kiss her and Louis.

'Go for it!' she tells me, as if she's sensed my mission, then cuts cake for Louis and everyone else at the table as I head out of the door, rubbing Ralph's head as I leave and telling him to be a good boy. I am going to get Henri's up and running today if it's the last thing I do.

My spirits lift even further as I approach the bistro to see the new window being installed and the sign-writer's van parked at the end of the narrow street. 'Yes!' I say. Thank God! It's all going to be okay. The window is going in, the signwriter is here. We can re-open! I'm practically jogging towards the bistro now, eager to be back to normal.

I can see Zacharie standing outside, just like he was when I met him. Hands in his cream trouser pockets, staring at the outside of the building. He doesn't turn to me when I arrive, hot and out of breath.

'This is wonderful! You should have called me. I would have been here to meet the glaziers,' I say, fanning my hot face.

'It's all in hand.' He still doesn't face me, just watches the men at work on the window. For a moment, I'm distracted by the company name and can't help but think it wasn't the one I booked. I must have misunderstood. I decide to take this moment to build some bridges and see if I can get Zacharie on board with inviting Henri's friends to the funeral.

'Actually, there was something else . . .' It seems like a window of opportunity. A bonding moment, getting Henri's name back on the bistro window and planning to open again. 'I wanted to talk to you about Henri's funeral, or service, whatever it is. People are still asking. I know you said about keeping it small, family only. But it really would help people. Henri was family to a lot of people around here,' I say, watching his reaction, hoping to have good news for Rhi and for Fabien. I know he'd want to be there, and as soon as we have the date, Fabien will be on his way home.

He says nothing, just stares at the front window and the signwriter at work.

'Well, as I say, let us know when it is. We're all keen to give Henri a good send-off. He's very well thought-of.'

I can't bring myself to say '*was* well thought-of'. I swallow. 'It would be very good of you to include us, the community, in it.'

He still doesn't respond. Slowly he turns towards me. 'And so, Del,' the use of my name so pointedly catches me off guard, 'I am here and you wanted to speak to me. Was that it?' He seems to smile.

I was ready for battle, but perhaps he's softened – and we could be on the same page. He's here having the window fixed and painted, getting ready to reopen, and so am I. Let's hope.

'The most important thing is to reopen the bistro. This place brings in a good income. Not massive, but it sustained Henri and me. I know you had a valuation done—'

'Just for my personal information,' he cuts me off. 'The valuation,' he clarifies.

'Oh . . . good.' I heave a sigh of relief. 'So, you're not intending to sell the place.'

'I'm not, *non*,' he confirms, with a brusque nod.

'Oh, that is good. *Bon!*' I gush. 'I was getting worried, what with you meeting Rhi and asking for the ashes yesterday, but I'm guessing it's grief. We're all grieving, which is why it will be good to have the funeral or service or whatever you call it. We all say things we don't mean in the heat of the moment.' I think about me idiotically insisting that Fabien go on this tour and wishing I could turn back the clock.

I smile at him, but he doesn't smile back and turns to the window.

'Right. Let's get this place sorted and ready to open,' I say, clapping my hands. As soon as I'm back in the kitchen the recipes I know and love will come back to me. I'll be where I belong, feeling Henri by my side. Life can go back to the way it was, even if Henri isn't actually in it. I'll make sure his name is written bigger and bolder on the daily blackboard so no one ever forgets why this place is called Henri's and who was at the heart of it. He changed people's lives around here and we won't let anyone forget that.

'We just need to decide how this is going to work,' I say. 'I mean, are you planning on helping out or hands-off, as Henri was?' I'm hoping for the latter, a sleeping partner, so that I can carry on as I was.

The glaziers finish putting in the new glass and I step forward to thank them, but Zacharie beats me to it, thanking them for coming so fast. Not fast at all, I think. I've been waiting since the mistral. Then I realize, it's not the same glazing company I had booked, or the signwriter, who steps forward to start on the window, stencils in hand. The glaziers leave and Zacharie returns to his spot, watching the work on the window.

'The thing is, this town has money,' Zacharie says slowly and thoughtfully. I'm not even sure if he's talking to me or to himself. He's staring straight ahead.

'Well, yes, there are some wealthy people here, big holiday homes, but there are also the ordinary ones who want to eat affordable home-style cooking, like Henri has always done. There's room for all here.'

'It needs more proper French restaurants, not Italian recipes or, God forbid, anything British.' I wince, wondering if he's referring to the fish and chips I've put on the menu on a Friday sometimes.

'This place is crying out for high-quality classic French cooking.'

'Well, yes, and Henri's does all the French classics: coq au vin, beef *daube*, ratatouille . . .'

He laughs, surprising me. I start to smile with him, hoping this is his way of going forward working together. It might take some getting used to but . . .

'Peasant food,' he says suddenly, repeating his description of Henri's dishes, practically spitting out the word with disgust. Then the smile returns to his lips.

For a moment I'm stuck for words as if I'm standing on sand and it's shifting under my feet. I try to find my way back into the conversation.

'Well, the customers seem to enjoy it and that's what counts,' I say. 'If you have any dishes you'd like to add . . .' I attempt to move things forward again. It's like herding a cat down a street full of alleyways for it to turn into.

He takes off his sunglasses and stares straight at me. 'They will all be new dishes,' he says decisively.

'Well, um, I think we should include some new ones but definitely keep the favourites,' I say, keen not to be walked over and overruled, but also to include him in the business. After all, we're partners now and we need to try to work together.

'*Non*,' he says flatly. 'There will be nothing of the old left behind.' He walks towards the window where the signwriter is at work inside.

'Well, hang on a moment. *Un moment, s'il vous plaît*,' I say, trying to appease him. 'I think people liked—'

He interrupts me. 'For it to be a high-end Michelin-starred restaurant, it will need a completely new menu.'

'Michelin-starred?' This time it's my turn to laugh. He doesn't. I stop and look at his face. He's not joking.

'I have no doubt,' he says, with confidence, 'for the cooking that we will produce, you will need deep pockets to eat here and, in time, I will expand.'

'Oh, it's good of you to rate me like that, but I'm not sure I could cook Michelin-starred food. I haven't had any formal training.'

He looks at me as the signwriter is finishing, wiping down not gold but grey writing. My eyes blur as I try to read the lettering. 'But there must be some mistake.' I look between him and the window. The sun is creeping up into the sky and bearing down on me, the back of my neck. I feel hot and light-headed.

'Like I say, this place will become a Michelin-starred restaurant.' He turns to look at me. 'I don't see a place for you in that, do you?' The familiar look of Henri yet with a cold expression is confusing me even further.

'What? But— Hang on! I'm Henri's business partner! You can't just push me out!'

I stand and watch as the signwriter finishes with a final rub of the window, eradicating any trace that Henri's was ever there. It now reads 'l'expérience'.

'You are partner of what was the business, Henri's. Not the building. And from what I see, Henri's doesn't exist any more,' he says, pulling his sunglasses back on and nodding at the signwriter.

I point at the sign with a shaking hand. 'What? No. You can't.'

'*Oui, je peux*,' he says. 'It's over and it's time to go home, back to where you came from. Leave the cooking to the professionals. *Au revoir.*' He turns away and starts to walk towards the car, parked opposite Fabien's *brocante* at the end of the narrow street. Suddenly the Sunday bells from the church are ringing. The bells I have become used to, that somehow make me feel this is my home. I'm not going to be bullied out of it. I may be a migrant, but I'm part of this community. Henri made sure of that. Everyone was welcome. I won't be pushed out. We all have a right to be here, however much Henri's son would like to see this turned into a high-end, money-making, no-peasant-food-allowed place.

'Well,' I say, a red mist descending in front of my eyes, 'we'll see about that!' I storm forward, practically knocking the signwriter off his feet. He tidies his belongings and makes to leave as I head straight for the kitchen.

'L'expérience!!' I say, furious, banging pots from their hooks onto the counter. The counter I have cleaned and polished every day since Henri handed over the keys, which now seem to be in Zacharie's possession.

I pull large spoons from the pots beside the hob.

Outside I hear a shout. Someone calling Zacharie's name. But I'm in my own world and everything outside it is just noise.

'Hey!' Zacharie is standing in the doorway of the kitchen, surprised and irritated. 'What are you doing?'

'Taking what's mine!' I say, standing in the middle of the kitchen with my hands on my hips. I feel as if my home is being repossessed so I'm grabbing what I can, while I can. 'I may not own the building, but I am still a partner in this business, Henri's! And these pots and pans belong to me, as much as they do to Henri, a part of the business.'

He sighs as if he's dealing with a petulant school-child, which infuriates me even more, making me pull every pan I can off its hook and slamming them onto the functional kitchen work surface with a satisfying clatter and a bang.

'I suggest you put everything back where it was and leave.' He holds out his hands in front of him. 'You're clearly upset.'

177

I spin round and glare at him. 'Upset?' I snap. 'I don't think you have any idea how I'm feeling, but upset doesn't quite cover it.'

My frustration moves up another notch and, with renewed vigour, I carry on, stripping the kitchen of the herbs and spices on the rack, the whisk Henri taught me to use, and the ladle he always served with. Henri's son Zacharie might own the bricks and mortar and Henri's personal items, but he's not having the pans Henri cooked with, the whisk, the ladle, or the ancient bottle-opener he loved. No way! These are the pans where he made enough for the bistro and the riverside clearing project. These are Henri's. The business's.

'If you want half, you'll have to come and take them off me!' I say, clasping the items to my chest.

He throws back his head and laughs. 'And what do you plan to do? Set up a little home-cooking bistro somewhere else?'

I say nothing. I have absolutely no idea what I'm going to do. But I'm not letting him have the tools that made Henri's what it was.

'Well, good luck,' he says, standing aside as I attempt to walk to the door, holding the pans and other utensils in my arms.

I stop and try to say calmly, 'It doesn't have to be like this. Your father would hate it.'

He screws up his face. 'What do you know about my father?'

'I know the good he did here, the people he helped.'

'Yes. He was so busy helping others he didn't notice the family he had under his nose. My mother left him and he should have done more to stop it happening, to stop our family falling apart.' I can see the anger flashing in his eyes.

'You're right. I know nothing of Henri before my time here. But—'

'Don't. Don't tell me water has passed under the bridge or whatever you say in the UK. If I am erasing all trace of Henri's maybe it's because that's what I want. I want to erase the memories of when I wanted my father there for me, and he wasn't. He was there for everyone else, though. Good old Henri! Now, please, leave!'

I grapple for a large wooden spoon that's slipping from my fingertips and catch it between my knees. Then, slowly and steadily, I waddle towards the door, trying to keep my dignity, which I may not have achieved, judging by the laughter of the signwriter, and the pointing of other shopkeepers who, as yet, have no idea what's going on. I head for the end of the street, tears rolling down my face and my dignity dragging along behind me in the gutter.

16

Back at the farmhouse, in the outside kitchen, with its saggy, comfy sofa to one side and festoon lighting across the high ceiling, there's bunting now too, making it even more homely. I'm wondering if Jen added it. I'm sitting at the table, nursing a glass of rosé that someone has put into my hands.

'He's taking over Henri's?' Rhi is flabbergasted. 'He's not selling it, but going to run it himself, just not as Henri's?' She throws up her hands angrily. 'I don't know which is worse. Selling up or just eradicating Henri from the building and business.'

I nod and shake my head, not sure in which order, and gulp some wine. My cheeks burn with humiliation, which is compounded by having had my bank card rejected in the small supermarket when I went in to buy groceries for the pickers' dinner. Dear Françoise on the till told me to come back later to settle the bill when I was less upset and to borrow the trolley, which was loaded with the equipment from Henri's as well as the food. I pushed it along the riverbank, past the clearing, feeling as if I'd become part of the homeless community there. I barely heard the shouts and jeers from a group of schoolboys who had gathered there, clearly having decided to play truant from school. Shocked, without a mooring, I pushed the trolley back to Le Petit Mas. Now I feel lost. If I'm no longer part of Henri's, who am I?

After a couple more glasses of wine, feeling fuzzy, with a headache coming on, I head to my bed for a siesta, knowing I won't sleep.

I wake with a start to the smell of something delicious. I'd fallen into a deep sleep, with nightmares about Henri's place burning down and nothing I could do to save it. It's not burning I can smell now, though. It's a barbecue. On the one hand I want to thank God that Henri's hasn't burned down. On the other, it might as well have done. I throw myself back onto my pillows, pick up my phone from the bedside table and try to call Fabien. It goes straight to voicemail.

'Phfffff!' I drop my hand and the phone into the softness of cotton covers and let the smells from outside fill my nose and head. The scent of the freshly cut lavender from the field, in the cooling afternoon, with the initial smell from charcoal heating reminds me of something. It reminds me of . . . Fabien and me here, with Stephanie, JB and Tomas, Henri and Rhi, Carine and our other friend Lou with her new partner. Stephanie and JB's wedding! The evening barbecue here at the farmhouse.

Voices and laughter are reaching me from the barn now, just like they did on that day, when Ralph ran off with the rings, as ringbearer, and Tomas chased him. A day of laughter, love and hope . . . when the future seemed full of possibilities and the celebrations went on for days. How have we come to this, with me here on my own, scared and worried, the business whipped out from under my feet, an empty bank account, wondering about Fabien, our feelings for each other, and no Henri to show us that everything would be fine in the end? Everything has changed. Even Stephanie and JB have moved into their own little place and are here less and less often.

Everything changes, seasons come and go. Like the lavender harvest. What will happen when it's finished? *If* we finish it, because if I can't find a way to bring in some money, I'll have to let the pickers go.

I try ringing the bank to talk to someone about an extension to my overdraft or a loan, but I recently helped Stephanie pay for the bakery unit and the van so it's no-go. I'm maxed out on credit.

I try Fabien, but the call goes straight to voicemail. I

go to the window at the side of the house, following the smell of the barbecue, then head downstairs. Ralph is lying in the cool. Three years ago he would have been outside causing mischief, but everything moves on. I step out onto the terrace towards the lavender there. I grasp a stem and break off the head, its flowers separating in my hand.

Graham is prodding the charcoal with long tongs, looking thoughtfully into the flames. 'What are you cooking?' I ask, wondering what I can sell in the *brocante* from the farmhouse to bring in some cash.

'Um, just sausages,' he says.

Maria is making a spicy potato side dish. Jen has put up more bunting and is photographing it on her camera and posting it.

Marco is seemingly playing a game on his phone.

'Damn!' says Ed, tossing a spoon into a pot on the gas hob.

'What's up?' I say, rolling the lavender blooms in my hand.

'I was making a Provençal chicken dish, but it's just not quite there.' He puts his hands on his hips. 'It doesn't . . . stand out.'

'Don't be so hard on yourself,' says Jen, putting down her phone.

'That's what Henri would say,' I remember. 'He'd tell you exactly that.'

And then I sprinkle a few of the lavender blooms from my hand into the sauce.

'Try that,' I say, and Ed stares at me as if I'd smeared Marmite over his caviar on toast.

He leans forward and sniffs, picks up a spoon and tastes. Then he looks back at me.

'Well?'

'It tastes of Provence,' he says.

'Exactly.' I smile. 'It's the flavour of here,' I say suddenly, as if Henri was speaking to me. 'It's one of our *herbes de Provence*. But be gentle with it. It can be overpowering if you use too much.'

The others turn to me.

'Looks like Henri isn't going anywhere by the sound of it,' says Jen.

That brings a smile to my face. It was just a tiny chink, a memory of him and me in the kitchen, but it's still there. I just have to find a way of reaching it and getting back into the kitchen.

Rhi appears from the drying room and joins us. She puts her hand over mine and squeezes it. We smile at each other.

The smell in the barn is fabulous against the backdrop of the drying lavender from next door. It reminds me of everything Stephanie and I learned together when she first arrived at the farmhouse with Tomas, where this journey began. I'd refused to go back to the

UK and was left here with nothing but an overnight bag and Ralph. Stephanie and I were thrown together by a twist of Fate and the only way I could think of getting through those early days was to bake my way through a lavender cookbook. Stephanie helped with my French and I helped her learn to bake. Just as my mother had taught me. That's the cycle of life, isn't it, the memories we hand on?

The table begins to fill. Stephanie, JB and the children arrive. Rhi takes a seat next to me and tries to persuade me to sit. 'I can't. I should be cooking, helping.' But Ed and Maria are managing perfectly well in the kitchen and Keith is taking over the sausages from Graham as he pours drinks.

Maria smiles. 'Sit. There's plenty of us here to help. You have enough to think about.'

'Yes! Like how you're going to get your restaurant back,' Jen says firmly.

'Don't make a fuss. I'm fine!' I hear Graham say to Keith.

'Have some water, a sit-down,' Keith says.

'You're fussing. I'm not a child!'

And with that Keith, upset, disappears to their bedroom.

I go to stand, but Maria beats me to it. 'Here, let me help,' Maria says to Graham, who's beside the barbecue, embarrassed and cross.

'After all, I'm from Australia, sort of. Barbies are what we do!' She goes over to stand beside Graham, who is a little relieved.

'Australia, UK, France, Spain ... No idea where you're really from, have you, Mar?' says Marco, making me wince.

'Might be good for us all to have some water,' Maria says, pointing to the jug by the sink and the glasses. Graham heads to the jug, fills it and puts it on the table.

'And it's really hot,' says Jen, passing round the glasses as the sun, despite dipping in the sky, is still fiercely beating down.

Graham takes a glass of water and drinks it.

'Everything okay?' I call over.

'Yes, yes. Just hot. We're not used to it in the UK, are we?'

'No,' I agree. 'And Keith?' I gesture towards the room that Fabien and I created, filled with antiques from the *brocante*, a wrought-iron bed, and hooks on the wall to match. Simple but homely.

'I'll go and see him now,' says Graham, smiling at Maria who is turning kebabs made from all the veg in the bottom of my fridge, peppers, tomatoes, onions and mushrooms. She brushes them with oil, then sprinkles them with fiery spice from her tin.

I watch Graham go, hoping the pair haven't had a falling-out. But it's hot and hard to sleep. And the mosquitoes. Which reminds me: I go to the farmhouse kitchen and bring out the last of the lemons for everyone to cut in half and rub over themselves.

I remember my humiliation in the shop earlier, my cheeks burning at the memory, and I'm still wondering how I'm going to pay the bill. I'll have to find some cash from somewhere. Zacharie has cut me off from the income I was relying on. With immediate effect.

I gaze at the happy group in the barn. I feel like the baddie in a cartoon about to burst their balloon.

I have to tell them I can't pay for them to be here any more. I can't afford the food. I need to tell them, and soon, so they can make new arrangements. Clearly getting back into the bistro isn't going to happen. I have no idea what to do. I can't move in on Stephanie, who is running the business that's supporting her and her family. JB doesn't make much from the *brocante*. Fabien would like to pay him more, but there just isn't the money. Whatever Fabien makes from his tour will be the most he's earned in a long time. And he needs it.

As we're rubbing ourselves with lemon, it's Tomas who hears it first. 'Fabien! Papi Fabien!' he shouts, jumping up and down. His younger brother does an excited dance on the spot.

'*Non, cheri,*' I tell him. 'It's not . . .'

Suddenly I can hear it too. My heart leaps. The familiar sound of Fabien's truck coming down the long drive. Then my heart does a triple somersault, like an

Olympic diver off the high board, as I see it pulling through the gates. I stand and watch as Ralph barks frantically.

The truck comes to a standstill, clouds of cream dust gathering around the wheels on the hot stony drive. I stand for a minute under the shade of the open-side barn as he steps out. He stares at me, then takes in the busy scene in the barn. I'm tense. What if . . . what if he's come back to tell me face to face that he doesn't want to be with me any more? What if he's come for his stuff?

After our last phone conversation, I'm not sure where we are. Suddenly I feel like the Del who was first getting to know Fabien and really hoping he liked what he saw. God, what is wrong with me? When did I become so troubled about our relationship, so bloody insecure? When the mistral took away everything I had. Well, when she took away Henri and brought in Zacharie. The mistral that changed everything, just like it had three years ago.

'Well, this looks busy!' he says, and suddenly smiles. The smile I love that comes with a bucketful of reassurance. I rush forward and wrap my arms around him. 'Good to know I was missed!' he says.

'Very much,' I say quietly into his neck, breathing in his familiar smell and then, in a rush so the words tumble over each other, 'And I'm sorry . . . things are going to be different. We need to make time for each other.'

He looks down at me, holding my arms. I want to kiss him and kiss him.

'I'm sorry,' I say again. 'I'm so glad you're back.'

'Ah,' he says, still holding my arms. 'Actually, I'm only here for one night. We weren't too far away, so rather than go out for a meal, I wanted to come home and see how you were doing with the harvest. We've barely been able to talk. I'm sorry. I just needed to see you. I have to go back later. I missed being here.'

'Oh.' My heart sinks. 'But you'll stay for tonight?'

He smiles. 'Yes, of course. But I'll have to leave early.'

And he kisses me, just like I've been dreaming of for the last couple of weeks. Finally we pull apart. I feel a rush of colour to my cheeks and my tired body suddenly feels alive.

'Come and meet everyone,' I say, as we wrap our arms around each other and walk towards the group. Keith has reappeared. He looks like he's been crying, but has washed his face and joined the gang, standing with a glass of rosé in his hand, next to Graham.

Maria is serving with Ed.

'Everyone, this is Fabien!' I say, and Ralph stands proudly at his side, chin lifted as if we're talking about him.

'Well, we did hope you don't go around kissing all male visitors to the farm like that!' says Keith, making everyone laugh.

'This looks like a feast!' says Fabien, having shaken hands with everyone. He's carrying little Louis on his hip and Tomas is attached to his leg. He hugs and kisses Stephanie warmly, JB too, then Rhi, saying he hopes she's doing okay and that being here at Le Petit Mas de la Lavande is helping.

'Has she told you?' Rhi asks him.

'He's only just arrived, Rhi,' I chide. 'I've only just heard the news myself. We haven't had a chance to talk.' I think back to the snatched phone calls over recent nights, tired and snippy with each other. 'And that's why I couldn't get you on the phone earlier. You were driving here.'

He turns to me with a sudden worried look. 'What news? Is everything okay?' He gently puts Louis on the floor, despite his protests.

'Yes, well, no. I'm fine, it's not me. It's Henri's.'

He frowns.

'Henri's son, Zacharie, has arrived, as you know. He came to collect Henri's ashes from Rhi.'

'Okay,' he says slowly and evenly.

'And to close down Henri's bistro as we know it,' Rhi rushes in.

'Close it down?' Fabien gasps.

I sigh.

'He's turning it into a high-end classic French restaurant, apparently. Called l'expérience.'

Fabien screws up his nose. 'L'expérience?'

I nod.

'He's hoping for a Michelin star. He's a trained French chef.'

'But what about Henri's?'

'He says we served peasant food. And that he owns the building, so he can do what he likes.'

'And the funeral for Henri?'

I let out a long sigh. 'A private family-only service, apparently. I tried to change his mind but he wouldn't hear of it.'

'*Oh, là*,' says Fabien, reverting to French to express his disgust, rubbing my arm. 'And the bistro now?'

I shake my head. 'Locked.'

'You should have rung me sooner. Told me to come back. I would have been here,' he says, his eyes darkening with fury. 'I should speak to him.'

'I only heard this lunchtime. And there is nothing we can do. He's right. He does own it.'

'In the eyes of the law and all that,' Ed puts in.

'Dinner,' says Maria.

'Come on, let's sit,' I say. 'You'll love the food these people put on the table.'

'You're not cooking?' he says in surprise.

'No. I'll explain later.' Although I don't quite know what to say. I'm like a racehorse that can't run, a bird that can't fly, a frog that can't jump. I'm a cook who can't cook. But I can still eat.

And we do: we sit, eat, drink, and Fabien gets to know a little more about the people around the table. Their travels, where they've been, where they're going.

'Jen knows her way around the engine of a camper van,' I tell Fabien.

'Had to! Lived in one in Spain for long enough,' she says, and we quieten. This is something we've not heard from her before.

'I thought you lived in London?'

'I did. With my second husband Trefor. But before that I lived in a caravan on a small patch of land with my first husband, Dan, when we took the big leap of faith and moved to Spain to run a bar there.'

The rest of the group don't know the full story yet.

'We were building a house, near the bar. But between running the bar and building a house, we lost our way. I met someone else, a holidaymaker, and we ran off together. I'm full of shame about it now. My family didn't want anything more to do with me when I left Dan. But Trefor and I had each other. Until . . .'

'He died,' Rhi finishes.

Jen shakes her head. 'He didn't die. Trefor left me. I was mortified. I had caused so much hurt, giving everything up for him. I should never have had my head turned. It was a moment of madness and I got caught up in the excitement of it all. After he left, I thought the only thing I could do was keep moving. I think it's the guilt that's kept me moving all this time. Not having to think about it.'

'We can't help who we fall in love with,' I say, taking a small sideways glance at Fabien. He's there to catch my glance and my cheeks colour.

'But it wasn't love. It was the excitement. Life had got busy with the bar and building the house. It was like the box of chocolates you're not supposed to open because you're on a diet. The temptation was too much for me.'

'And then comes the feeling of sickness and the guilt,' Keith finishes.

'And now?' I prompt her.

She looks around the group. 'Van life. People think it's cool and I've got it sussed, but the truth is I hate it. I absolutely hate it,' she says, and we stare at her. And then she lets out a little laugh. 'We always said that once we retired we'd go on the road. I thought it was exactly what I needed. Turns out it isn't! I should never have left where I was in Spain. I loved having friends and staying in one place.'

Then Maria says quietly, 'I wonder if I should have left the UK . . . or if I should go back.'

Marco frowns. 'Why would you?'

'Because it was my home,' she says.

Marco peers at her as if she's talking a different language. 'Yeah, but Australia is like the best place ever.'

She shakes her head. 'You think that. Maybe I don't.'

'Tsk,' he says, and tuts loudly. 'Don't be ridiculous. How can you compare anywhere to Australia? I said we'd do a tour of Europe, but I assume you'll make the right decision and want to go back to Oz as soon as. I can't wait to get back.'

Maria's eyes fill with tears. 'We cooked differently when I was growing up and my grandmother was alive. I miss it,' she says, and I haven't heard her speak like this before. 'I miss her. I just have no idea of who I am or where I fit in. I'm not Australian, I was born in the UK, and my parents have mixed heritage. I miss my grandmother, even though I know I'm not of Indian heritage, because I was adopted.' She shrugs. 'I can't work out *me* and where I fit. I thought cooking with the spice tin would make me feel more like her, like I belong.'

'That was *magnifique*!' Fabien leans back in his chair. 'It must be very hard for you.'

'It is,' she says. 'Thank you.'

'I think you've fallen on your feet,' says Marco, 'your parents taking you on and moving to Oz.'

'No matter where we've come from, we don't forget the past,' I say. 'Or want to. It's part of the journey.'

I have a feeling that Marco and Maria aren't on the

same journey, and from Maria's face, I have a feeling that she may be realizing it.

We turn to gaze across the lavender field and the valley: the sun is setting and the sky is painted with colours that reflect those in the field.

'I tasted lavender in there tonight,' says Fabien, and Ed beams.

'Del suggested it. She says it was how she'd learned to cook when she arrived. With lavender.'

'There's so much left. We'll be eating this for days,' says Jen.

'I'm not sure it'll keep that well,' says Maria, looking at the vegetable kebabs.

'No,' says Fabien, and we look at each other. We know what the other is thinking.

'Henri's may have been taken over, but Henri is still here, in spirit, in all of us,' Fabien says, his eyes on the table and the food.

I nod, a tiny spark trying to reignite in the pit of my stomach. I don't know if it's the warm night, the clear sky, the cicadas singing louder than ever, the fact that Fabien is here, or that it feels like Henri is with us in the chair next to Rhi where he should be. Maybe I won't tell them tonight that I have to cut short the harvest and their stay. Just one more night to enjoy the food and the company.

'Shall we?' Fabien raises an eyebrow, making me smile.

I stand, then Fabien, Stephanie, JB and Rhi follow. 'Henri may not be here, but his legacy is. Grab a bowl or a dish, everyone, and come with us.' I'm smiling as I lead the way down the drive towards the riverbank.

17

At the riverside clearing the solar festoon lighting has come on, strung from branches of the big larch tree there.

Heads turn as we arrive. There is a small group, some standing, some sitting on the blue settee, some with cans of beer. Dogs mingle with people who have either nowhere else to go or anywhere they want to be. There are some new faces. I stop, feeling overwhelmed. What if this place isn't the same as it was when I put the sign up and left to start the harvest? What if it's changed in that short time? Lots of things have. What if we're not welcome here? Fabien looks at me and smiles.

'No one ever turned down good food,' he says, and I know Henri would have said exactly the same. I smile at him and remind myself all over again how lucky I am to have him. I just hope he still feels the same about me.

I take a deep breath and stride towards the little whitewashed hut – frankly, it could do with a lick of paint. There's rubbish in the doorway, sweets packets and bottles. Not something I've seen here before. I kick at the mess and plan to clear it up once my hands are free. I balance the dish of kebabs on the little lip to the hatch and grapple for the key to the padlock with my other hand. The door swings open and I let myself in, happy to be back in the little workspace with a warming hob and small sink. It feels good to be back. Then I open the hatch. Familiar faces are smiling at me. 'Welcome back,' they say in French.

'*Merci*,' I reply.

'Henri is still here,' one says, putting a fist to the chest.

'He is.' I usher those carrying pots into the shed, the makeshift kitchen where for years Henri brought the dish of the day from the bistro to offer to those who couldn't afford a meal. Before he died, we were serving lots of people, many paying what they could for the food. Now, it seems, it's just those in need.

Fabien explains to the pickers how this all started and how Stephanie came to rely on it as a place of safety when she was struggling as a young mum. Henri and the riverside clearing were her lifeline. Without it, who knows what would have happened to her and Tomas? It was the people here, looking out for one another, who helped us find her again when she went missing from Le Petit Mas, when life got too much for her. This place has a heart all of its own. Let's just hope we haven't left it too long to come back to it.

We serve bowls with a mixture of tonight's dishes, the barbecued kebabs, the spicy potatoes, the fabulous chicken, with bread made by Keith. Jen quietly puts out pots of knives and forks as if she's been a part of this all her life, and I suppose, from having worked in her Spanish bar, it comes naturally.

'And you would come here often?' I hear her asking Stephanie, who is helping her.

'I knew there would be a hot meal for me and Tomas and no one would ask questions. It felt safe. Henri had a way of doing that.'

Graham and Keith look less sure of themselves, as does Maria, who stays in the kitchen with Ed.

'No one ever turned down a hot meal, especially not one as good as this.' I repeat Fabien's words. Fabien is talking to the men he recognizes, telling them why he's been away. It sounds as if he'll be continuing the tour with the band. But this isn't something we've discussed. Our eyes meet and my stomach flips.

This place holds a lot of memories for all of us. Some good, some bad.

We hand round the bowls of food and I put out the honesty box for those who can afford to contribute, but I'm pretty sure it'll stay empty tonight. We're just giving people who need it a good meal. As they sit at the long table, just a few at one end and the odd one or two spread along it, it's very different from when I left it. I've neglected this place, like I've neglected Fabien and me. And who knows if that can be brought back?

When the food has been eaten, the diners thank us, with a smile and a few words, and right now, that feels good enough for me. There may not be money for me to do this again until I can find a way of working. I kiss Stephanie and the sleepy children, who peel off to their little house in town.

'It's good to see you back here,' says Samuel, whose face I recognized. '*Merci.*'

'You're welcome, Samuel.'

'But be careful,' he says, and my smile drops. 'A new crowd have moved in.' He indicates a group who are laughing loudly and drinking from cans. 'They are not like us,' he says. 'Less peaceful. A group of young lads, using this place to gather. Mostly they are bored. But it's not always a good place at the moment.'

I smell smoke in the air, not cigarette smoke, something different.

'A few older people have moved in too. They are here to do business.' He shrugs. 'Money passes hands, deals are done.'

I feel myself go cold.

He looks over his shoulder. 'Just take care, you and

the little ones,' he says. 'It's not as trustworthy a place as it once was.'

'*Merci*,' I stammer.

I can feel the atmosphere change as more people arrive and join the group at the table. Lighters are passed around and silver-foil packaging laid out. There is a mix of ages, and the banter is loud and crude.

'I think we should leave now,' I say to Samuel.

He nods sadly. 'Thank you again for all you have done here. Let's hope this passes,' He gestures again at the group. There's a shout, an argument, dogs bark. 'Maybe they will move on soon and this place can go back to being the safe space it once was.'

Fabien is already shutting and locking the hut. The lights on the tree flicker and go out. I find myself wondering how long the lock will last and if the hut, too, will be taken over, like the seating area, as more familiar faces move off into the shadows of the night. There's another shout, a tirade of swear words, and suddenly this place feels anything but safe.

I'm anxious, heart thumping, when Fabien catches my eye and we share an understanding look. We gather our things, say goodnight to Samuel, then head back up the riverbank, with the pots and pans, under the bright white moonlight to the farm. In the distance I can hear raised voices, shouts, arguments, and barking from agitated dogs.

'It's changed a lot,' I tell the pickers. 'A new group is

using the area, youngsters for drug deals by the look of it. Maybe I should have been there more.'

'Sssh,' says Fabien. 'You're doing plenty for lots of people. You cannot do everything for everyone,' he scolds, but there is firmness in his voice too, and I think back to our snapped conversation, the row we had. He's trying to make me feel better but I still feel that I've let people down, by allowing the riverside clearing project to lapse. First the bistro, now this.

'*Bonne nuit.*' We wish each other a good night. Graham and Keith head off to bed, arms round each other. Jen goes to her van where she puts on the fairy lights. It looks cheery, but there's sadness too, the loneliness of life on the road.

Maria and Ed stop their debate about ingredients over technique, simple southern-Italian cooking against the learned culinary skills of a trained chef, and wish each other a good night. Maria runs to catch up with Marco, who is striding to their room.

As the moon shines brightly, the stars beside it, Fabien lets us into the farmhouse and drops his keys onto the kitchen table. 'I've missed you,' he says.

'And I've missed you,' I reply, kissing him on the lips, my worries about the two of us melting away. Then he takes my hand, tells Ralph to stay where he is, and leads me up to the bedroom, where the moonlight is streaming through the windows.

He pulls back the white mosquito netting that hangs

over the bed and kisses me slowly on the lips, then down my neck, making me shiver. It's hot, very hot. He takes me to the bathroom and we shower together, massaging and soaping each other, enjoying the familiarity and the way our bodies fit together.

In the silver moonlight, under the canopy of the white netting, we make love, like I never have with anyone else. It opens a floodgate and I weep, overcome with love for the man I'm with, and the man we've all lost. I weep until my pillow is wet, with Fabien there to kiss and wipe away my tears.

In the early hours of the morning, I feel Fabien untangle himself from me and slide from beneath the sheets.

'I wish you didn't have to go,' I say.

'I wish you could come with me,' he says, and we kiss until he pulls away.

'I have to be here,' I whisper. 'I have to find a way to get Henri's bistro back. If we don't, all trace of Henri will be lost for ever. It's like Zacharie's wiping him out of the town he was a part of.'

He brushes the hair from my forehead. 'I have to go. I promised. But soon we will make time for each other. Soon,' he vows, and slips out of the bedroom before dawn to rejoin the band for the next leg of the summer tour, heading for a festival in the Loire.

I let my tears soak into the pillow until dawn breaks. It's a new day, and there are people to feed. Henri would have made sure they had a meal, and I intend to do the same. I need to start cooking again. And now the tears have fallen, maybe I can. I have to find a way of remembering Henri's recipes. I can't let him disappear. I just have to get the restaurant back.

I lie there wide awake, trying to find a way to make this right, but in my heart of hearts I know I can't. I haven't any money. Without the bistro, I can't keep going and I'll have to let the pickers go. Tomorrow. I can't keep them here under false pretences. I can't even pay for their board. Is my time at Le Petit Mas coming to an end? The only income we'll have will be from the lavender sale, and that's not a lot. Getting a still to make oil and such would make it far more profitable. Right now, it's just bunches for sale in the market. How will we make ends meet at Le Petit Mas? Will I have to put it up for sale? And where that will leave me and Fabien I have no idea. I have to tell him I can't keep this place going. There is so much more that Fabien and I should have talked about. After all, Le Petit Mas is Fabien's home too. First, though, I must talk to the pickers. I'll do the rest of the harvest on my own.

18

The next morning I'm on the terrace, waiting for everyone to appear for breakfast. I had to scrape around for the money to buy the bread this morning and decided against cinnamon swirls. Fortunately Keith has made another cake he brings to the table to the pickers' delight.

'Banana cake,' he says. 'Thought it might be a breakfast thing, with a hint of lavender. And great with butter – especially French butter!'

And suddenly I want to cry. But I won't. I've cried enough. I can't believe any of this is happening.

'So, here's the thing,' I start, just as Stephanie arrives carrying little Louis on her hip. He holds out his arms to me. I take him from her, and Tomas hugs me. She kisses me on both cheeks. I clear my throat and wish I'd talked to her about this but now I've started I need to carry on. Everyone is looking at me, waiting.

'So . . .' My palms sweat and I place Louis on the floor. He immediately hugs Ralph instead. 'As you know, things have changed since you all arrived here.' I feel hot, light-headed, sick.

'I was running the bistro, Henri's, but with Henri's recent death, and his son arriving to take over the building, it looks like I'm out of a job for the time being.' My mind is whirring. Where will I find another? I'm not qualified to do anything else here. 'I don't have any income right now, and won't until the lavender starts to sell at the market. Offering to have you all here and feed you in return for your work on the harvest is proving . . .' I clear my throat, '. . . prob-lematic. So, I'm afraid I'm going to have to let you all go.'

'Oh, no!' There's a universal cry of dismay.

'I'm so sorry.' There's a lump in my throat. I take a big swig of coffee.

Marco shrugs and Maria glares at him.

'Well, it was nice, but I can't wait to get to the coast!' He smiles widely.

'Marco, I thought you said you were happy for me to come here, find my roots, what I was looking for?'

'Yes, but, Mar, that was when I thought we were going to be sunning it in St-Tropez, watching football in Barcelona, or drinking beer in Rome. You're the one with the permanently itchy feet, trying to work out where you came from!'

I see her eyes smart. She tosses back her dark hair and sniffs, looking upwards, then back at me. 'It's complicated,' she says. 'I'm complicated. I just . . . This trip was about taking some time off from work. I sort of—'

'Went doolally!' Marco laughs. No one else does.

'I was burned out,' she says quietly. 'I gave up my business. I'd become just about the business and nothing else.'

'What was it?' I ask.

'Holiday lets. Running them, advertising them, dealing with the owners and the renters. It was a lot.'

'So you sold the business?'

She nods.

'Some mug paid well over the odds,' Marco interjects.

I'm already feeling prickly towards him this morning.

'We're on our way to Italy to see if I can feel that's where I'm supposed to be in life, if that's where my roots are. My true home.'

'We don't have anything other than an empty nest to go home to,' says Keith.

'I still need a new clutch,' says Jen. 'Don't think the van's going anywhere. Bit like my life in it – looks idyllic on the outside, but knackered and miserable under the bonnet!'

They all laugh.

207

Then Maria speaks. She may have sold her business but her business brain hasn't left her.

'We could do what the mayor suggested and start a supper club,' says Maria. 'We all pitch in and cover the bills with the money we make.'

There's agreement around the table.

'Oh, I don't know,' I say. 'I couldn't let you do that.'

'Why not? It's not like any of us have anywhere we're rushing to.'

Ed agrees. 'I'm happy to stay on here as long as I can. Last thing I want is to have to go back and start working at the law firm.'

'Isn't that what you've always wanted to do?' asks Graham.

Ed shakes his head. 'It's what my parents wanted me to do. It'll make them very proud.'

'Wouldn't you rather be a chef?' asks Maria.

'I can't. My parents . . . It's complicated. They're very proud of me becoming a lawyer. I can't let them down. This is just my summer out, before I have to start working with the firm. It's a deal we sort of made . . .' He waves his hands as if he's juggling. 'After I left, when I told them I couldn't go through with the wedding, I said I'd be back in September to start my new job. The cooking thing, like I said, I was watching these programmes and they helped. Y'know, when you have stuff going on in your head . . .'

'So you never really wanted to be a lawyer?' asks Keith.

208

'It seemed like a good choice when I was picking courses. My parents were delighted. First person in the family to go to uni.'

'And now?'

He shrugs. 'I can't not. It would break them. I just have to enjoy this summer.'

There's a lull.

'It's a lovely idea but I think it's best if I just call off the harvest. I'm sorry. There's no rush, it's just I can't afford your keep.'

'You should charge people to come and stay here. It's a wonderful place. I've never felt so calm,' Maria says.

'Nor me,' says Jen, checking her phone. 'Oh, saying that, looks like I've found a clutch and it's on its way. Do you mind if I stay on until it arrives? I'll keep myself to myself.'

'It's fine. I'm happy to have you here. All of you! It's just that, without Henri's bistro, I've no income, and the lavender won't bring in much, even once it's dried.'

'And what will you do now? Without Henri's?'

I let out a long sigh. The words 'Sell up and go home' are on the tip of my tongue. But where's home? Certainly not with my ex-husband, his new partner and their baby in England. 'I don't know. I – I had nothing when I decided to stay here. Apart from a bucketful of debt and a daft dog!' I look at Ralph, who lifts his head and pants.

'Sounds like you've come a long way,' says Keith.

209

'I have,' I say slowly, feeling that each of the people staying here now is feeling in some way how I felt when I first came here, at a crossroads in life, trying to find the right path forward.

'But something about this place just made me feel safe. As if I was at home. I took it day by day, and, with the help of people like Henri, I started to find my feet. I've tried the bank for a loan, but they refused. Remortgaging was a no-no. I need to find another job.'

'Or get the bistro back,' Jen says.

'There must be a way,' Maria agrees.

I shrug. 'Right now, I need an income. I can't rely on the lavender.'

'You can work with me on the lavender cakes and bakes,' Stephanie offers. 'You started the business.'

'No,' I say firmly. 'You need the money. You have a family and a home to pay for.'

'What about new premises? Somewhere to rent?' says Maria. 'A pop-up restaurant?'

'Well,' I start to think, 'I suppose I could ask my friend Carine if she knows of anywhere.' But even if I found somewhere, could I actually cook? Out of the kitchen at Henri's, I haven't been able to.

They all smile.

'In the meantime, we'll do some more of the harvest,' says Keith.

'I'll look at trains,' says Graham, sadly.

'I guess I'll look at flights,' says Ed.

'Best I get that new clutch in,' says Jen.

And I feel wretched. I've let them all down.

I step into the cool of the kitchen and wash my face. When I turn away from the sink, I see Keith and Graham have followed me.

'We could lend you some money, if it would help,' says Graham.

'No, no, thank you, but I couldn't.'

'We really don't mind. This trip and being here is just what we needed. We'd be happy to help out.'

'We would,' agrees Keith, although I'm not sure that he agrees this trip is exactly what they needed.

And as much as I would love to take them up on the offer, I really can't.

'Are you sure?' Graham says. 'A bridging loan?'

'I've come this far without taking handouts. I can't start now. But thank you.'

These people, whom I've only just met, feel like life-long friends.

19

'I'm sorry, *chérie*. There's nothing,' Carine says, when I tell her I'm looking for a restaurant to rent. 'Certainly nothing reasonable.'

'I don't know why I thought there would be. I haven't even the money to feed the pickers.' What was I thinking of?

'I'll keep my ear to the ground. And talking of an ear to the ground, I hear there is a service at the church this morning.'

'For Henri?'

She nods slowly.

'How early?'

'I just heard it was early.'

'But hardly anyone will be able to make it – they'll be at work or in school.'

'That is exactly the point.'

'What?'

'From what I hear, it's just a small service for the family, as Zacharie said it would be.'

'But what about Rhi? What about his friends, the community?'

'*Non*. Not invited.'

Then I hear the church bells ring and stare at her. 'It's now!'

'He is trying to do it before anyone is open for business!' Carine looks as enraged as I feel.

'Well, I'll see about that!' I march out of the office. Carine scoops up her jacket and follows me, her kitten heels clipping on the pavement behind me.

I can hear the church bells and I quicken my pace. Down the alley, past the bistro, towards the church in the square.

There is a dark car with blackened windows. The doors to the church open. I step forward to rush in, but it's Zacharie and a woman, both in dark glasses, and the priest who step out. Zacharie looks around. I stare straight at him.

He's done it. We've missed it. I'm seething, my hands clenched.

'He's had the funeral service,' I say to Carine, staring at the car as they step into it. He'd completely ignored everything I said and everyone who cared about Henri. 'How could he?'

The car drives away and the priest glances at Carine

and me on the far side of the square. He has the decency to look regretful.

'No one was there. No one!' I cry.

'Let's go and get a brandy,' says Carine, and we turn up the alleyway towards her office, passing what used to be the bistro.

On the outside it's unrecognizable. And then I see it. A sign, welcoming people to the restaurant's opening . . . tonight.

'Tonight! The day he said goodbye to his father. This is too much! Something needs to be done.' But I still have no idea what.

I stand and stare at the new awning, the minimalist writing on the new window, 'l'expérience' all in lower case.

The red-and-white-check tablecloths are nowhere to be seen.

'I know where there's a really good bottle of brandy,' I say. 'Henri's brandy.'

'I thought Zacharie took the key from you.'

'Yes, but he doesn't know there's a spare, just in case.'

I go to the geranium pot and lift it to see the key still sitting there.

'Bingo!' I'm fired up and angry.

For a moment I wonder if it will still work. I look up and down the street, then push it into the lock and turn it. It works. My heart is thumping. Looking over my shoulder, I push the handle, no longer brass but chrome, and let myself in.

'Grab the brandy from behind the bar,' I tell Carine, pointing. 'The good one!'

While the front of the restaurant is practically unrecognizable, there are still reminders of the bistro in the kitchen, the bones of the place, the shape of it, the eyeline into the restaurant and the street beyond. I run my hand over the work surface. Here, I was happier than I have ever been. This place, Le Petit Mas, Stephanie and the children, I felt like I had it all. Now everything seems to be crumbling around me, as if I'm being punished for being happy.

Don't wait until life stops being hard to be happy. I hear Henri's words. A saying he lived by.

I look around the little bistro, taking in the changes. I walk upstairs. The pictures on the walls have gone, and in the apartment, there are more tables and chairs, more dining area. Nothing of Henri left at all.

I walk down the stairs. Carine is standing at the bottom, holding the brandy.

I slide the key onto the side, next to the trays of champagne flutes ready for tonight's opening. I grab two of the bottles lined up there and head out into the alley as the day begins to heat up.

'Let's go back to Le Petit Mas, get drunk, angry and make a plan. There has to be a way to persuade him that he's making a very big mistake in pushing Henri's friends out. I'm not going to let that happen!'

20

'Put on all the old favourites,' says Rhi, buoyed up by her champagne cocktail, a favourite of Henri's. 'One sugar cube, two dashes of Angostura bitters, cognac and champagne,' she says, pouring them for everyone. And we all raise a glass. I take a snap and send it to Fabien.

'And some new ones.' I'm looking at Maria and Ed. 'Are you sure you all mean this? You're happy to stay on and give the supper club a go to raise some money?'

'Yes!' they say, except Marco, who isn't with us.

'If Zacharie sees how popular our dishes are, he'll know this is the sort of comfort food people want. Not high end with high prices! They want value for money, company and good food.'

'What about the night market at the weekend? We could go and see if people like our cooking, hand out samples,' Maria suggests.

'Well, we could but that still doesn't help us on where to hold the supper club,' I say.

We spend the rest of the day going through recipes online, looking at the classics that Henri taught me, aiming to recreate them. If I do this, perhaps he won't entirely have left us.

'So, let's decide how it's going to work,' says Ed. 'We need this to pay for our keep and food. Don't forget, the mayor said he thought we could.'

'So, it's like a pop-up. We cook, people come and eat as if they were in a restaurant and pay . . . a suggested figure, as a donation.'

'We could do it here. Just like we do every night. We eat together. We just cook and make sure people have a nice time,' says Maria. 'Jen could put up more bunting.'

'But who would come, once the mayor and Carine have been? We can't get that many people around the table in the barn and people won't drive up here. We're a good stretch out of town.' All the reasons why we shouldn't do it are tumbling into my head.

'This is about putting food on the table to pay our way, but it's about remembering Henri too, isn't it?' Ed says.

'And it's about making us feel at home, even though we're here . . . we're home,' says Keith.

'A Friday-night supper club!' Maria agrees.

'What about going back to the riverside clearing?' asks Jen.

'It's a good idea, but it doesn't feel safe now the kids have muscled in there,' I say, wishing I could think of somewhere we could rent.

'What address is Henri's registered to?' Ed says.

'The bistro.'

'So, effectively, it's still where the business is based . . .'

'You mean I could go in and claim my space?'

'You could indeed,' he says.

'But it's a very small kitchen.'

'We could do the next best thing and serve meals outside it – like we did when we first started the lavender bakes,' says Stephanie, warming to the idea. 'Hit them right where it hurts!' she says, with a sharp twist of her fist.

'We need somewhere people can sit to share food and conversation,' I say.

'What about your Romani caravan? We could take it down to the market,' says Ed.

'Wouldn't be easy,' I say. 'It hasn't moved in years.'

'We need somewhere bigger,' Maria says.

I'm beginning to think this just isn't going to happen.

'I know somewhere,' says Stephanie, flicking through the old lavender recipe book.

'Oh, no, not your unit. You need that for your baking. I'm not going to let you give that up.'

A rare smile pulls at the corners of her mouth. 'No, better than that. You need somewhere with tables and chairs, right?'

'Yes,' I say.

'With French charm? Antique furniture?'

'But we're not going to . . .'

'In the heart of the town, not far from Henri's?' She's grinning.

My eyes widen. 'Are you saying what I think you're saying?'

She nods. 'The *brocante*!' She beams.

'A pop-up supper club at the *brocante*?' Rhi repeats.

'*Oui*, of course!' Stephanie says excitedly. 'Cook the food here and take it there.'

'Or barbecue! I love to barbecue,' says Graham.

'Henri loved a barbecue,' says Rhi.

'It's perfect,' I say slowly. My heart lifts and soars.

'We all cook, different dishes from different backgrounds, a mixed bag. Everyone is welcome,' says Maria.

'Yes!'

'Here's to Henri's supper club! Now to get the word out!' says Jen.

While Maria and Ed return to talking menus and Keith talks styling and bunting with Jen, I can see a hole in our plan. 'Just one thing. How are we going to do all this without a vehicle?'

'You could use my work van,' Stephanie suggests. 'But it is going in for a service at the end of the week and I'll need it again on Saturday.'

'You can use the camper!' Jen says. 'It won't take me long to put in the new clutch.'

'We couldn't do that!' I say.

'It's fine!' She waves a hand.

'I don't want you to feel pushed out!'

'I've told you I hate living in this van! Can't wait to get out of it.'

'Well,' I smile, 'there's a spare room in the house.'

'Perfect! I'll take it!'

'So, we're on. Friday-night supper club!' Maria can hardly contain her excitement.

'Zacharie won't like it,' says Rhi.

'All the more reason to do it!' I raise my glass.

21

Carine squeals when I tell her the plan on the phone the next morning.

'We're on our way to the *brocante* now, to sort things out.'

'And Fabien?'

I chew my lip. 'We didn't have time to talk last night. He was at a noisy festival but I texted and asked if I could use the *brocante*. He said, "Anything." I hope he doesn't mind. I wouldn't ask if it wasn't important.'

'Fabien will think this is a fabulous idea. You can send him photographs when everything is set up.'

We all walk down towards the town, past the riverside clearing, all except Marco. Samuel is there on his own.

'*Bonjour, Samuel.*'

'*Bonjour!* How are you?'

'Good,' I reply. 'How are things here?' So much rubbish on the ground, the debris of a lively night.

His mouth pulls downwards. 'Not so good.'

'I'm sorry,' I say.

'There's people here who'd come to rely on Henri's for their evening meal. It's hard for them, especially now this place isn't what it was. They don't know where to go.'

'I'm sorry,' I say again. It wasn't just me who was relying on the bistro.

'I wish I could help. I feel useless here,' he says.

'Actually, Samuel, I have the lavender harvest going on. If you or any of the other regulars wanted to help out . . . I can't pay, but I can guarantee a home-cooked meal at the end of the day. Not made by me, but the other pickers staying. Everyone is pitching in and it's wonderful.'

He looks at me.

'Don't decide now. But if you want to, join us at Le Petit Mas.'

He nods, and I have no idea if that means he will or he won't. '*Merci*,' he says.

I leave him to his thoughts.

We walk on towards the *brocante* – I pause at the alleyway to the bistro. It's almost as if your husband has a new younger lover and has moved her into your life. She's changed everything and it hurts. I think back to when Ollie left me for his lover and went back to our old life, where I used to belong. But the happier I became here, the less I worried about what I'd lost when he'd gone. I have to recreate here what we had at Henri's to make Zacharie realize we need Henri's at the heart of the town.

I turn to the big cream gates, rusting in parts. JB is there to meet us with a big grin, his arms folded across his chest.

'So, Stephanie told you the idea?'

'She did!' he says, unusually animated.

'What do you think?'

'If it's okay with Fabien, then it's fine by me! Sounds like a great idea,' he says, beckoning us all into the *brocante*'s courtyard.

'It's perfect,' says Maria, who has been quiet since Marco refused to join us on our reconnaissance mission to the *brocante* and was suggesting they move on. Now, though, it's a joy to see her face lit up as she glances around the courtyard and the warehouse, piled high with second-hand treasures. It's hard to see what anything is, unless you know what you're looking for. Fabien found all the essentials I needed for Le Petit Mas when I first discovered this place. He collected them together, made me coffee and gave me an excellent price. Even delivered them as I was still contemplating my next move and showing some second-home owners around the property with Carine. It was there and then I made the decision to stay, to make Le Petit Mas my home. And I don't intend to leave. I'm not going to let Zacharie push me out by taking away my business. The *brocante* is helping to save me all over again and I intend to do it justice.

'Okay, let's get started, shall we?' I say, studying the crammed warehouse and trying to work out where everything should go.

'Look at that lovely candlestick,' says Keith, who is straight into the dark recesses of the space. 'And this rug! We could go vintage, mix and match plates. Oooh, my auntie used to have doilies like these.'

I see Graham smile. 'He's happiest creating a home,' he says quietly. 'Hang on, my love, let me help,' he says, as Keith inspects the piles of tables and chairs, clearly planning to unpack them.

'I'm thinking we could go for a front-room feeling. Like when you visit family. Rugs, lamps, teacups . . . and look at all these glasses. They'll polish up beauti-fully,' Keith calls.

'And some bunting,' says Jen. 'Bunting makes every-thing better,' she cries, as she joins in the scavenger hunt. JB is helping to reach higher-up tables and chairs, and Keith has moved on to tennis racquets to create the feel of an afternoon turned evening by the river. He finds boules sets and a box of board games.

'What should I do?' asks Ed.

'Work out where to serve the food from? Create a serving area? There's a small kitchenette in the office,'

I say. 'Or we could barbecue in the open air. We can bring the one from Le Petit Mas. See what would be best for you.'

He nods. 'Maria? Coming?'

I swear I see a touch of pink in her cheeks.

And there in the courtyard, as we rummage through boxes of cutlery, unwrap glasses from newspaper, and Jen irons napkins among the tables and chairs that Keith and Graham are setting out, our first supper party starts to come together. And I need it to happen quickly if I'm to get money in to cover our costs.

As the sun starts to set, the *brocante* has become a festive outdoor dining room, comfortable and cosy. Carine turns up to check on progress. 'This looks great!'

Keith places a mirror against the stone wall, which adds warmth, like a fireplace, as the sun bounces off it, giving a focal point to that end of the courtyard. It stands next to the chestnut tree, which now has bunting hanging from it.

'I have something for you,' Carine says. 'Come with me.' She walks towards her car, parked by the gates, and opens the boot. 'I found it in the skip at the bistro as they were clearing out the upstairs to make more seating there. I didn't know if you'd want it or not. As you know, I'm not one for clutter.'

She reaches into her car and from the back seat pulls out the sign that once swung from outside Henri's living-room window.

'Of course I want it!' I shout. The blood rushes to my head and I don't know which to hug first, her or the sign.

'So, tomorrow is your first night?' she asks.

'It could be our only night if no one comes,' I say.

'They will come,' she says confidently.

The *brocante* courtyard is beautiful. I take some pictures on my phone.

'Get it across social media,' says Carine.

'Let me help.' Jen takes my phone. Her thumbs work fast for a few moments. Then she hands it back to me. 'There!'

'Wow! That was quick!'

'I wish! Young people are so much better at it, with nimbler fingers than mine. I'm a dinosaur, a slow one trying to keep up with the pack.'

I hear a ping and JB takes out his phone. Then there's another: Carine's. They both start typing.

'Shared!' Carine beams.

'Done!' says JB.

A warm sensation fills me. Maybe, just maybe, this will work.

Later, back at the farmhouse, I check my phone. There are lots of likes and comments on the *brocante*. We're ready for tomorrow night, the big event. I go to bed and fall asleep.

Damn! I missed a call from Fabien last night. I call him back but it goes straight to voicemail. It's early morning and I know he's probably not awake yet. He called me late last night. I'll ring him after the supper club, tell him how it went. I carry on mindlessly scrolling through Facebook, as I wonder about tonight's event.

And then I see a picture Fabien has posted of him and the band. At first it makes me smile. Then I look closer. The woman, with blonde hair and cowboy boots, short skirt and tight white T-shirt, has her arm firmly around Fabien's waist and is leaning in to him. She must be Monique.

My hackles rise. I have no idea why. She's just an old friend. But she's there with him, when I want him to be here with me. I know that if I carry on like this, I'll drive him away.

Outside, by the barn, Samuel is waiting with two others.

'Is it okay?' he asks tentatively.

'Of course! We need all the help we can get, what with our supper club starting at the *brocante* this evening.'

They smile and I show them where to leave their bags, then the outdoor kitchen. I take them to the shed for secateurs and show them how to cut.

I spend the next couple of hours out on the field, cutting and gathering lavender. As the sun rises high in the sky, I call time on the picking. And as we go from the field to our showers, it can mean only one thing. It's time to get ready for tonight's supper club.

*

Jen and Maria are back from the market. They've been shopping and handing out leaflets for the supper club with lavender biscuits that Stephanie has made. Stephanie takes leaflets with her on her morning rounds and Keith has joined her to help – with little Louis more than anything.

Jen has made a Facebook page for Henri's pop-up restaurant and there are lots of likes and comments. 'We met so many people who wanted to talk about the food,' Jen says excitedly, when she and Maria get back from town. 'And they loved the biscuits! I must tell Stephanie.'

'I have to let Marco know I'm back,' says Maria, and heads towards the accommodation barn.

'He said he was coming to town to find you,' I tell her. 'Just as I went to meet the bakery van. Said he wasn't up for working in the field today. I presumed he was coming to help you. Didn't you see him?'

She frowns. Then, her excitement seeping away, she stares at her phone. We watch and say nothing.

She reaches out a hand. Rhi and I move forward to catch her arms as she wavers and guide her to sit on one of the chairs on the terrace. Jen grabs a glass, fills it with water and puts it in front of her. I think we all know what's coming.

'He's gone.' She lets out a long sigh and drops her hands with her phone into her lap.

We suck in our breath.

'We had a row last night that was still going on this morning. He wanted to move on. I wanted to stay for the supper club. He said he'd go anyway. I didn't believe him. I didn't think he'd really go without me. But he has.'

None of us knows what to say. I put a hand on her shoulder.

Ed runs in from the outdoor kitchen. 'There's a food blogger, Lulu Likes. She's in the area and has seen the Facebook page. She's coming to eat tonight! At Henri's pop-up!'

We're all momentarily distracted from Maria. Suddenly the pop-up feels real for the first time. We're doing it.

I look at my phone. 'He's right!'

'There's loads of interest,' he adds.

'Perhaps we should have done a booking system,' I say.

'Well, we didn't know. We'll just have to find more chairs.'

'And make more bouillabaisse,' says Maria, distracted as well.

'Are you sure?' I ask. 'If you need to go after him . . .'

'It looks like I'm needed here. He'll have to come back and find me if he wants me.'

'If *you* want *him*,' says Jen.

And I see Maria snatch another look at Ed.

'It's okay to realize something isn't right, y'know,'

Jen continues. 'I wish I'd had the guts to understand that. I should have tried to go back to my first husband, tried to find a way to make it work, not keep going with a relationship that was making me unhappy until it was too late. He left me, and my first husband had moved on. There was no way back. It's okay for it not to be okay,' she says.

We surround Maria in a group hug.

'I'm not going anywhere right now,' she says.

'I'm not sure we could have done this without you,' I say.

'You would have. You have Jen and Ed.' She sniffs.

'We have a supper club to prepare for.' Keith has rallied.

And with that, Maria stands. 'Actually, there's something I'd like to say.'

We hold our breath.

'I came here, travelling to find out who I was . . . where my roots are. But it's not about where your roots are, it's where you choose to put them, isn't it? Since I've been cooking here, it's like my wings were hidden and now I've found them. It's not about a place I want to be, maybe just about being me.'

We hug her again and head into the kitchen to prepare our ingredients. Graham and Keith are heading down to the *brocante*. Before they leave, Keith says, 'He'll come back. He'd be a fool not to.'

'I think maybe *I* was a fool, kidding myself we still

had a life together. We've become different people – well, I have. I was just too busy trying to find myself to realize it. Now, let's get cooking,' says Maria, with a smile and a hug from Keith. They move as one to the kitchen.

'You know your side dish? I think you could lose some ingredients,' Jen says softly to Maria. I've never seen Jen like that: it's as if she's leading from behind. I love it. 'Keep it simple. Just let it be you,' she says.

I hold my breath, hoping she hasn't scared Maria off, making her decide to chase after Marco.

'Just be me?' Maria wonders.

Jen nods. 'Beautiful, just the way you are. You don't need to try so hard,' she tells her and Maria gives a wider smile. I allow myself to breathe again.

22

I'm so nervous that my hands are shaking. I don't know why. I've been working as a cook in this town, just down that lane, for three years! At 'l'expérience' as it's now called. It will always be Henri's to me. I look down the pretty lane, with cream stone buildings either side and wisteria clinging to its walls, to where the olive tree once stood. All trace of it has gone, with the sign that used to hang over the bistro door.

I take a deep breath.

I look at the sign, surrounded by fairy lights, propped in pride of place on the far wall. I'll make sure Zach-arie sees that it should be back where it was on the bistro. His dad's place. Back to how things were around here. I refuse to let him wipe out Henri's legacy.

I have an idea.

I pull out a pen and find a piece of paper in Fabien's

office. I'm enjoying sitting at his untidy desk, taking comfort from it and remembering drinking coffee here on our first meeting. Now it's full of crockery, and there's a hotplate as well as the small gas burner. I take a moment to think what to write, then put pen to paper. When I've finished, I find an envelope and put it in. I stick down the flap and walk out of the office into the hot afternoon, out of the worn cream gates and down towards the bistro.

My chest tightens as I reach it, slowing, taking in the effect its makeover has on me. It's strange seeing the place active at night. When it was Henri's we just opened at lunchtime. By evening the bistro was closed, as if it had been tucked up for the night. Now it sleeps all day and is awake at night. I step forward quickly and slide the envelope into the letterbox. At least that's still in the same place. Then I look up at the building.

'I'll see you again soon,' I say. 'Hang on in there.'

The door opens. 'Have you come to book a table?'

It's Zacharie.

'Erm, no.' I clear my throat and lift my chin. 'I came to bring you something.' I point at the envelope on the mat by his feet. He bends down to pick it up.

'It's an invitation,' I tell him. He holds it in one hand and taps it in the palm of the other. 'To our supper club.'

'This evening?'

'Yes.'

'But I have a restaurant to run.'

'Yes, I know. But I thought if you could get away just for a bit. You may like to see what we've done in memory of Henri. Join us for a glass of wine.'

He smiles again. 'Of course. I wouldn't miss it! How do you say . . . "Wild horses wouldn't keep me away"?'

I'm not sure if he's being sarcastic or if this is some kind of olive branch. 'Good. I'll see you there,' I say, and hurry away. I don't want to prolong the conversation. I've said what I need to say in the envelope, why it matters. A partnership between Zacharie and Henri's could be fantastic. A blend of old and new. I just hope he takes in my idea for us to work together, blending ideas like we have here tonight. Nothing stays the same. Everything changes. We could make it work at Henri's with change from both of us.

I hurry back to the *brocante* where the excitement is building.

'Okay, let's do this! Let's get this fusion feast on the road!' I say to Ed, who smiles.

'Henri would have loved this!' Carine says, behind me. She's carrying a bunch of flowers held together with curling ribbon.

'Oh, Carine, they're beautiful! *Merci!*'

'They're not from me. They're from Fabien, sent to wish you luck for tonight. He wishes he could be here.'

And my heart leaps. I wish he were here too. The longer he's away, the more I seem to be falling into a routine without him and I don't want that. I want him with me! I want everything back to how it was before the mistral. Henri's, Fabien, me and our little stitched-together family. Just as it was.

But everything is changing: Stephanie and JB are in their little house, him helping her with the business, partners in life. I'm so proud of them, yet melancholy that everything has to change. But I can't let that happen to Henri's. That sign needs to go back to where it was. I need to prove to Henri's son that it's the best thing for the business and the town, and that we can work together. And this is how I plan to do it. Tonight will be a great success, serving Henri's meals, classics, with a twist, a fusion of flavours from all of us and our food memories. It's about feeling at home around the table, wherever you have come from.

I inhale the scent of the flowers, wishing Fabien was here. But I'm determined to make this happen, to get us all back to how we were, whatever it takes.

'I found a beautiful vase,' says Keith. 'Thought it would work a treat for those blooms!'

I turn to him.

'In fact, I've found a few vases. I thought we could separate the bouquet and add them to the tables. Spread the joy, so to speak.'

'That would be perfect!' I say, and hand him the

235

flowers. That way Fabien will be here in spirit, at each of the tables. Suddenly music is playing.

'I found an old record player and some vinyl,' says Ed. 'Reminds me of Sundays at home before lunch. My father loved to play his records in the front room on a Sunday.'

'He sounds lovely,' I say.

'He is. He and my mum both are . . .' He hesitates. 'Just a bit stuck in their ways.'

'Traditionalists,' I suggest.

'Yes. Church, Sunday lunch. Working at the factory. Taking their two weeks' holiday in the same cottage every year. They just want the same security for me. And something to brag about to their friends!' He laughs. 'A lawyer for a son!'

'I'm sure they'd be even better pleased to know you were happy,' I say. 'It's hard to live your whole life just trying to make someone else happy. You have to live with yourself. Make sure you like the life you've chosen,' I say, without stopping to think. I hope I haven't offended him.

'Like you?'

'I don't have children of my own, but I do know that what I want for Stephanie is for her to be happy, whatever she does, and the little ones.'

'Sadly, it's not quite like that in my family. And I've already let them down once by walking away from the house and the wedding. I'm not sure they could live with any more disappointment.'

I put my hand on his shoulder. 'That makes you a very kind and thoughtful person,' I say. 'But be kind to yourself too.'

'I will,' he says, and we turn to help Keith.

The old rugs are pulled out and we add more mismatched crockery from the fifties to the collection Keith has arranged on an old dresser to give the place a real front-room feel.

'This is looking amazing,' I say, as the outside space is turned into something resembling a vintage tea room, with lace tablecloths, ironed and weighted down with worn but beautifully patterned plates and side plates. There are water glasses of differing heights, knives and forks of all different shapes and sizes. On each table there's a vase of the flowers and a jug of water. There are tea lights in jam jars, waiting to be lit. Intricately woven rugs lie on the floor and each chair comes with its own history. Some are ornate, perhaps from a local château or a *maison de maître*, others from humbler backgrounds, from the heart of a French country home, a little like mine, where families have joined together for meals at the kitchen table. And at the heart of this scene? The table. There are long farmhouse tables, where workers like the pickers would sit after a morning in the sun. There are dark-stained stately ones from formal dining rooms, smelling of beeswax, and some that would have had another purpose, like the sewing-machine tables with their ornate wrought-iron legwork. Machinists would have sat at them to create their garments, either in the home or the château, mending the linen, or in shops, running up local fashions. All of this, the tables, chairs, silver cutlery and worn patterned plates, is part of the history of the town, of the people who have lived and worked here, whose stories are woven into the fabric of the place. This is what Henri would have wanted. A place where everyone is welcome.

'Is everything okay?' Keith asks.

'It's fabulous,' I tell him.

'You haven't seen it with the candles lit!' He beams.

'Let's just hope people come,' I say.

'They will,' he says. 'Make somewhere welcoming and they will come.'

And they do.

The candles are lit, making it look like a magazine lifestyle shoot. The festoon lighting is twinkling. Bottle-openers and corkscrews of all varieties are lying on the tables, and people are opening the wine they've brought with them.

By eight o'clock, three nervous chefs are waiting inside the cool of the *brocante* warehouse. Outside, the barbecue charcoal has been lit, and my heart lifts and swoops as I see the mayor and his wife arrive with neighbours and Carine with Clémentine. They all come in with oohs and ahhs, taking in their surroundings and sitting at the long table Keith has reserved for them, with pressed napkins on top of the patterned plates.

The sound of popping corks heralds another table arriving. It's the bakery-van owner, Adèle, with her husband, elderly mother and children. And they keep coming. Serge, the old lavender farmer, arrives on his own, and Rhi seats him next to Carine at the mayor's table. The neighbours from the shops next to what was Henri's bistro are here too. Samuel and his two companions, who helped on the field, arrive shyly and I usher them in, insisting they're welcome especially after their work in the field that morning. My friend Lou and her partner, who live on a smallholding a few towns away, arrive with armfuls of flowers and produce from their land.

We hug each other hard, then Rhi is in Lou's arms. 'I'm so sorry about Henri,' Lou says to Rhi. 'And I'm sorry I haven't been here sooner. But with the harvest . . .'

'It's fine!' Rhi says, smiling. This is the old friend who would never have got her hands dirty, let alone chip a nail, before she met Alain at the riverbank clearing. He'd lost his way in life after his wife died but, thanks to the riverbank project and spending time at Le Petit Mas when I moved in, planting lavender, he and Lou had got together.

I put all the produce in the cool of the barn, and suddenly I'm wondering what to make with it, turning over ideas in my head as if I were having a conversation with Henri. Just like that, I'm remembering the dishes I made with him. The fog is lifting. I turn to Rhi. 'He's here. I'm thinking about what I can make with these courgettes and tomatoes. The ideas haven't gone! He's still here!'

'And this is where we want him to stay!' she says.

'Very much so. And I need Henri's son to see that too.' I just hope my invitation to come tonight will do the trick.

As Edith Piaf sings from the old record player, Maria and Ed start to plate up her salad starter. It's a mix of different flavours and styles, green leaves and edible flowers. She and Ed are working in harmony together. Jen is behind them, washing up. Graham is helping guests pour their wine and refilling water jugs.

'Everything you see is for sale,' says Keith, revelling in his role as scene-setter. One or two people raise their hands and ask about particular pieces, the gilt mirror and the candelabrum, and he writes 'sold' labels to tie on them.

I keep watching the gates, open and welcoming, as are the lights, the candles and the cheerful conversation over the music. But as we all pitch in to hand round the starters and baskets of bread, then take seats with our guests to eat with them, I take one final glance out of the gates. Zacharie is standing, arms folded, next to his new sous-chef, in chef's whites. Just for a moment I wonder if he's going to come and join us, even just briefly, to raise a glass to his dad. He stares back at me and I'm willing him to come and see what we're doing. He lets his arms drop to his sides. Then, to my disappointment, he shakes his head and turns to go back to the bistro, laughing and slapping his sous-chef on the back. He's not coming. My heart sinks as my fingers curl into my palms, frustrated by his refusal to see what this place is all about. His father, Henri.

The barbecue is served with *carottes râpées*, grated carrot in a thick French dressing topped with poppy seeds, chickpea salad and garlicky potatoes with a hint of cumin and coriander. Baskets of bread are replenished and I feel as if I'm back at the bistro. Food is enjoyed and diners ask to meet the chefs who cooked it and tell them how much they love it. Keith has sold two more mirrors he hung outside, reflecting the festoon lighting, the candles, and another pair of candelabra he's used on the centre table.

'Everything is for sale,' he repeats happily, giving people prices for large tureens and jugs.

After cheese and a glorious trio of desserts, including Keith's marvellous *macarons*, our diners reluctantly leave, promising to come back as soon as we're open again. The wooden till drawer is full: everyone paid the suggested price and more. I grab some wine glasses from the box inside the barn and open two bottles of *crémant*, sparkling wine, a gift from the mayor, and take them to the nearest table.

'I've loaded all the washing-up into boxes,' says Jen. 'I suggest I come back down in the morning, test-run the new clutch and pick it up.'

'And the tablecloths and napkins for washing,' says Keith.

'Just the tables and chairs to go away.'

'It'll be like we were never here,' I say, and hope that's not the case.

There are a few desserts left that Keith made with Stephanie earlier today. I pick up two plates and two glasses of wine. The dessert that had the mayor in tears, reminding him of his childhood. A chocolate mousse, with nuggets of nougat, soft vanilla ice cream and a drizzle of warmed honey and crumbled almonds on the top, like the bar of Toblerone his father would bring him, taking him right back to his childhood, where most of us feel happy, safe, and where the troubles of today are a long way off.

'What about same time next week?' Graham says, enjoying the dessert.

'I don't know,' I say. 'We've made a lot tonight,

enough to keep us going. The harvest will be over in a week or so.'

'I'd like to stay for next week,' says Maria. 'I feel I'm only just starting to find myself.'

'I'd like to stay too,' says Ed, pushing away his phone as a message heralds its arrival. He tuts. 'It's my dad, wanting to know when I'll be back. He saw the man who owns the law firm I'm returning to today.'

'I love this. It's just like being at my nan's,' says Maria.

'My nan used to make us mulligatawny packet soup with extra curry powder and pretend she'd made it herself,' says Keith.

'*What?*'

'And our parents would sit there glaring at us not to say anything. It was disgusting.' He laughs.

'Well, I don't think we should put that on the menu,' says Jen.

'But barbecuing is what I loved most. I loved barbecuing when I was a child. We'd go camping in the woods. My dad would light a fire to see off the mozzies, and we'd sit in silence and watch the flames. I think that's when I felt closest to my dad. Just us, in our thoughts, feeding the fire and cooking on it, fish we'd caught mostly. I felt happy then,' says Keith.

'Do you and your dad still barbecue now?'

He shakes his head. 'No, we don't really talk. He didn't find my life choices very easy to accept. So sad.

He missed out on so much with our son growing up, being a grandparent.'

'Maybe you should invite him to barbecue again.'

'Maybe I should . . .'

'Well, we should definitely barbecue again next Friday for supper club,' says Ed.

'Maybe get some live music,' says Jen.

'Music?'

'Yes – we saw someone busking at the market. Invite them here to play for the supper club.'

'Del, are you okay?' asks Ed.

'Sorry, I was in a world of my own. Just thinking. About Zacharie. He didn't come.'

'No, but lots of locals did,' says Rhi.

'We haven't persuaded him to change his menu yet,' says Jen. 'I say we keep going until he comes.'

This group, who were strangers not long ago, are now supporting me and each other as friends. I owe it to them at least to try.

'I'll be back,' I say, standing, picking up two plates of desserts.

'Where are you going?'

'If the mountain won't come to Muhammad . . .' I march off towards the big gates, then across the road, looking both ways, the flash of the green cross of the pharmacy the only sign of life now. It's hot. The ice cream is starting to melt.

I walk towards the familiar building that looks like

someone I used to know but who has had fillers, a facelift, and changed their face completely. I reach the outside and stand there, trying to pick out features that used to be my old friends. Everything is . . . grey. It's not warm and welcoming, like it used to be, more formal and standoffish. And, by the look of it, empty.

I take a deep breath and push open the door.

23

'You didn't make it to the supper club this evening,' I say, frustrated.

Zacharie is sitting at a table with his sous-chef. The restaurant is empty and closed for the night. They each have a glass of cognac in front of them and are discussing menu ideas, with an iPad and a few ingredients in front of them.

He gives a smile that doesn't meet his cold blue eyes. They are the same colour as Henri's but without any warmth behind them.

'Ah, the home cook! How was your supper club?' He grins.

He has the ability to leave me feeling very small and insignificant, just like my ex-husband. I'm not going to let that happen to me again. I attempt to picture him naked, then blush. That's a very bad idea. He may

246

be a bully, but he's physically very fit and attractive. Instead, I remember he's the son of one of my best friends. And he's behaving badly.

'You didn't come, despite my invitation and you saying you wouldn't miss it for the world. Wild horses wouldn't keep you away.'

'Ah, yes, but they did! There were too many of them! I'm sorry.'

His sous-chef sniggers.

'And how was your little dinner party?' He leans back in his chair and sips at the cognac in his balloon-shaped glass. There on the table is the envelope I pushed through the bistro's door, unopened.

I won't be intimidated by this man. I want to get him on side, get him to see why this place should go back to being Henri's.

'Good. Excellent, in fact. I wish you could have tried it all. I think your father would have loved it. I brought you a couple of desserts.'

'Ah, from your kitchen in the barn?'

'Actually, they were made in my house this morning.'

'Thanks, but no thanks. We have slightly different hygiene standards here.'

I look through to where the old kitchen used to be. Now shining chrome, spotless and sparse. No pans bubbling on the stove, or large ceramic pots with uten-sils to grab easily. The whole place has been stripped of character, including the upstairs, with an arrow for more seating under a row of very modern paintings. Probably worth a fortune but lost on me. I preferred the photographs that Henri had hanging there of fête days in the market square and the night markets.

'As I say, we're not doing peasant food here.'

I lift my head. 'Your father would have loved it.'

'Well, that says it all.'

My eyes flash as I remember the hurt in Henri's eyes when he talked about his children. 'Look, I don't know what your problem is, but there are a lot of us around here whom your father helped and looked out for. We just want him to be remembered. For his bistro to serve the food he was known for. For it to be a hub for locals again.'

He gets up, walks towards me and stops, face to face. I can smell his hot skin, cognac and a mix of scents from the menu tonight. Many I don't recognize. None that remind me of somewhere happy.

He looks back at me, challenging me, and suddenly I feel heat between us. Suddenly there is excitement, electricity in the space between our bodies. I can't believe it's attraction. But all of a sudden I feel on fire. He knows it and I know it. It's an unpleasant mix of attraction and challenge.

'I said,' he says slowly, and I find myself watching his mouth, *'non, merci.'* And laughs. The swirling attraction disappears, like the plug pulled out of a sink, leaving a nasty scum where it once was. Then he steps around me and walks towards the door, reaching for the handle and pulling it open.

His face is fixed. He does not look happy.

I look down at the brandy he was drinking and pick it up.

'To Henri's,' I say, and down it. It burns, calming the fury that had built in that mad moment of seeming attraction. I put the glass down firmly on the table, pick up the desserts and walk towards the door with them. I am not going to let this young man mess with my emotions or my head. He is a game-player and I intend to beat him at his game.

'Same time next week?' I raise an eyebrow as I pass him at the door. I hold his gaze, which darkens. 'I'll take that as a yes, then,' I say, holding my nerve. And without looking back, I walk as steadily as I can out onto the narrow lane and hear the door shut behind me. I lean against the stone wall, in the shadows, hands shaking, looking at where the olive tree once stood. I need Fabien. I need him to tell me this is worth fighting for. But I know it is. I look up at the space where Henri's sign used to be.

'Damn you, Mistral. Damn you!'

24

'I should go away more often,' Fabien says, later that night, when I tell him how much we've sold from the *brocante*.

'No, you shouldn't!' I say, joining in with his laughter, just a tiny bit of me worrying that he might have meant it.

'And do you plan to do it all again?'

'Yes, I think so. Maybe next Friday. Do you think you could be here?'

'It's hard. We're back in my parents' town and a lot of people here want to say hello. But I will try.'

'Okay. What about now? Getting an early night?'

'A few of us are meeting up, going to a party, after the gig.'

'A few of us?'

I feel something unpleasant crawl across my skin

again. Something I've never thought I would feel that is a lot like jealousy. I try to shake it off. I'm an adult in a relationship. Why would I suddenly feel jealous? Or is it guilt? I remember how Henri's son made me feel when he looked at me tonight, before he humiliated me. The frisson, the teasing, the anger and repulsion we feel for each other. How he held my gaze and my insides melted, like the desserts I was holding. And how stupid I felt when he laughed. He was like a cat playing with a mouse, teasing it, knowing it can squash it with one paw. Well, I'm not going to be squashed and made to feel stupid.

Firmly I say to Fabien, 'Well, you deserve a good night out.'

Because he does. He's been working hard. I'm so cross with myself. There's nothing to feel jealous about, nothing to feel guilty about. It was just a look from a man I'm coming to dislike, even loathe, for what he's doing to his father's legacy.

Don't ask, I tell myself. I look at him on the screen. 'So, who's going to be there?'

Damn! I hate myself.

'Just the band. And some old friends we used to hang out with when we were younger. Now they all have children or divorces and are moving into second-time-around relationships.' He gives a light laugh. I remember the call of 'Grandpère', and teasing him.

I think of my ex-husband Ollie leaving France and

starting again with his new partner, having a baby. I had no idea any of it was going on. What if I get hurt again?

'Fabien . . .' Don't say it. Don't poke the nest. Don't say what doesn't need to be said. 'You would say, wouldn't you, if you were unhappy? If you didn't want "us" any more?'

'Of course! I mean no! Yes! What? Jesus Christ. Where's this come from?'

I'm not sure. Why did I have to say that? We rarely get to speak at the moment. Why spoil what time we do have?

'Look, forget it. I didn't mean—'

'Maybe, Del, it's me who should be worried. Maybe you're getting tired of our relationship?'

'No, Fabien. I didn't mean that.'

'Why else would you say that?'

I hear the beep of a car horn at his end of the phone.

'I have to go,' he says, and I can tell he's hesitant to hang up.

'Okay.' I'm unsure what to say next. I'm cross with myself for rattling the bars of a cage that didn't need to be rattled. It's just a party, with friends, one of whom may be Monique. I wish Carine had never sown that seed of doubt. But it wasn't Carine. It's me. Thinking that what happened with Ollie will happen again. I'm pushing Fabien away. And I don't know how to get us back to where we were.

'If you want me to come home, I will . . .'

How can I make him do that? It wouldn't be fair.

'Go! And have a lovely evening,' I say.

'*Au revoir, chérie*,' he says, and I wish the words weren't ringing in my ears as the phone goes dead.

Days pass. Fabien and I swap text messages but don't really speak. I don't know how to start the conversation. Somehow the gap between us has widened. All I can do is get ready for Friday night, the supper club, and make sure it's as good as last week's. It's the only thing I can do to get things back to how they were. I'll put things right with Fabien when he's home.

I need to focus on cooking. I need to find me again. How can I expect Fabien to come home to me if I've lost myself?

I pull out the pan in which Henri always cooked the *daube*. It's early morning and the mist has lifted. Ed, Maria, Graham, Keith, Rhi, Jen and Samuel, with a different companion but one I recognize, are heading out into the field with secateurs and sun hats. There is just a week left of the harvest. Two-thirds of the field is cut. This is the final section.

I put the pan on the hob and look at the beef and vegetables I've brought back from the town. I picture myself at the *brocante*, with all the happy faces around me. This is what food does: it makes people happy, makes them feel at home. And that's how I feel in my kitchen, imagining Henri here, Fabien too, Stephanie, JB and the children. With that, I pick up Henri's old wooden spoon, take a deep breath and look at the pan. The fog starts to descend again but I push it away with images of the supper club, the 'sold' stickers on the furniture, and I know I have to keep going. I turn on the flame and begin to cook. I brown the chunks of beef and smoky pancetta in bubbling butter and oil, set them aside, then soften the onion, carrots, leeks and celery. I add garlic, bay leaves from the garden, tomato purée and stock. I pour in the wine, a whole bottle, loving the sound it makes as it sizzles. There's parsley to go in and a drop of Henri's favourite brandy, the smell filling my nostrils and making my mouth water, giving me the nod that I'm heading in the right direction. I season the dish, and sprinkle over the dried lavender. As soon as the familiar aroma reaches my nose, I'm back in the zone and I couldn't feel happier.

I add the meat to the pan and put it into the oven. Then I fry off the shallots and mushrooms in more butter. I'm nearing the end of the process and I know I've finally got back in the saddle. I put the shallots and mushrooms to one side to add later, with a little slaked cornflour, and chop more parsley to garnish. Then I stand back and regard the work surface, *mise en place*. I hear Henri's voice, *Everything in its place . . . as it should be*, and my heart swells with joy. Life is starting to return to normal.

'So, that's the menu. Are we all agreed?' I say, leaning back in my chair and glancing at the empty plates around the table, wiped clean with baguette. A huge piece of me is back. 'I'm going to cook Henri's beef *daube*,' I say nervously, hoping I don't freeze again and it tastes like the *daube* I've just served, with a hint of lavender among the other *herbes de Provence*. An aromatic mix of thyme, parsley and rosemary. The taste of home. Here. Where I want to stay. A smile pulls at my lips. I intend to fight to do that every step of the way, and feel the fire burning inside me, for me, Fabien, Stephanie, JB and the boys, for our home together.

'Agreed,' they all say, including Samuel, who confirms that Henri's *daube* is a firm favourite with the locals, and we start to talk about all our other dishes for the menu.

We're doing Maria's spiced potatoes and Jen is making a starter of Spanish tapas while Ed's on desserts. Once again a fusion of flavours, heritages, backgrounds and stories are coming to the table . . . with a sprinkling of lavender. Samuel is helping Jen with the tapas. Keith is keeping us fuelled with more homemade cakes and biscuits to go with our coffee.

'Here's to Friday-night supper club!'

'I remember when I first went to Spain,' says Jen, 'I didn't even know what tapas was! It was all such an adventure. I loved it. But that was then,' she says. 'I've come a long way from those days.'

'And where do you want to go?' Graham asks.

It seems she's never really thought about it. 'I don't know. That's the problem. I've just kept travelling, thinking that if I could keep planning a route, I'd be able to avoid the hurt,' she says, and her eyes fill with tears. Rhi places a hand on hers. 'I can't go back. Dan, my first husband, has moved on. I just have to live with losing him. It was my silly mistake. I should've put the effort into being with him, instead of looking elsewhere for my happiness.'

I feel all my senses standing to attention. I just hope there's still time for Fabien and me to remember what we have.

'I suppose we have to learn to find a way to live with sadness,' she says, looking at Rhi.

'And feel lucky we loved them that much.' Rhi's voice cracks.

Come Friday morning, we gather on the terrace overlooking the lavender fields for a trip to the town to visit the grocer and then the *brocante* to set up later this afternoon when the food is prepared.

'Any news from Marco?' I hear Graham ask Maria. She shakes her head. He puts his arm around her and squeezes her to him. No words, just a gesture of support and she seems to appreciate it.

'He's probably waxing his windsurfer as we speak,' she says.

Everyone sighs.

'We had good times. He was fun. He knew who he was, what he liked, what he didn't like, and I liked that in him at the time. But now we may have come to the end of our journey together. I don't hate him. I just think I lost me.'

'Well, I suggest you sharpen your knife and make the best dish you can. You know what they say about revenge,' Keith says.

'A dish best served cold!' everyone choruses, then laughs, like the sun breaking through and the mist lifting over the lavender field.

'A few of us will stay behind and carry on in the field and another couple will go to the shops,' says Ed, taking control.

'I'm happy to stay and harvest,' says Samuel, in his deep, rich voice.

'If that's okay,' Ed adds, turning to me.

'It's perfect.'

'Right, let's make a list,' he says.

Perhaps waiting and wondering if Fabien will make it home tonight won't be so hard after all. I can't wait to show him what we've done with the *brocante*.

*

We walk past the riverside clearing in the fresh air. Later in the day it will be hot. It's quiet. I pick up the debris of beer cans and other detritus and shove it into my bag to put in a bin when I find one.

In town, the sun is shining and the cream walls of the shops look brighter than ever. Jen and I make our way with keen eyes to the outside stalls. I remember Henri doing this with me, pointing out the sellers to buy from and those who were more geared towards the tourist, happy to pay a little more for a slice of Provençal life.

Heads down, we look over the tomatoes in the shade of a parasol. The heat of the sun warms the backs of our necks.

'I'm thinking pork and peaches,' says Jen.

As well as the *daube*? Lovely, with *herbes de Provence*, just a hint of lavender, I think, feeling Henri with me, talking through his idea for a recipe, always with the herbs including the lavender. It's comforting, like I'm walking in familiar shoes.

'And a splash of crème fraîche. Or a peach *tarte*,' I say, 'like *tarte Tatin*, but with peaches.'

'Perfect!' She smiles.

'Roasted peaches, one of Fabien's favourite things.'

'Sounds just right!' says Jen. 'And we'll make plenty, if last week was anything to go by.'

I'm starting to feel this might not just be beginner's luck.

I reach for the peaches, imagining them caramelized in dark sugar sitting on a buttery pastry served with vanilla ice cream just as another hand reaches for them.

'Del.' The familiarity of that voice, which fills way too many of my thoughts and sounds taunting, sarcastic and dismissive.

My heart dips. My chest tightens and twists. Suddenly I'm feeling the heat on the back of my head, racing around my neck and up into my cheeks. I snatch my hand back, feeling like I've touched an electric fence. I straighten.

'Zacharie.'

'We meet again,' he says, as if I'm some traveller passing through.

'Yes,' I say tightly. 'Well, it is where I live and shop.'

'It's a good town. A little pricy maybe, but once the sellers know what we're doing, I'm sure they'll come down a little, to be associated with l'expérience. In the meantime, I shall be bringing in produce from elsewhere. Higher quality.'

'But this place has everything from the local area!'

'Then they should up their quality and lower their prices if they want local business,' he says, peering down at the peaches. 'However, for now, I'll have to make do with what's available.'

He points to the peaches and calls to the seller.

'Oh, actually, *excusez-moi*,' I say. I point to the peaches. '*Pour moi*, Renard,' I tell him.

But Zacharie has already scooped up the box and is holding out a note, pushing it on the seller. Renard looks between him and me. Zacharie puts the note on the scales. 'Like I say, they'll need to learn who to prioritize around here. I'm a restaurant attracting high-class clients. Yours is just a hobby that cannot compete.'

I'm left with my mouth waggling up and down.

Renard picks up the note and puts it into his money-belt.

Then he looks at me. '*Désolé*,' he says.

'We need to have a rethink,' I say to Jen, who is waiting in the shade across the road.

'Why?'

'Zacharie took the peaches.'

'We can get more.' She looks around. 'Or we stick with a *tarte Tatin*. An apple one. We don't need to over-complicate things.'

We wander the market a little more, but the wind has left my sails.

Later that afternoon when we're setting up for dinner, my spirits lift. The *tartes Tatin* are beautiful, amber and golden. And the homemade ice cream is fabulous. Rich and creamy, with flecks of vanilla, served with a sprig of lavender.

This time I'm less nervous. In fact, we're all in high spirits as we load the camper van with food and plates to take to the *brocante*. But curiosity is scratching at my door. I want to find out what Zacharie is up to with the peaches he stole from under my nose.

'Graham and I can walk down the alley and look at the menu, pretend we're interested diners,' says Keith, giving the cushions on a chair a final plump.

It shouldn't matter really. We're doing the dishes that Henri served, with added twists from everyone's past. *Patatas bravas*, small cubed potatoes with a fiery tomato sauce to go with the melt-in-your-mouth beef *daube* and buttery green beans. Roasted artichokes for the vegetarians. For starters there is duck *rillette*, made locally, soft like pâté, with wine and thyme, served with bread and cornichons, or baked Camembert, drizzled with honey and scattered with rosemary and lavender.

Everything is in its place. I wait anxiously for Keith and Graham's return, polishing the cutlery that has already been polished to within an inch of its life, and glasses that shine in the hot afternoon sun.

Finally, they're back, walking hand in hand across the courtyard, heads down.

'Well?' I stand up to meet them. Neither of them is smiling.

'He's doing a tasting menu,' says Graham, slowly.

'With drinks included. A special offer he's calling it!' Keith is clenching his fists angrily.

'What?' Rhi stands and joins us.

'He's doing what?' I'm trying to process what's going on.

'He's doing a special evening, a tasting menu of his experimental dishes. He's got the local press there and bloggers. He clearly wants to make sure no one sees what we're doing here this evening.'

'Phfff!' is all I can think of saying.

'And the peaches?'

'Peach bellinis with a twist for an aperitif,' Graham confirms. 'And then . . .'

'A trio of peach desserts, including peach *tarte Tatin*, with gold leaf.'

I take a deep breath. 'He's stolen our idea. He must have heard me talking with Jen.'

Keith and Graham tut. The mood has nose-dived.

Samuel drops his head. 'Gold leaf? *Non*, just *non*! That isn't a meal, that's a jewellery store!'

I lift my head. 'He may have stolen my idea, but that suggests our ideas are good and he should be working with me. Now, let's show him what the people around here really want. We have plenty on offer. Let's write out a menu and pin it up outside,' I say. 'Keith, do you have any kind of board we could use?'

'Just the thing.' He goes into the warehouse and comes out with an artist's easel and a gold frame.

'Great,' I say, and leave him to write out the menu for the supper club while the rest of us carry on getting ready for the evening, with a little less excitement and more nerves than earlier. I keep checking my phone, but there's no word from Fabien, and I'm thinking he won't make it now.

At seven o'clock the church bell rings to let us know that it's the end of the day. The sun is dipping in the sky, and I hear people walking down the street.

'Here they come,' I say. 'People know we're open tonight. You did lots of canvassing in the market. Well done,' I say to the others. 'And giving out the samosas and lavender cookies at the night market yesterday was a great idea!'

The voices get closer and I smile at the gate, ready to welcome people to our second pop-up night. The candles are lit and we're playing a scratchy but atmospheric tune. The *daube* smells amazing and tastes just as it should. I'm relaxing by the second.

The voices are by the gate. I smile to welcome them, but they walk on and are now passing the gate.

I frown, then shrug. We stand and wait.

But no one comes.

From the far end of the alley opposite, I can hear voices, welcoming and greeting each other, convivial conversation and corks popping. There is music too, some sort of modern jazz, being played by a cellist if I'm not mistaken.

Finally, by ten past eight, with a pot of *daube* on the stove and the candles burning brightly on the empty tables, I pull off my apron and march out of the gates towards the top of the alleyway. Then, as if drawn by the strange music and smells, I walk down it and stand beside where the olive tree once was. Sitting outside under the awning, in front of the newly painted l'expérience window sign, are the mayor . . . and Carine. And the shop owner from across the road, and Renard the greengrocer! It's full! Of locals! My locals! People who supported me and Henri! What are they all doing here?

'Carine!' I say, and she turns.

'Del, are you coming to join us?' she says, with only a hint of surprise in her eyes.

'*Non!*' I say crossly. 'I have a supper club to run . . . an empty one! What are you doing eating here?'

'I was invited,' she says, and nods at the mayor.

'It is hard not to support all the businesses in the town,' he says.

'B-but he closed down Henri's,' I splutter.

'I know, I know,' the mayor says. 'But I must be seen to be supportive of all ventures,' he says, sipping his peach bellini with a twist, whatever the twist might be.

'It's just one meal,' says Carine, trying to calm me. 'Del, he is Henri's son. I think he would want us to be here for him.'

Hurt, eyes stinging, I turn away.

'Ah, Del. Come to experience the real taste of France?'

I turn back to see Zacharie standing in the doorway, smiling, looking far more attractive than he should for someone who is quite so infuriating.

'I have not,' I say, with just a tiny shake in my voice.

'What are you serving tonight? Fish and chips or shepherd's pie?' he scoffs.

'At least I don't have to resort to bribing customers to come in with cheap menus. The people at my table are there because that's where they feel at home,' I say. Just as this place was for me.

I walk away, feeling his eyes on me.

'Del! Come back! Try the bellinis,' calls Carine. But I keep walking, feeling let down, hurt and betrayed. Henri was their friend too.

Back at the *brocante*, I wipe away the tears of frustration on the apron I left there.

'They're not coming. No one's coming,' I tell the group, with a hiccup, and start to blow out the candles and scoop up the cutlery.

'No one?' asks Jen. 'But I thought they all said they'd be back next week!'

'Zacharie's event is heaving. He has the local press, and bloggers, celebrating the street and the local businesses on it. I think most of them are eating there for free tonight.'

'So they're eating for free and getting publicity.'

I take a moment. 'Yes,' I reply.

'What are we going to do now?'

'We may as well pack up and go back to the farmhouse. It looks like our supper club isn't quite the success we thought it would be,' I say. They are all as down-hearted and dejected as I feel.

'Wait! We're part of this supper club, aren't we? This is why we started it. Somewhere we all felt at home, sitting round the table,' says Ed.

'Yes!'

'Then what we should do is sit and eat,' says Ed, firmly.

'Ed's right. We should remember why we started this in the first place,' says Maria.

'I agree,' says Jen.

'And we do! I haven't felt so much at home since our boy left. It's like a hole in my heart has been filled,' says Keith.

So, we relight the candles and lay the tables with the mismatched cutlery, the polished glasses, and start to serve dinner, the baked Camembert and duck *rillette* with bread and cornichons. Graham pours the wine.

'*Âllo?* Am I too late?' It's Serge, the old lavender farmer. 'I fell asleep and forgot the time. Have I missed the dinner?'

'Not too late at all!' I grin. 'Come and join us.'

'First people I've seen all week,' he says. Samuel brings another chair and I move him to the middle of the group, then pour wine into his glass. He beams as the group take seats around him and pass the *rillette* and Camembert, talking animatedly about the flavours, then asking Serge about the lavender harvest when he was young. He's delighted to tell them about long days in the fields, cutting and drying the lavender and making oil. The lunches that would take place in the fields in the shade. Siestas afterwards and swimming in the river.

This is why we're doing this, I think. Not for the bloggers or the journalists, but for the people who want to come to the table and feel among friends, at home.

'*Bon appétit, tout le monde,*' I say, just as I'm about to lift my glass. 'To the chefs!'

'*Âllo?*' I hear, and my wine nearly shoots into the air, as my heart swoops and I whirl around.

'Fabien!' I run over to him and hug him hard. Then I pull back and gaze into his face.

He beams, pulls me back to him and kisses me.

'I missed you!' I say.

'And I you!' He tilts his head. 'I have a favour to ask.'

'A favour?'

'I have the band here. We are on our way to the next festival so I told them of a place that makes amazing food. They are desperate to try it.'

'Oh, Fabien. Thank you!'

'You don't mind?' he checks.

'Of course not! I'm delighted. Tell them to come in!'

He kisses me again. 'I knew you wouldn't mind.' He waves at the people by the gate. This is . . .' He introduces them all. 'And Monique.'

So, this is Monique.

'Pleased to meet you,' she says, shaking my hand, and I feel I'm being give the once-over, sized up, as I'm doing to her.

We pull up more chairs around the table and glasses are filled. Serge couldn't look happier, with Ralph lying at his feet waiting for food to fall.

'This *daube* is amazing,' he tells me, dipping his bread into the sauce, which dribbles down his unshaven chin. 'Just like Henri used to make.'

Samuel grins. 'It's home.' Fabien agrees wholeheartedly with him and they high-five. That makes my night.

We move on to dessert. The *tarte Tatin*, simple and classic, little custard tarts that Ed made, and Maria's chocolate mousse with the slightest hint of chilli, with fondant red chillies.

Graham puts his spoon into the custard tart, takes a mouthful and stops. 'Oh, my God!' He drops the spoon and claps his hand over his mouth.

Keith looks at him, worried. 'Gray?' he says.

Graham's face falls, and suddenly he bursts into tears.

'*Gray!*'

25

Graham's face is in his napkin and he is weeping openly.

None of us knows what to do or say.

Finally he lifts his head. 'I'm so sorry,' he says, reaching with a shaking hand for water.

'Don't be sorry. We're just worried about you,' I say.

'Was the dessert that awful?' Ed is concerned.

Graham gives a little laugh, and Keith hands him a tissue, telling him to blow.

The candles flicker on the table.

'It wasn't the dessert, not in that way. It just . . . it reminded me of being seven. At boarding school. I was very lonely and lost. But I remember the custard tarts and the cook. She was fabulous. It made my time there bearable.'

'You were sent to boarding school at seven?' Jen says.

We're all horrified.

He nods. 'It's how you learn to keep things to your-self. Not to show emotion. Not to show weakness. Not to show you're hurting.' He turns to Keith. 'I'm so sorry.'

And we all hold our breath, praying it hasn't come to this, that they're going their separate ways.

Keith is staring, wide-eyed, at him. His bottom lip is quivering.

'I know I don't say how I feel very often, and that annoys you,' Graham goes on. 'And I know I'm too critical of you when you cook for me, and you're just trying to make nice things, and I'm always too worried to eat them in case I put on weight. And I know you didn't want to come on this trip and really want to go home . . .'

No one moves.

'. . . but I miss him too. I miss our boy so much. I thought, like Jen, that travelling would help ease the pain. I know you miss being at home, and if you want to go back, we will. I love you and I don't tell you enough. I'm sorry . . . I love you, and the home you've built for us.'

'And I love you, you silly sod!' Keith says. 'I love the family we made, even if he's not with us right now. We still have each other.'

'Yes,' says Graham, his voice catching. 'I'm sorry I made you come away.'

'It's okay. I'm glad you did. I like it here.' Keith smiles, plants a kiss on his lips and they stay like that for a moment or two. Then, as they break apart, they smile and we find ourselves clapping and waving our napkins as if they had just married.

'Now, who's for another custard tart?' asks Ed, and everyone puts up their hands.

We move on to coffee and stories from the band – and the pickers, all sharing their tales of travel, life on the road.

Something is flapping over the wall. Another napkin. Maybe one of ours flew off when we were waving them. I see it again, like a . . . white flag?

The gates to the courtyard open and the mayor and Carine come in, their napkins clearly stolen from l'expérience.

'May we come in?' says Carine, contrite.

I fold my arms like a stern head teacher. 'How was dinner?' I ask.

'Small!' they say at the same time, and laugh.

'Is it true you cooked Henri's *daube* tonight?' the mayor asks, looking pitifully pleading through his round glasses.

'Among other dishes.' The smile returns to my face.

'What else?' the mayor asks.

Jen tells of the dishes on the table. Who they belonged to and why they're there.

The mayor nods, understanding.

When I've let them salivate a little, I say, 'Come on,

there's plenty left,' and pull up another couple of seats at the table.

'This is proper home cooking,' says Serge, having another helping to keep the mayor and Carine company.

This feels like a battle. One I want to win. Clearly this town isn't big enough for me and Zacharie.

But what am I going to do next?

As the meal draws to a close, Fabien kisses the top of my head and follows the other band members to the parked van. They return with their instruments. And in no time, there is jazzy blues playing out from the courtyard. Faces pop in around the gate, people leaving l'expérience, and soon the courtyard is filling with people dancing and clapping.

Fabien presses me to him between songs and whispers in my ear, 'I have news.' I look at him curiously. 'I will be home soon. One more week. They have found a guitarist.'

Suddenly I want to cry. 'You're coming home?'

'Yes, in a week. At the end of the harvest.'

I hug him tightly, then let him rejoin the band for a final number.

Later that night, as Fabien joins me in our room, and the rest of the band bed down in the barn and the minibus, it's the joy that I remember most about the evening. The fun and the laughter.

*

'A complaint about the music?' I'm staring at the local *gendarme*, having waved off Fabien and the band the following morning. I'm still wondering about Monique doing her early-morning yoga on the terrace and trying to shake away the image of her supple body. Mine aches.

The *gendarme* is looking out over the lavender field as the team pick in the early-morning sunlight.

'Who complained?' As if I need telling.

'I can't say, I'm sorry.'

'No licence? It was just Fabien, in his own business, with his band.'

'*Oui, je sais,*' says the *gendarme*. 'But I'm obliged to tell you. No more live music without a licence.'

The sooner I get the restaurant back, the better. But how?

26

'Okay,' I say, as we all gather on the terrace. The bakery van has just been and there are freshly baked baguettes, a pile of buttery croissants, an almond swirl for Graham, a chocolate croissant for Maria and another for little Louis, who is eating with Keith while Stephanie makes her deliveries.

'So, what's the plan?' Ed asks.

'We can't have live music, but they didn't say anything about recorded music. We still have the record player and Edith Piaf.'

'We need to make sure l'expérience knows we're not going anywhere,' says Maria.

'We've got a write-up on a blog!' says Jen. And then her shoulders drop. 'So have l'expérience. It says that both are great places to eat but for different reasons.'

'Let's open two nights a week, double our takings,' says Maria. 'More even!'

'Different set menu on each night,' says Jen.

'How's the harvest doing?' I ask. I haven't been in the field for a few days.

'We're nearly done,' says Graham, who's taken up the reins on getting the last of the lavender in with Samuel and a couple of the other men from the riverside clearing.

'I say we give it a go, for a week, open every night,' says Maria. 'It's our final week here.'

'Show l'expérience we're as busy as they are,' says Ed.

There's just one week left until Fabien comes home. Until the harvest is officially over.

'I'm in!' says Jen.

'Me too!' says Keith.

Ralph gives a bark and little Louis claps, raising his hand too, and everyone laughs.

'One big push to show him we're more popular than his fancy tasting menu,' Jen says.

'To see if he can be convinced to work with me, and put Henri's back at the heart of the town. Just until Fabien comes home at the end of the week,' I say.

'Let's do it!'

27

'You're joking! Another complaint? What about this time?' I say, a couple of days later, to the young *gendarme* at the *brocante* gates.

'He says you're operating as a restaurant without a restaurant licence. You have been open every night this week.'

'It's a supper club! On private property. People make a contribution.' I'm reminded of the group of expats who tried to close down the riverbank project, saying we were running it illegally. 'It's all above board.'

'I had to tell you. And the curried goat was amazing last night.'

'*Merci!*'

'But he's right. You can't operate as a restaurant here.'

'What? It's just a few friends sharing food. A taste of home for travellers on a journey. Come back again tonight. I'll save you some of the Spanish chicken. And there'll be some Moroccan flavours too from Jen's travels.'

She smiles. 'I'll pass on the message. And, as a friend, I'll be dropping in tonight.'

The only thing I can do is have it out with the man. I storm down to the restaurant, push open the door and stride in. We may have only one more night ahead of us, but I'm not going to let him spoil it.

'This has to stop!'

The delivery man takes the signed paper from Zacharie's hand and makes a hasty exit from the restaurant.

There's no time for fake niceties. He retaliates straight away. 'You cannot operate your home-cooking kitchen as a restaurant,' he says, leaning across the pass from his kitchen.

I throw up my hands. 'It's a supper club! Friends gathering!'

'Phffff!' He throws up his hands. 'Friends gathering!' He turns down his mouth in disgust. 'You are open every night! Advertising in the town! Handing out samples and pointing them towards your "supper club".' He makes speech marks in the air. This time he's more irate than I am. 'Trying to recreate Henri's bistro just a few feet from where it used to be. But you need to accept that Henri's is gone! There is a new place here now. L'expérience!'

He comes out angrily from behind the kitchen counter and indicates the new chrome and grey interior. 'We are cutting edge. With great reviews. Not plates of food you would get in your granny's kitchen. Going out to eat should be an experience.'

'Home cooking, made with love! Not tiny pipettes of food, too pretentious to be called a meal,' I fire back.

He puts his hands on his hips. 'It is high-class French cooking. Something you would know nothing about.' He takes a step forward, confronting me.

'I know it's not what Henri would call French cooking.' I stand my ground.

'What do you know about my father?' He inches further forward.

'I know he loved you.'

He leans in. 'He abandoned us!'

'He was trying to give you space when your mother met her new partner. He told me about it when he taught me his recipes here in the kitchen, how much it pained him, but he did it for you, to help ease you into your new life.'

'Is that what it was? Space!' he spits. His face is angry, and close to mine.

'And I know that when you were growing up he would cook for you, cook your favourite *moules frites* on a Saturday, followed by crème caramel and on Sundays you'd join him in the kitchen . . .'

Tears are rolling down his cheeks. He brushes them away.

'I'm sorry,' I say, and touch his arm. He lets me.

I hug him. He lets me do that too.

Then he pulls his head back and looks me straight in the eyes. He's so much like Henri. He's not Henri, I remind myself. He's someone who is missing his dad and is too proud to say so. I don't know what to say to make him feel better. I've said all I can.

He stares at me, with angry, searching eyes, and I finally feel I'm starting to see the real Zacharie, Henri's son. Slowly he leans in to me and I feel the connection between us. I want to tell him I understand his pain. I want us to work together, celebrate his father's life. I want us to be friends. Suddenly he leans in a little more and his lips are on mine. They rest there for a moment, offering some comfort, before I come to my senses and pull away.

'Whoa!' I say, stumbling into a chair and table.

'What?' He doesn't move and raises an eyebrow. 'You don't want to kiss me? I knew you did when you came here the other night shouting and fighting. It's okay. I get it. It's foreplay.'

I'm feeling hot and queasy. 'No, it is not. And I don't,' I say, wiping the back of my hand across my lips.

'Are you sure? I heard you like younger men!'

I'm so angry I could— I don't know.

'I do not want to kiss you!' I say firmly.

'So, you're not inviting me to bed?' He's back to where he was before I saw the chink of damaged young boy.

'No!' I snap.

'You are a tease.' His face becomes red and angry. 'You keep turning up here, wanting my attention, and when you have it, you think you can play with me.'

Suddenly I'm nervous. 'No!' My face is reddening too. I need to leave.

'Really? So it's not just younger men you have a thing for. Maybe it was my father you were secretly in love with, seeing as you're so keen to remember him here.'

'I wasn't in love with him! He was – he was like a brother!'

'So you say! My father had a habit of breaking hearts.'

I turn and see Rhi in the doorway behind me suddenly looking as she did when she first arrived: confused and in shock. She turns to hurry away.

'Rhi! Come back!'

'And your home-cooked café? I will get you shut down! I don't need any reminders of my father around here,' Zacharie calls after me.

I storm out after Rhi.

'I promise you, I was never in love with Henri. Only like we all loved him, as a family member, perhaps the head of the family.'

'You were close,' she says, sitting in the shade at the *brocante*.

'We were. But that's just Zacharie trying to sow seeds of doubt. He's trying to destroy anything that remains of Henri's legacy. Trying to wipe out the friendships he forged, all the good he did. We're all missing him and wishing him back. Zacharie is trying to destroy everything.' I sit next to her on the town-hall steps.

'I just came to see if you were all right,' she says. And I wonder if she saw him kiss me. I feel sick. Did I encourage him? No! I just wanted to comfort him. What a mistake.

'If only we'd had a funeral service for him. I think it would have helped,' Rhi says.

I nod. *You have to know when the journey ends*, I say to myself. I can still taste the unpleasantness of Zacharie and this battle.

'And the new beginning starts,' she says.

'Let's go back to the farmhouse,' I say. 'Fabien will be home any time soon.' And every bit of me wants to hope this is where our journey ends and begins, at Le Petit Mas. Together. I just hope he does too.

28

I push back the thin sheet after a heavy afternoon nap, and head to the bathroom. I use the loo, wash my face and stare at myself in the mirror. Everything I've built here is rapidly falling away in front of my eyes. The day we moved in together, I dreamed of spending our lives here with our unconventional but happy little family, but that is gone. I retch into the sink. I drink a glass of water from the tap, refill it and walk back into the bedroom, passing the lavender field on one side. There is barking and laughter, and there on the drive is Fabien.

I run down the stairs and outside. 'You're here!'

'Hey!' He smiles. 'Where have you been? Meeting your lover?' He laughs. 'A final fling before the old man gets home?'

'You're hardly old.' I'm blushing, thinking of Henri's son.

He goes to put his arms around me and I'm stiff – Zacharie's cologne is still suffocating me. 'I need to shower,' I say, pulling back.

'Okay.' He loosens his embrace around my waist. 'Shall I come and shower with you?'

'No, no! I'll be back in a minute. Pour some wine. Then we have to get to the *brocante* for supper club.'

I rush upstairs and turn on the shower. Scrubbing vigorously until my skin is red, I'm trying to get rid of the smell of Zacharie.

I arrive back on the terrace and Fabien is reading a message on his phone.

'What's that?' I ask, not wanting to ask but the words come out of my mouth. This is Fabien's homecoming. I planned to do so much more. I should have been focusing on that instead of Zacharie.

'Just the band. A few pictures from last night. I wish you could have come. It was a great final gig.'

I tip olives into a bowl, then pick it up with my glass of wine and carry them across to join him. I look over his shoulder at a picture of him next to Monique, shoulder to shoulder, him on bass, her on saxophone, smiling at him.

He types a message back and sends a laughing emoji.

My cheeks are flaming, trying to push out the memory of Zacharie. Fabien puts his phone away and we stand in silence, looking out over the cut lavender plants. For a moment we are two strangers, with different paths ahead of us, who have come together just for one part of their journeys. I stare at the glow of the golden sun setting over the town, wondering if this is where our journey together ends.

I take a deep breath. 'Is this enough for you, Fabien?'

'What do you mean?'

'Will you miss life on the road? Is this, at Le Petit Mas, what you really want?'

Zacharie's words are ringing in my ears. *I heard you had a thing for younger men!*

'We've been through this!' Fabien sighs. 'Maybe you're so busy worrying about other people and their lives you don't have time for ours any more.'

I feel hot and sick. I have to tell him what happened between me and Zacharie. 'Look, there's something I need to tell you . . .' at the same time as he says, 'So, let me just tell you.'

We both give a little laugh.

'You first,' we say in unison.

'It was just a kiss!' we say together, then stare at each other as if time has stood still. As if we've just hit the end of the road with a bump.

'A kiss! You kissed her?'

'Who did you kiss?' He scowls.

'I didn't! He kissed me! But I let it happen. You kissed her? Monique!'

'You kissed who?'

'Zacharie.'

'You kissed Zacharie? Henri's son? *Oh, là!*' He slams down his wine glass and holds his hands to his head.

'No. Yes. Not really. Sort of! And you kissed Monique?!'

'Yes! And I realized straight away she wasn't the person I wanted to be kissing! I wanted to be with you! That's when I told them I was leaving. Last weekend. But you were busy kissing Henri's son!'

'Because you were away! I was confused, lonely. And it was him kissing me! I was just trying to talk to him about Henri when he suddenly cried.'

'Crocodile tears to get you into bed!'

'No. It was just a heat-of-the-moment thing. He just leaned in and kissed me.'

'And you let him!'

'No! I stopped him.'

'Eventually!'

'You can talk!'

Suddenly there is a cough. We turn.

It's Carine.

'I can see this is a bad time. I'll come back later,' she says.

Fabien and I glare at each other, neither knowing what to say. He picks up his glass and drains it, then grabs his bag and storms upstairs.

At the *brocante*, everyone is ready for service. The candles are lit and it's hot, really hot. There hasn't been any rain for weeks.

There is a strange atmosphere in the courtyard tonight. Everyone is looking at me and each other and I can't help but think they must have heard our argument. Embarrassed and broken inside, I walk to the gates and write up the menu. This is all Zacharie's fault. If it hadn't been for him starting this war between us none of it would have happened. Outside l'expérience braziers are burning brightly, despite the heat of the night, dramatic against the cream walls of the alleyway.

I won't let him win. He can't destroy everything.

'Let's get cooking!' I call to the team. 'And bring in as many as we can, perhaps go out onto the square and point people in our direction. Let's do what we can to get them into Henri's and away from l'expérience!'

Jen and Graham go out into the alleyway and the square, pointing people towards us, offering them a glass of wine on the house. The place is buzzing, lots of happy diners. Ed and Maria are exhausted, serving from the tiny kitchen. At the end of service, I'm dead on my feet. We load the plates into crates with the cutlery and dishes.

'So, last night tomorrow,' says Graham, as I sit fanning myself.

He's right. We agreed to do this just for the week.

'We'll have to make sure it's a goodie!' I try to smile.

Back at the farmhouse, it's silent. Fabien is either asleep or avoiding me. I check my phone. Nothing from him.

I try to think of a message to send to him. But what can I say? He's not wrong. We took our eye off the ball. We strayed from the path and now it looks like there's no way back. We've hurt each other. And what should have been his first lovely night home ends with us in separate rooms, so close, but so far apart.

29

The next morning, I'm awake early. I listen for sounds of Fabien moving around, but there's nothing.

'Oh, Fabien! How did we get here?' I say aloud, checking my phone again to see if he's messaged. He hasn't. I have to speak to him, see if we can put things right. But what if we can't forgive each other? What if we can't get over this?

I get up and head down to the kitchen, my head turning to dishes we could make for our last supper club at the *brocante*. We need to make it our best ever.

I let Ralph out into the field, now harvested, ready for a rest until next year. And right now, I feel I could sleep for ever. I put on the coffee and when it's ready I pour myself a cup.

We may not have been able to convince Zacharie to take on Henri's recipes and ethos, but the supper club showed the town that there was room for both sorts of cooking, the trained French chefs and the home cooks, sharing their generosity on the plate. If only we could have worked together. I look down at my pad, my pen hovering over it, wondering what to make for tomorrow, a huge final feast.

As I'm sitting on the terrace, the smell of my coffee turns my stomach and I push it away, craving something fresher. I head back into the kitchen, take a few sprigs of lavender and pour boiling water on them, lavender tea. I hold it to my nose, inhale its soothing scent and take it back out on to the terrace.

'Hey,' says a voice behind me.

It's Fabien, his hair messy from the pillow he's just left. He looks tired.

'Couldn't sleep?' he asks, and I shake my head.

'You?'

He shakes his head too.

At least we're being civil to each other, but I'm overwhelmed with sadness. How did we get here?

'*Café?*' he asks.

'I have lavender tea,' I tell him.

He goes into the kitchen, returns with his own coffee and sits down. And here we are, back where we started, on the terrace.

289

'He would have hated seeing us come to this,' says Fabien, looking out over the field.

'He would,' I agree.

And we fall into silence.

'I didn't mean to kiss him or let him kiss me,' I say. 'I was angry. He was in my face and it just sort of happened. It wasn't a kiss, it was more like a challenge. He was challenging me, seeing if I was stupid enough to fall for him and go to bed with him. He was laughing at me.'

I can see Fabien's fists curl, his jaw set.

'And what about Monique?' I'm not the only one in the wrong here.

'It was just a kiss,' he says quietly, his face set.

I feel the distance opening between us once more. Like the tide that comes in, then recedes. 'So you said.' I wait for more.

'I stopped it before it went any further.'

'The night of the party?'

He nods.

This time it's my turn to feel angry and hurt.

'I stopped it because hers were not the lips I wanted to be kissing. I knew it as soon as they landed on mine. It just told me everything I needed to know, to be sure. I just wanted to be with you.'

Tears spring to my eyes.

'And me you,' I say, my hand reaching across the table to meet his.

'It's always been you, just you,' he says, and stands.

'And it's always been you,' I say, as he pulls me towards him, like a magnet.

'I shouldn't have gone on the tour,' he says.

My body is feeling more alive than it has in weeks. The aches and pains of the last few days are forgotten.

'I should never have told you to go, but I wanted to make sure you didn't feel being with me was some kind of a mistake, that you missed being with your friends.'

'I have never regretted for one moment being with you. Well, maybe when you sent me off on that tour bus so that I had to sleep in a van and a tent for the past four weeks.'

'If I've learned one thing, it is to appreciate what we have here.'

'And that we need to make time for each other,' he says.

'I agree. Now the harvest is over, the pickers are leaving. We can spend time together, just us.'

We laugh, and then slowly lean in to each other and kiss, and I know these are the only lips I want to taste again. Our bodies mould together and we turn towards the house and climb up the stairs, still kissing.

There's a cough.

'*Bonjour*,' says Carine, with a smile and a knowing look. 'I'm glad to see you two have made up.'

I blush. 'Carine!' My body is on high alert right now,

but I pull my silk dressing-gown around myself. 'You're early.'

'I wanted to see you before I went to the office. I came last night, but you were otherwise engaged.' I think back to our argument and the despair it stirred up. I want that to be behind us now. I want us to move on together. I hold Fabien's hand and he holds mine tightly. It feels so good.

'*Café?*' says Fabien, leaning towards her and kissing her on both cheeks.

'*Non*,' she says. 'How was your trip?'

'Tiring.' He smiles. 'I'm not as young as I was.'

'How was Monique?'

I smart at Carine's boldness.

'Still wishing she could get you down the aisle?'

He laughs. 'Yes, but there's only one person I want to be with,' he says, making me feel that everything I ever wanted is here with me. My world is back on its axis.

Carine raises an eyebrow as if that's not a concept she's familiar with.

'So . . .' says Fabien, as Carine lights a cigarette and blows the smoke out towards the fields. 'Is there something you wanted?' He wants to hurry this along. Our bed is calling to us.

Carine blows out smoke and takes her time.

I'm like a cat on a hot tin roof.

'I thought you'd want to know . . .'

Know what? I'm yelling in my head. Despite my frustration, I let her take her time.

'Zacharie . . .'

His name throws cold water over us and my excitement melts away.

'What about him?' I frown.

Fabien drops my hand, reaches for his coffee and takes a restorative sip.

'He's selling,' she says flatly.

'*What?*'

'He's going to sell l'expérience. The building too.'

I reach for a chair and sit on it.

'Wh-what? Why? I thought he wanted to make a name for himself around here.'

'And he has,' she says, stubbing out the cigarette. 'And now he feels he has made a name for himself, for the brand, he can expand and move to bigger premises.'

'So . . .' I slowly process what she has said, '. . . he's selling.'

She nods.

'Which means,' I look up at Fabien, 'we could buy it.'

He throws his hands into the air. 'We just said we need to make more time for each other.'

'I know, I know, but this is the bistro! This is my

chance to get it back! For it to be Henri's again! Everything back to how it was!'

'And how are we going to afford it?'

'I – I'll run the pop-up for longer. Try to get a deposit together. Don't you see? We can get Henri's back! We can do a fundraiser night, a memorial night, for Henri. We'll get a licence for the band. We'll do an auction. Just give me a chance to raise the money. Or try to do it.'

'He's asking top price for the place,' Carine warns.

'Then we sell here,' I announce, without thinking it through. 'We can live above the bistro. We'll sell Le Petit Mas.'

'And live above the bistro. You will live in your work. Where is the balance?' Fabien says crossly.

'But, Fabien, it's everything!'

'And your life will be nothing but the bistro. It seems to me you care more about Henri and the bistro than you do about what is happening to us.'

And with that he storms out again. And any of the bridges that had just been rebuilt are blown apart.

'I know one thing for sure. There is no way Henri would have wanted this. You two still have each other. Don't let it slip through your fingers,' says Rhi. I hadn't realized she'd joined us on the terrace. Or that Stephanie had arrived in the kitchen. 'That's why he wanted to leave. He had been tied to that one place for too long. He wanted to live while he still had the time. Yes, he loved the bistro but he'd realized there was more to life than that.'

I look at Carine. She shakes her head. 'If you two can't make it work, I was right not to believe there was one man out there for me.'

'Go after him, Del. You have to!' says Stephanie.

30

I knew exactly where to go to find him. When I realized he wasn't at the *brocante*, I knew where he'd be. Where we've all found solace at one time or another: down at the riverside, clearing up around the hut, sweeping the litter from the doorway. I watch him for a moment, then walk up behind him. He's deep in thought. I reach out and touch his arm. He stops sweeping, and I don't know if I made him jump or just interrupted his thoughts. I wish I knew what they were. It's quiet here at the riverside. Just a couple of ducks on the water, paddling along, making it all look easy, while under the water they're working hard. 'Be like a duck. Remain calm on the surface and paddle like hell underneath!' Michael Caine said that, and Henri liked to quote it when service in the restaurant got busy. I smile at the memory.

'I thought you might have gone,' I say quietly.

'Gone where?' he says.

'I don't know. Back to find Monique? To the band. Maybe I drove you away.'

He leans the broom against the shed and turns to me. I'm trying to read his face while wanting to hug and kiss him. He hasn't gone. Not yet. A tiny glimmer of hope is flickering in my stomach.

He sighs and looks up at the larch tree. 'I told you. I realized what I knew all along. I didn't want her. I wanted you. But you just don't have room in your life for me.'

I shake my head and reach for him.

'You told me to go, Del, so I went. I thought you needed space to work things out for yourself. See if you wanted "us". I just don't know what to think any more, except that the only thing that seems to matter to you is the bistro, getting it back. Getting one up on Zacharie, even if it means climbing into bed with him.'

'I did not climb into bed with him! It was a kiss. One kiss and I regret it more than anything. But I was alone, thinking you were with Monique. Which you were!'

'It was just a kiss.' He reaches for my fingertips. 'And one I regret very much. It's in the past. All of it. I need to know about now . . . the future.'

The little glimmer of hope is becoming a growing flame inside me, warming and comforting me. 'Me

297

too. I want us. Wherever that may be. If you want to go on the road with the band, I'll come with you.'

He laughs. 'You'd hate the sleeping arrangements.' And I get a glimpse of Monique undressing in a tent and shake it off. I'm not going back there.

'I mean it. Henri's was part of the journey, my journey. And you have to know where the journey ends.'

He hesitates. 'Are you talking about us?'

'No. It's not about Henri's. It's all about us being together, wherever.'

He takes a moment and the flame dies a little. 'I can go. If that's what you want. If it was just part of the journey. The band has another tour coming up, America. Hoping for the big-time. The door is open for me.'

'And do you want to go?'

'Do you want me to?'

'I want you to do whatever you want to do that makes you happy. If that's going back on tour, so be it. I'll support you and be here for you when you come home.'

He lets out a long sigh. 'What do you want, Del? I want what makes you happy.'

Without realizing it I have taken his hands.

'Del, if you want Henri's, I'll support you. We'll sell Le Petit Mas. Live above the bistro.'

'You-and-me is far more important, Fabien. I just need to know that you want to be with me.'

'There is nobody else I ever want to be with.'

'Nor me, only you.'

'And is it what you really want, to sell Le Petit Mas?'

'No.'

'If it is, I'll support you. We'll go for it.'

'Do you want to be back on tour?'

He shakes his head, and we move closer, our foreheads touching.

'There'll be other restaurants. Or you can keep going at the *brocante*, get a licence for the summer, making it a more permanent feature. Do weddings maybe,' he suggests.

'I like that idea.' We kiss as the wind weaves through the trees, making them whisper, like passing on a message, letting us know the mistral is on her way back into town, like a returning diva to her home.

'Le Petit Mas is our home, Stephanie, JB and the children's too. Henri's bistro was about me, not about us. It was part of my journey to find myself.'

And I think about Maria, finding her wings. Maybe I found mine, too, in this year's lavender harvest.

'I don't ever want to lose you.'

'But you were in love with Monique.'

'Monique and I were a thing of the past.'

'But you loved her.'

'Maybe once. But not now.'

'But she's your age . . . I'm older.'

'More beautiful and way more intelligent. I love the way you are a mother to Stephanie, how you help others, not thinking of yourself, how you are there for people when they need you. I promise you, nothing happened. I enjoyed revisiting my past, being with the band, remembering the times we had, but that's all. You and I, we need to slow life down. Take time for each other. Anyway, my back aches from sleeping on bad beds during the tour. I never want to do that again. I want to wake up every morning with you beside me.'

'I don't want you to regret being with me.'

'No regrets, ever! Think of all the men you could have settled with. Instead you went for a penniless *brocante* owner, who plays bad guitar so has to play bass.'

'I love you for your guitar playing. The way you play with the children . . .'

'I want us to grow old together.'

I look at him. 'But right now, we have a supper club to organize and we need to make tomorrow, the last night with everyone, really special. The end of a journey. A goodbye to the pickers. And a celebration of Henri's life. We have not had a funeral so this will be our way of saying goodbye.'

At last he leans in and kisses me, and I kiss him back.

'Now, let's get to the *brocante* and get ready.'

'Tomorrow is our night to say goodbye to everyone,' I say sadly. I'm going to miss the pickers, my new friends.

'I won't invite the band,' he says. 'It was great to go back, but I want to move on. I can start a teenagers' band – get some of the youngsters who are hanging out down at the riverside. Get them playing music. I'm going to talk to them. We don't need a licence for a youth project. My days of being on the road are done. I'm happy to be home.' He kisses me gently but fully on the mouth, and my whole body comes alive, despite the exhaustion I've felt of late.

'Come on, let's go and tell the others. Tomorrow night is for Henri! A celebration of a life well lived.'

That evening we run the supper club as usual. There's a relaxed feel to the evening. The harvest is at an end, and soon we'll be moving into autumn. The place is calm, despite the wind slowly building, bringing with it a welcome coolness.

We fight a losing battle with candles on the tables and the bunting is attempting to take off, but none of us seems worried, perhaps melancholic at the end of our time together.

'No regrets about not going for Henri's?' Jen asks me.

'I've barely thought about the place this evening,' I tell her. And although Graham and Keith have taken their nightly stroll to look at the menu at l'expérience and report back on the people sitting there this evening, I haven't wanted to go and see for myself. I haven't stood at the top of the alleyway to count how many customers they have. According to Graham and Keith, there are hardly any tonight.

A napkin takes flight. Ed catches it and attempts to pin it down with a heavy silver butter knife. Another follows the first. Glasses clatter on the table. Suddenly we're chasing napkins and picking up glasses as table-cloths lift.

'*Putain!*' I say. '*Le mistral!*'

As we run around to try to save everything and gather it safely into the warehouse, I gasp, 'I don't think we'll be having many diners here tonight.' A hat lifts off a man's head and flies down the road. Dogs bark and the chestnut tree sways and waves.

'Maybe we should take a plate of food to Serge,' I suggest.

'I'll go,' says Fabien. 'Then we can all eat together in here, out of the way of the wind.'

'Good idea.' I kiss him.

Maria serves a plate of food, a selection of all tonight's treats. Spanish prawns and chorizo, Greek salad, pakoras and chicken *pot-au-feu*, followed by Ed's trio of desserts that he and Keith made.

As Fabien takes off, Serge's dinner wrapped in foil, we lay a table for ourselves out of the wind.

Graham sets out glasses, fills them and kisses Keith as he passes, much to Keith's delight.

Keith makes sure the table is laid to perfection.

Maria and Ed are studying their phones.

'Everything okay?'

'Yes . . . just, y'know, getting ready to go home,' says Ed. 'My new job's in touch to welcome me.'

Maria looks downcast. 'And I'm just working out where to go next.'

'It's home for us,' says Graham.

'I don't mind,' says Keith. 'It's hard to go home to an empty shell. Maybe we should look at renting for a while. Somewhere I can enjoy being, and make a home. Not always moving.'

'We could.' Graham smiles.

'Somewhere with an oven so I can make custard tarts!' Keith beams.

'And you won't stop cooking, will you?' Maria says to Ed.

'Not likely! Just a matter of finding someone to cook for.' He looks up at her and she smiles.

'Or share the cooking maybe.' Then, 'But I'm not sure there's much I could be doing in South Wales. I should head home really.'

'And me.'

I want to dive in and tell them they're perfect for each other and need to follow their hearts, but that's for them to work out. Not me . . . not any more.

I promised Fabien that it's time for us to think about us. We'll let others work things out for themselves.

'And what about you, Del?' asks Keith. 'What will you do when Henri's sells?'

I frown. 'I'm not sure.'

'You don't mind not getting the place back?'

'I thought that was all I wanted, until I realized it's not about the place but the people. That's what's important. Henri brought us together and that won't change. We don't need the building to tell us that.'

The wind whips up stronger and harder. The warehouse doors slam shut.

'Whoa!'

'Gosh, I don't know what Zacharie's cooking tonight, but it smells like he's burned it!' says Ed.

'Yes,' we all agree, sniffing.

'Definitely like burning!' I say.

And we laugh.

'It's all about l'expérience!' I smile. I breathe in the smell again and suddenly I'm not smiling. 'It's burning!'

I run out of the gates and to the end of the street, but I don't need to be told twice what's happening. The wind whips up my hair and the edges of my dress. The blood drains from my face.

'No, no, *noooooooooo!*'

I hear someone's voice behind me. It may be Jen, calling to the others. 'Henri's is on fire!'

31

I start to run down the street.

'Oh, no, oh, no!' I'm repeating, as I stumble over the shiny cobbles.

I can see smoke billowing from the front windows. The air is now thick with the smell of burning.

Outside, a few diners are staggering, leaning on each other, catching their breath and watching the smoke as it builds inside the restaurant. The wind is whipping it up. The fallen brazier has set alight the awning and flames lick up the walls to the shutters above.

Suddenly there's a bang, and flames appear from the roof. People around me jump backwards, diners who are coughing and clinging to each other, along with kitchen staff and waiters.

'Who's in there? Is everyone out?' I shout. I can see the sous-chef, but there's someone I can't see. It seems everyone is out, except one person. I can feel the anxiety in the air.

'Zacharie! Where is Zacharie the chef?' I ask.

Behind me the whole group from the supper club have arrived and are standing watching the scene unfold, holding each other's hands. There is a hand on my shoulder. I don't know whose it is.

'Fabien – where's Fabien?' I look around all the faces, trying to spot him.

'Not back from Serge's?' says Graham.

'Are you sure he's not back?' Keith says. 'He's not in there, is he?' His panic is growing.

'You don't think he's gone in to help the chef, do you?' I hear someone say.

'What if he saw the fire and didn't go to Serge's? He could have come straight here! Fabien!' I shout. 'Zacharie!' I try to push through the crowd. There's another bang.

'No,' says Graham, grabbing my arm, holding me back. 'You can't!' The group closes around me for comfort, support and my own protection. The seconds tick by.

'Has anyone called the *pompiers*?' I shout.

'They're on their way.'

I hear footsteps.

The mayor has appeared from one direction and Carine, running in her kitten heels, from the other.

'Is everyone out?' says the mayor.

'I don't know where Fabien is! And no one has seen Zacharie the chef, Henri's son! Fabien! Zacharie!' I shout.

Suddenly sirens are blaring and the growing crowd moves back. Adèle from the bakery arrives and touches my arm. 'I heard . . .' She's looking up at the building as the flames increase. The neighbouring shopkeepers have gathered, and I can see familiar faces from the riverbank slipping off their hats and bowing their heads. More and more people are arriving at the scene as word spreads. Henri's is burning down.

The wind whips and twists and fans the flames, reaching higher and higher.

'Where's Fabien?' I try my phone but my eyes are blurred as I punch in his number.

Suddenly I can feel him. 'I'm here!' he says, out of breath from running. Behind him, moving slowly, is Serge. It seems the whole town is here to watch Henri's bistro burn.

'Is anyone in there?'

'Zacharie, Henri's son!' I shout. The air is full of agitation and anxiety.

'Zacharie is in there?' Fabien moves forward.

'No! Fabien, don't!'

Stephanie arrives with JB. They are carrying the children. 'What's happening?'

'It's Zacharie. We think he's still in there.'

'Idiot!' Fabien says, and again steps forward.

'No! Fabien!'

'But I have to help!' he says.

I couldn't love him more than I do right now for his selflessness, but I am not about to lose him to the fire. I tug at his arm. Frustrated, he looks back at me but doesn't pull away.

'Let the firefighters do their job,' says Stephanie, firmly. He understands. He means too much to us. He looks back at the door, and as he does, it opens. Plumes of smoke pour out. Then Zacharie is there, coughing and spluttering, barely able to stand.

The firefighters and medics move in to support him and the items he's carrying. Under his arm is a stack of the pictures that, I'm guessing, used to hang along the wall of Henri's. He looks at me, tears streaming down his face. It looks like a small boy is still inside Zacharie, just wanting to remember his father for the good times, not the bad.

Suddenly there is another huge bang and we all step back as the front window blows out, with the last of the l'expérience signage, and the *pompiers* get to work dousing the flames. We move back. And with them is Rhi, tears running down her face. She walks to the front of the gathered group, with us behind her. The firefighters move us back, but we don't leave. No one is leaving.

'It's the end,' I hear myself say.

'Or maybe a beginning,' Fabien says, and I fall against his chest. He hugs me hard and kisses the top of my head. He's here. And I know I have everything I want and need.

In the distance I can hear music from the *brocante*, carried on the wings of the mistral wind.

'Je Ne Regrette Rien' by Edith Piaf.

'*Au revoir, Henri. Merci pour tout,*' says Fabien, and everyone around us says, '*Au revoir,*' and '*Merci.*'

Don't wait for things to get better, to be less complicated. Learn to be happy right now. I hear his words as the sparks and flames rise higher. And then, as I lean against Fabien, my head swims, my knees give way and my whole world goes black.

'Medics!' I hear, then no more.

32

I wake in bed in the hospital. Fabien is beside me, holding my hand and stroking my forehead.

'I fainted,' I say.

'I know.' He smiles. 'And they brought you in just to be sure everything was okay. You fell asleep once the doctor had finished his tests. You must be exhausted.'

I feel like I could sleep for ever.

'Is everyone okay?' I ask, in a husky, rasping voice from the smoke, with a banging headache.

'Always thinking of others!' He smiles, his longish hair falling over his face. 'Yes, everyone is fine. Zacharie is recovering.'

I think back to the ambulance journey we took together.

Him, coughing from the smoke, clutching the pictures, me light-headed from fainting. 'Henri was a good man,' I told him. 'He made mistakes, but he always wanted the best for others, mostly you.'

At first he said nothing. Then, 'Always crème caramel,' he says, as if reliving a memory that had long been hidden away. Perhaps the fire had made him see it again for what it was.

'You don't have to like me, Zacharie, or work with me, but I want you to know how much we loved him because he helped others. He might not have used words to say how much he cared for you, but I'm thinking he said it with crème caramel. It was his way of showing he cared. Just like your anger has been about wiping out everything he cared for.'

Zacharie pulled the oxygen mask over his face and said no more.

'I'm guessing we won't see him again,' I say now. 'The building is burned to the ground. He did what he came to do and wiped out Henri's.'

'But not Henri or his spirit,' says Fabien. 'If this has taught me anything, it's to grab the moment.' He strokes my forehead. 'I love you, Del. Only you. I want to spend the rest of my life with you. Will you marry me?'

'What?'

'You are my present and my future. Marry me!'

'What? But we always said—'

'I want everyone to know you are my beautiful wife.'

I swallow. 'You may want a rethink after you've heard what I've got to tell you.'

'What? Is something wrong? I thought the doctor said you were fine. You just needed rest. Is there something else I should know? Are you ill?'

'No,' I say quietly. 'Pregnant.' The word catches in my throat. The word I'd thought I would never be able to say. A word I had put into a little wooden box at the back of my mind, where it has stayed for a very long time. Along with my hopes and dreams.

'Pregnant. As in with baby?' He's staring at me and we're trying to read each other's thoughts.

I nod, my eyes filling with tears. He straightens, runs his hands through his thick dark hair, his face screwed up tight.

Worry washes through me. 'Look, I know you said we should take more time for each other and I know it'll be busy. If you want to rethink the marriage . . .' I babble on. 'We agreed, and now I'm—'

'Sssh.' He rushes to me, eyes full of tears that trickle down his face. 'I cannot think of anything more wonderful. You, me, Stephanie, JB and the children, and now this one.' He touches my stomach. 'I love you. Marry me. You are my now and my future. Both of you adding to our wonderful family!'

He kisses me, and I want that kiss never to end.

Eventually he leans back, still smiling, and says, 'Is it okay, with the baby?'

'Oh, yes, it's definitely okay! In fact, I would say doctor's orders!'

33

We set out the tables and chairs with care for our last supper. There is still the smell of smoke in the air from the fire last night, a reminder of yesterday, but also a reminder to live for today. The mistral did a good job of clearing away the dust as she blew her way out of town, waving goodbye to the chaos she'd caused once more. The skies are clear and blue today, and a fresh start lies ahead, like a clean page in a diary.

Everyone has a job to do, except me. I'm under orders to sit in the shade of the chestnut tree with a glass of homemade lemonade. A jug of it has been put at my side.

'Over a bit to the left with the bunting,' I call to Jen and Maria. They look at me. 'What? I can't help it! And I am taking things easy!'

Earlier today, after a night in my own bed, I walked

with Fabien to the bistro . . . or what had been the bistro. Now it's a burned-out shell, the roof fallen into what was Henri's sitting room above the restaurant. L'expérience lies in ruins.

'It was never about the building,' I said to Fabien, who was pushing his hair off his face. I gaze at his square jawline. 'I shouldn't have let it be about the building.'

I looked at the ruin.

'No. Henri's not only here, he's everywhere in this town,' Fabien said.

'And that's what we must celebrate, every day. He brought people together. Made them feel safe and supported. Made us the community we are. Our past, present and future.'

'He did.' He squeezed my hand.

'He'll always be part of us all.'

At the *brocante*, we light the candles, put on the record player and set the table for whoever wants to join us in our final supper. Ed, Maria and Jen are serving all of Henri's specialities that I've talked them through, with their own twists and side dishes. Keith has been baking with Stephanie, making lavender sourdough and little biscuits to go with lavender ice cream. Graham is on wine duty, making champagne cocktails with Henri's brandy. Fabien is rigging up lighting, so the walls of the *brocante* are uplit, creating wonderful areas of light and shade. And there are speakers so the music plays loudly, with JB's help.

'They can shut us down after tonight, if they like.' I laugh.

Oh, and Keith has helpers in Tomas and little Louis, who adore him. He is making sure they help with the baking and laying the table. They are both determined to hand around the baskets of bread.

Now, we just have to hope people come for our final supper club. In some ways it feels like the wake after the funeral, as if yesterday we said goodbye to Henri and today we celebrate everything that was good about him.

And as the church bells ring out for seven o'clock, they arrive – the mayor, Carine, Serge, the shopkeepers, Adèle from the bakery, Samuel and the regulars at the riverside, who helped bring in the harvest. Fabien visited them and insisted they come.

We even run out of chairs and have to find more in the warehouse. There are bundles of lavender hanging from the walls and stems in vases on the table, filling the air with their soothing scent, helping to clear it of the fire.

As we start to serve, I notice everyone is helping, taking long platters of sharing starters to the tables. There is the oven-baked Camembert, soft and melting, drizzled in honey and sprinkled with thyme, little terracotta pots of chorizo and prawns in garlic and olive oil, bite-sized onion bhajis, more of the duck *rillette* and cornichons with baskets of bread that Louis and Tomas hand around. There are bowls of spicy salsa made from ripe tomatoes and lemony guacamole from avocados bought that morning on the advice of Renard, at peak perfection.

When we have shared, passed, dipped, scooped and popped the last piece of bread into our mouths, everyone helps clear the tables.

Then we put out platters of spicy merguez sausages, lamb cutlets in garlic and rosemary, and barbecued vegetable kebabs, all cooked by Ed. Jen and Maria serve salads, crunchy carrot and celeriac, dressed in homemade mayonnaise, green salad, dressed in olive oil, red wine vinegar, garlic, mustard and a little sugar, as Henri showed me. There are big bowls of steaming new potatoes, in melting butter and showered with chives. Maria has made ratatouille, of aubergine, courgettes and tomatoes, cooked in peppery olive oil and garlic with *herbes de Provence*. There is something for everyone, cooked by everyone. Graham has even helped with custard tarts for dessert.

I sit quietly, drinking in the atmosphere. There is a wonderful sound that carries over the courtyard, the music, the conversations, the laughter, the memories and stories of Henri, who is still very much at the heart of our table. We are here. We are at home. It's not about where you are, it's about who you are. It's about where we've come from and where we're going.

Fabien looks at me and smiles. I smile back. Life may have hard times for us ahead, with the bistro gone, but Henri was right: don't wait for life to stop being hard to be happy. I am happy. Whatever the future brings, I know that this is where I belong, and that Fabien and I belong together.

We eat and drink, then toast a terrific harvest.

'To friendship old and new.' Ed lifts his glass and holds it up to everyone around the table.

'To Henri, for bringing us together, as he always does,' says Fabien. Maria and Ed are holding hands under the table where they think no one can see them.

We raise our glasses again, and as we do, I spot a figure standing by the gates. I catch my breath. Everyone turns to look in the same direction.

The figure hesitates and I wonder if he's going to leave.

Fabien is the first to stand and speak. 'Come in. Everyone is welcome here.' He holds out a hand.

'Yes, come in, join us,' I say, wondering how he'll respond.

He looks around the group, who have fallen silent. Even the record has ended.

We shuffle up on the bench to make space for him, and my eyes prickle with pride. He steps forward and accepts a glass of wine that Graham has poured for him. 'It's just the local stuff,' says Graham.

'It's fine. Perfect. *Merci*.' He takes a sip and stiffly, with a gash on his forehead, he hands a cardboard box to me. 'Crème caramels . . . like Henri used to make, on a Saturday night for me,' he says. 'Henri. Papa.'

I take the box from him, open it and peer in. Everyone is watching me. A smile grows across my face as I reach in and take one out. 'Hardly like Henri used to make!' I laugh at the beautifully crafted little morsels, breathing in their caramel scent, with other miniature desserts, beautifully crafted.

'Well, a blend of the two of us. The classic tastes and flavours, and the flair of the new,' he says, with a respectful nod.

'The past, the present and the future,' I say. It's perfect.

'There really is room for both of us in the town. All of us,' I tell Zacharie, as he sips his wine.

'I know. I'm sorry. I behaved badly. I was angry, letting the past cloud my judgement of what is right here, under my nose. The love for my father is real. I'm sorry,' he says, turning to Rhi, who stands. 'Would it be all right if . . .' She doesn't let him finish before she's hugging him hard and he slowly, as if taken a little by surprise at first, hugs her back in a clumsy but still well-meaning gesture.

'Please join us,' I say, and Fabien brings another chair, placing it next to mine.

Jo Thomas

Graham tops up the drinks and Ed repositions the record player arm so Edith is singing 'La Vie En Rose'. We clink glasses, 'To Henri,' and sip.

Then Zacharie says, 'The bistro is gone. Once the insurance comes through, I'll be looking at new premises. We could always talk about some ideas, working together in a new venture.'

'Ah, it's good of you, but I don't think that's going to work now,' I say. 'I'm not sure I'm a Michelin-star sort of cook. But that's okay. Like I said, there's room for everyone.'

'There is.' He nods and smiles.

'You could carry on with the supper club here,' Fabien says. 'My profits have never been so good! However, you will be taking things a lot easier from now on,' he says to me.

'I will.' I laugh.

'And I apologize for my behaviour, both of you,' says Zacharie. He holds out his hand to me, and I shake it, then to Fabien, who accepts it and shakes. They both know it's what Henri would have done.

'However,' I look around the table, 'the autumn is coming. Maybe we could do the supper club next summer, but in the meantime, I was thinking about events catering, weddings, christenings, first communions, even moving into catering for film crews or food festivals. Anywhere that needs us to feed people.'

Keith and Graham, Maria, Ed and Jen all look at each other and smile.

'That sounds amazing!' says Graham.

'Brilliant,' says Jen.

Maria's phone pings. She looks at it. 'It's Marco. He's heading for the airport tomorrow and wants to know if I'll be joining him to travel home.'

She looks at Ed. 'Well, I have to be going back, so . . .' She trails off.

'You could stay,' I say. 'If you wanted to. All of you. Us. Working as a team. Doing what we do now. It's a leap of faith. I don't know what work we'll get, but if we managed to pull this off, I'm pretty sure we can set ourselves up as an outside catering company. We can call it Henri's At Home! Chez Henri!'

And they nod in agreement.

'I'd like to stay on here for a while,' says Keith to Graham. 'Find ourselves somewhere to rent. Somewhere I can create a home for us.'

And Graham beams. 'Perfect!'

'We should let Bobby know,' says Graham, picking up his phone, his hands shaking with his excitement.

'What about you, Jen?' I say.

'Well, I was going to offer you a lift to the airport, Maria, but, actually, it's time for a rest. The van and I should stay exactly where we are. I'd like to think my travelling days are over, that this is where my journey ends. I can't run for ever. I messed up and there's no going back, but that's not to say I don't still have a future. Like you say, don't wait for it not to be hard to be happy.'

Then I look at Ed.

Maria's phone is beeping again.

And I know Ed is torn. If he could find a way of staying with Maria, of not hurting his parents . . .

Maria looks at him. 'There's nothing I want to get back to Australia for right now,' she says aloud. She's talking to Ed. She types a message and puts down her phone. It rattles with replies but she ignores them and smiles. She has her wings and she's using them. 'I don't know where I come from, but I do know that I've found myself here. And I like that. So this is where I'm going to stay.'

We give a little cheer, and Ed is wide-eyed.

Then Zacharie gives a little cough.

'Well, it'll be a while before l'expérience is open again, so perhaps if you need a chef, I could join the team . . .'

'It's up to the team,' I say.

'The more the merrier,' says Jen.

'Of course!' say the others.

I can't help but beam. These people who never even met Henri feel part of his world.

Everyone is smiling, except Ed, who is checking his phone. His flight is booked for tomorrow and I know he's working out just how long he has left here.

'Talking of weddings. There's one wedding that needs

to take place here . . .' Fabien says quietly to me. 'What's it to be?'

I nod, with no hesitation, then kiss him. He stands and wipes tears from his eyes.

'I know one event I'd like you all to cater for,' he says. 'Del and I are getting married. And we have a baby on the way. I couldn't be more excited about our future. So, we need you all here for that.'

Stephanie and Carine jump up to hug me, and Tomas joins in, as does little Louis, who hasn't a clue as to what's going on but doesn't want to be left out.

JB is shaking Fabien's hand and slapping him on the back.

Our family.

And then I hear a ringtone on a FaceTime call.

'There, it's easy. Nothing to be scared of,' says Maria, standing by Graham.

'I always email. I haven't done this before.'

'It's simple,' she says. 'And you'll be able to see him.'

'I don't think he'll answer,' says Graham.

'Don't worry, we'll try him again tomorrow,' Keith reassures him. 'He might be busy, seeing friends.'

Suddenly the ringtone changes.

'Dad! Dad?'

'Hello, son,' says Graham, his face full of love. 'Are we interrupting?'

'Not at all. I've just never known you to FaceTime before! You always email. Is everything okay?'

'A friend, Maria, showed me how to do it,' says Graham. 'Everything's fine.'

'That's brilliant! You two look amazing!'

'We feel it!' says Keith. 'We've got some news. We're going to stay on a bit in France. Find a house to rent.'

'Make a home.' Graham beams.

'In that case, I'd better come and see you soon.'

'We'd love that.'

'Because there's someone I want you to meet,' he says. 'This is Alexandra, my girlfriend.'

Keith's hands shoot up to cover his mouth.

'I'm sorry I haven't been home of late. I've been a bit busy,' we hear him say. 'We met in the lunch queue at uni and haven't been apart since. I just didn't want to say anything before we were . . . y'know . . . official.'

'Oh, my God! That's wonderful! Hello, Alexandra! I'm Dad.'

'And I'm Dad,' says Keith.

'I've heard all about Bobby's two dads. He's so proud of you,' says Alexandra. 'You brought up the man I've fallen in love with so that must make you pretty special. I can't wait to meet you in person.'

They talk animatedly together and to the young woman with Bobby on the screen. Then Graham turns to us. 'Everyone, this is our son, Bobby.'

'And his girlfriend, Alexandra,' says Keith, a blubbering mess.

'And this is the *brocante* where we're holding supper

club!' Keith takes the phone and holds it up for Bobby to see.

'It's exactly how you described it in your emails, Dad,' he says to Keith. 'Sorry, I should have sent more back. But I loved getting them. I felt I was there! I can't wait to visit the new house.'

'And bring Alexandra.'

They blow kisses and we all shout goodbye as they finish their call.

We sigh, the music plays, and Keith tops up everyone's glass when a woman standing by the gates, waving, catches my eye.

'More customers?'

Fabien shrugs. 'No idea.'

'Budge up, everyone! Make room. There's plenty of food left,' says Jen, welcoming them in.

This time it's Ed's jaw that drops. 'Mum, Dad, what are you doing here?' He stands and walks towards them.

I look at Fabien, who shrugs again.

'Mum, Dad? You don't fly! You don't even leave our town!'

'They do a lovely panini on the plane! Even had a glass of wine.' His mum is smiling, her cheeks rosy.

'And we thought maybe we should come and see this place that seems to have caught your interest,' his dad says, clearly proud of himself and his wife for having made the trip. 'We thought we'd meet you before you travel home. Just in case you were feeling worried about coming back or anything.'

'Actually, Mum, Dad, there's something I need to tell you,' Ed says.

'It's all right, son. We know – we've always known,' says his dad.

'What?'

'That you're different,' he says. 'Not like me and Mum.'

'Hang on, I don't know if you're on the right track here.'

'I'm just saying we need to accept you for who you are.'

'Are you gay?' says his mum. 'Because I love you just the way you are.'

'No, Mum, I'm not gay!' Ed blushes. 'Sorry,' he says to Graham and Keith, who laugh.

'I didn't think so. But Jean down the road said she thought you were and that's why you didn't go through with the wedding. I told her she was wrong. I said to your father, "We need to go and tell him we love him whatever. He's got no reason not to come home."'

'I'm not gay,' Ed says quickly, 'but I do want different things. I know you want me to come home. But . . .' he takes a deep breath, '. . . that's not where I want to be.'

For a moment no one says anything. The candles in the courtyard burn brightly in the warm summer's evening.

'No, son. We know. And maybe it wasn't you that

needed to come home, but us that needed to learn to spread our wings. I'm sorry. We realize now we were trying to get you to be what we wanted you to be, not letting you be yourself. With us only having you, we'd put everything on you and that wasn't fair. Sorry.'

His father gulps and Ed steps forward and puts his arms round his father, who is taken aback, but then embraces Ed. I have a feeling it's the first time they've hugged like this, but maybe not the last.

His mum puts her arms around them both.

'We were just so proud, what with your degree and a lovely girlfriend, but it's not about what we want. We don't want to see you unhappy. You have to follow your dreams. Like we did. They're just different dreams.'

'Now, come and join us,' says Ed. 'There's plenty of food, a lot of which I made.'

'You? Cooking?' says his mum. 'Well, that's a turn-up for the books.'

'I always thought you'd be creative. Your nan was a smashing cook!' says his dad. His mum nudges her husband in the ribs, looking cross. 'And your mum, of course!'

Keith helps seat them around the table and puts out knives and forks. Ed and Maria head to the kitchen where I can see they share the kiss they've been wanting to do since they first met.

More food is laid out, sharing plates and main courses, everyone helping again. The music and the conversation start again. Just as lively as before, with Ed's mum and dad being introduced to the mayor, Carine sitting with Zacharie and Samuel, and hearing about Henri's riverside project.

I look around the table. Everyone is here, the past, the present and the future, and that's all down to Henri. It's not where we are but who we are because of him and who we're with. Wherever there's a table, Henri will always be with us. I chink glasses with Rhi, and watch Fabien dancing on the old rugs with little Louis and Tomas, harmonica in hand. This is my future. We may not know what it will hold, but it is my future and I am happy.

ACKNOWLEDGEMENTS

A book is only an idea without the team behind it. This book was an idea I had and Francesca, my editor, trusted me to do my first follow-up. And I loved writing it. Thank you, Francesca, for your faith in me, your encouragement, and your insightful editing that always made each book the best it could be.

I'd like to thank all the team at Transworld for the effort they put into my books, and welcome back editor Sally Williamson on to Team Jo! I'm looking forward to exciting times ahead.

This book wouldn't have been written without me having a long-standing love affair with Provence, initiated and nurtured by my parents and the time they spent there. I love it there. Going back always feels like I'm returning to my happy place. So, thank you, Provence, for all the inspiration you've given me over the years and for being my happy place, and a place where I remember my Dad so well.

As always I'd like to thank my lovely agent David Headley.

And my writing friends who are always at the end of WhatsApp when life gets tough, or when there's something to celebrate, or we need encouraging or company. Our Friday Zooms and daily messages are so special to me. Thank you, Katie Fforde, Catherine Jones, Jill Mansell, Milly Johnson, Judy Astley, Janie Millman, Bernadine Kennedy and A. J. Pearce; and never forgetting Jane Wenham Jones.

Thank you to all of you for reading my books and staying in touch. And my Bookery Club gang who turn up on a Friday to see what's cooking in the kitchen, what I'm reading and writing, and telling me what they're cooking and reading too! I love it! Keep cooking and reading and letting me know. Until the next one . . .

With Love

Jo
x

*Read on for some delicious
recipes and more information
about Jo's uplifting and
heart-warming books . . .*

RECIPES

Bouillabaisse

This rich fish stew is a traditional dish from Provence which is an absolute must-try! It's best served with crusty white bread and garlic and saffron aioli – also known as *rouille* – which I like to make myself! While it can be a challenge, the mix of seafood is utterly satisfying and has the most wonderful aroma too!

Serves 6–8

Ingredients:

4 tbsp olive oil
1 onion, finely diced
1 fennel bulb, thinly sliced
1 leek, thinly sliced
2 carrots, peeled and diced
1 celery stalk, chopped
3 garlic cloves, minced
1 tbsp tomato puree
3 large tomatoes, diced

100ml dry white wine

1.5l fish stock

1 bouquet garni (bundle of herbs made from thyme sprigs, bay leaves and parsley stalks)

Small pinch of saffron

Pinch of chilli flakes

800g mixed fish fillets (such as monkfish, John Dory, gurnard), filleted

200g prawns, peeled and de-veined

200g mussels, cleaned and de-bearded

200g clams, scrubbed

Salt and pepper, to taste

Fresh parsley, chopped

Crusty white bread, to serve

For the rouille

Slice of white bread, crusts removed

25ml fish stock

2 garlic cloves, crushed

Pinch of chilli flakes

Small pinch of saffron

1 egg yolk

250ml olive oil

Method:

1. Heat the olive oil in a large pot over medium heat, then add in the onion, fennel, leek, carrots and celery. Cook this for about 10 minutes, until softened.

2. Add the garlic to the pot and cook for a further two minutes. Then add the tomato puree, diced tomatoes, white wine and fish stock.

3. Bring this mixture to the boil, then add the bouquet garni, saffron, and chilli flakes. Lower the heat and leave to simmer for an hour.

While the broth is simmering, I make the rouille.

4. Cover the slice of bread with the fish stock and leave to soften.
5. Place the bread, along with the garlic, chilli, saffron, egg yolk and a pinch of salt to a food processor. Blend until smooth.
6. With the food processor running on a low speed, gradually add the olive oil until you have a smooth mixture like mayonnaise. Store this in the fridge until needed.

To finish the bouillabaisse

7. For a rustic bouillabaisse, you can simply add the fish, prawns, mussels and clams to the broth, and allow this to cook until the shells of the seafood begin to open (normally around 5–7 minutes).
8. For a more refined version of the stew, remove the herb bundle and then using a handheld blender blitz the soup until smooth. Pass the blended soup through a sieve into a large, clean pan and bring to a low simmer. Then add in the fish, prawns, mussels and clams and leave these to cook in the broth until the shells open.
9. Taste the broth, and season with salt and pepper to taste.
10. Using a slotted spoon, carefully scoop the fish and mussels into bowls and then ladle over the rich broth. Serve with the crusty bread and rouille and enjoy!

Ratatouille

This classic French dish is one of my favourites – vibrant and full of flavour, it's packed with fresh vegetables and herbs, making it a super-healthy lunch or dinner. It's also a brilliant and easy way to enjoy the best of the summer veggies!

Serves 6–8

Ingredients:

2 aubergines
3 courgettes
2 red or yellow peppers
2 red onions
4 cloves of garlic
6 large, ripe tomatoes
5 tbsp olive oil
1 x 400g tin chopped tomatoes
1 tbsp red wine vinegar
1 tsp granulated sugar
¼ tsp dried oregano
¼ tsp dried thyme
Small bunch of basil
Salt and pepper to taste

Method:

1. Begin by prepping the vegetables. Trim the aubergines and courgettes, deseed the peppers and then chop them into chunks. Peel the onions and the garlic; cut the onions into wedges and finely slice the garlic. Roughly chop the tomatoes.
2. Heat 2 tablespoons of oil over a medium heat in a large saucepan. Fry the aubergine and courgettes for

5 minutes – you may need to do this in batches. Cook until the veg is golden but not completely cooked through, then set aside. Repeat with the peppers until they are softened, again making sure to not cook them through, and then set them aside with the other veg.

3. Add the remaining oil to the pan, then add the chopped onion and sliced garlic. Fry for 10 minutes on low heat until golden and fragrant.

4. Return the aubergine, courgette and peppers to the pan and stir in the chopped tomatoes, red wine vinegar, sugar, oregano and thyme. Tear up most of the basil leaves and add them to the pan, along with a pinch of salt and pepper.

5. Mix the veg and sauce well, then cover the saucepan and leave to simmer for half an hour, stirring every so often.

6. Season to taste and serve with the remaining basil leaves scattered on top.

Canard aux Olives

Just like the dish that Ed cooks in the story, I love to make this slow-cooked duck with green olives and plenty of fresh herbs. Beautifully fragrant and filling, it's a real treat!

Serves 4–6

Ingredients:

For the duck

2 medium onions, chopped
2 sticks of celery, sliced
8 garlic cloves, halved
1½ tbsp fresh thyme
30g fresh parsley, roughly chopped
1 whole duck (approx. 2.3kg), legs tied
2 tbsp unsalted butter
1 tsp *herbes de Provence*
Salt and pepper

For the sauce

1 tbsp olive oil
1 tbsp butter
Neck, wing tips and gizzard from duck
1 medium onion, sliced
1 tbsp tomato puree
200ml dry white wine
1½l chicken stock
1 bouquet garni (bundle of herbs made from thyme sprigs, bay leaves and parsley stalks)
350g pitted green olives (brine-cured)

Method:

1. Preheat the oven to 220°C/200° fan/gas mark 7. In the base of a roasting tin, spread the onion, celery, cloves of

garlic, fresh thyme and parsley to make a bed for the duck.

2. Score the duck all over with a small paring knife and rub the skin with the butter. Season with the *herbes de Provence*, salt and pepper.

3. Place the duck on top of the veg, skin side up. Place in the oven and roast uncovered for 15 minutes, then remove from the oven.

4. Reduce the oven temperature to 135°C/125° fan/gas mark 1. Cover the roasting tin with foil, then return it to the oven (you don't need to wait for the temperature to reach 135°C). Cook for roughly 3 and a half hours, until the duck is very tender.

5. While the duck is cooking, prepare the sauce. In a non-stick saucepan, heat the butter with the oil over a medium-high heat. Add the duck neck, wing tips and gizzard, season with salt and pepper and cook for 5–8 minutes, stirring occasionally.

6. Add the onion and allow this to fry with the duck until fragrant, then add the tomato puree and let it cook off a little.

7. Add the wine, stock, and bouquet garni and bring to a boil. Then reduce the heat and leave the sauce to simmer for at least 2 hours, occasionally skimming the fat from the surface.

8. After 2 hours, strain the sauce to remove the solids and return it to the saucepan. Add the olives, and stir over a medium heat, continuing to let the sauce reduce until it coats the back of a spoon (45 minutes to an hour).

9. When the duck has been in the oven for 3 and a half hours, remove and leave it to rest for a further 20 minutes.

10. To serve, carve the duck and pour the rich sauce over and serve immediately!

Banana and Lavender Cake

This banana loaf is made with a delicious lavender-infused twist. With a hint of lavender in the cake and a lavender syrup drizzled over the top, this utterly yummy, moist cake always goes down a treat!

Ingredients:

2 tbsp dried lavender
6 tbsp unsalted butter
200g self-raising flour
½ tsp salt
2 eggs, room temperature
150g plain yogurt
175g caster sugar
1 tsp vanilla extract
2 large ripe bananas, mashed

For the drizzle

65g caster sugar
80ml water
1 tbsp dried lavender

Method:

1. Preheat the oven to 180°C/160° fan/gas mark 4. Grease and line a loaf tin with baking paper.
2. In a non-stick saucepan over a medium heat, cook 2 tbsp of lavender until fragrant. Lower the heat and add the butter to the pan. Allow to melt and cook for a further two minutes, stirring occasionally.
3. The butter will begin to brown slowly. Keep stirring and cooking until the butter is a light caramel colour. Strain

out the lavender, catching the butter in a bowl. Save roughly 1 tsp of the lavender.

4. In a bowl, sieve the flour and salt. In a separate bowl, mix the eggs, yogurt, sugar, vanilla extract and the brown butter. Once combined, gradually fold in the mashed banana and the saved teaspoon of lavender.

5. Mix the wet mixture into the dry, and then pour the batter into the loaf tin. Bake for 1 hour, or until a knife inserted into the centre comes out clean.

6. While the cake is in the oven, make the syrup. In a small saucepan over a medium heat, make a simple syrup by combining the sugar and water. Once the sugar has dissolved, add the lavender. Cook for about a minute, until you can smell the lavender, then set aside.

7. Once the cake is out of the oven and has been removed from the tin, poke small holes into the top of the cake with a skewer or a cocktail stick. Place the cake on a wire rack and brush the syrup over the top of the loaf and then cover the sides with any remaining syrup.

8. Leave the cake to cool and serve!

French Onion Soup

There is nothing more comforting than a hearty bowl of French onion soup. Sweet caramelized onions, rich beef broth and topped with cheesy toasted bread – what's not to love?

Ingredients:

50g butter
1 tbsp olive oil
800g onions, thinly sliced
1 tsp sugar
3 cloves of garlic, crushed
2 tbsp plain flour
250ml white wine
2 tbsp brandy
1.2l beef stock

For the croutons

French baguette, cut into slices
1 tbsp olive oil
2 cloves garlic
200g grated gruyere

Method:

1. Melt the butter with the olive oil in a large saucepan. Once melted, add the onions and sugar and cook on a high heat until the edges of the onions have browned.
2. Lower the heat and leave the onions to keep cooking for around 30 minutes, stirring frequently until caramelized. In the last few minutes of cooking, add the garlic.

3. When the base of the pan is coated with a caramelized brown film, sprinkle the flour into the pan and stir to coat the onions and garlic.
4. Gradually add the wine and brandy, followed by the beef stock. Cover and leave to simmer for 30–45 minutes.
5. While the soup is simmering, prepare the croutons. Pre-heat the oven to 120°C/110° fan/gas mark ½. Brush olive oil on both sides of the baguette slices, then place the bread in the oven to toast.
6. After 10 minutes as the bread begins to turn crusty, remove the slices from the oven and rub the garlic clove on one side – be careful not to burn your fingers! Return the slices to the oven for a further 5–10 minutes.
7. When it's time to serve, season the soup with salt and pepper to taste. Ladle the soup into bowls and top with the croutons sprinkled with the grated gruyere. Place under the grill until the cheese is golden.
8. Serve immediately, and don't forget to warn everyone that the bowls will be very hot!

If you enjoyed *Love in Provence*, make sure to look out for Jo's next book . . .

CHRISTMAS IN THE SWISS ALPS

When Clara signs up for a month of chocolate-making in Switzerland, she imagines the stunning scenery of the magical snowy Alps, a cute chalet and a cosy workshop like something from a Christmas advert.

What she isn't expecting is chocolate-making bootcamp! In this stark laboratory, chocolate is *everything*. It's a very serious set-up, with master chocolatiers to be revered and where favouritism and fanaticism, subterfuge and scandal are rife!

Clara is way out of her depth. But caught up in the world of chocolate school, picking her friends – and her enemies – carefully, she discovers a newfound passion. Until a secret is revealed, and Clara has to decide whether to risk everything she has for a new life and love . . .

Let the queen of feel-good Christmas fiction whisk you off to the snowy mountains this festive season!

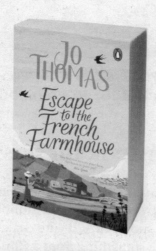

A place to heal broken hearts and find new beginnings . . .

Del and her husband Ollie moved to a beautiful village in Provence for a fresh start after years of infertility struggles. But six weeks after they arrive, they're packing the removal van once more. As Del watches the van leave for England, she suddenly realizes exactly what will make her happier . . . a new life in France – without Ollie.

Now alone, all Del has is a crumbling farmhouse, a mortgage to pay and a few lavender plants. What on earth is she going to do? After discovering an old recipe book at the market run by the rather attractive Fabien, Del starts to bake. But can her new-found passion really help her let go of the past and lead to true happiness?

Sometimes happy-ever-after is closer than you think . . .

A dream home

Beca Valentino is ready to escape the city. When she sees the perfect house for sale in her hometown, it seems like fate. Is this her chance to build the foster family she dreams of, on the beautiful Pembrokeshire coast?

A big mistake?

Returning home isn't as easy as she thought, however. Her family's beloved ice cream café is gone – turned into a soulless wine bar by her hateful ex-boyfriend. Reconnecting with her oldest friend, fisherman Griff, isn't straightforward either. And when, instead of the children she expected to take in, two wary teenage boys appear on her doorstep, Beca fears she's made a terrible mistake.

A recipe for change

But an old family recipe book is just the inspiration she needs. Soon, with a little help from friends old and new, Beca is selling mouth-watering homemade gelato from a pop-up café on the beach.

Then disaster strikes. Will the Valentino family legacy be lost forever? Or can Beca create a new recipe for happiness?

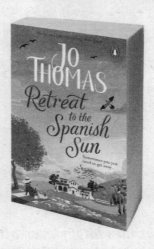

Sometimes you just need a getaway . . .

Eliza has a full house! When her three children grew up
and moved out, she downsized to a smaller property . . .
but now they're all back. Every room in the house is taken
and Eliza finds herself sharing her bed with her eldest
daughter and her daughter's pug. Combined with the
online course she's trying to finish, plus her job to fit in,
there just isn't the peace and quiet that Eliza needs.

So when an ad pops up on her laptop saying 'house-sitters
wanted', Eliza can't resist the chance to escape. She ends up
moving to a rural finca in southern Spain, looking after the
owner's Iberico pigs, learning about secret gastronomic
societies . . . and finding a new zest for life and love along
the way.